Have Yourself A Merry Little Romance

2015 Holiday Collection

Anthology: Sweet to Sensual

Stories to satisfy your romantic cravings

Linda Swift, Celia Yeary, Barbara Miller,

Teresa K. Cypher, M.C. Scout, Gerald Costlow

Have Yourself A Merry Little Romance
2015 Holiday Collection
Anthology: Sweet to Sensual

Presented by *Victory Tales Press*

ISBN-13: 978-1519743480
ISBN-10: 1519743483

Cover Art Copyright © 2015 Karen Michelle Nutt
Editor: Briana Nickol
Produced by Rebecca J. Vickery
Collection Coordinator Karen Michelle Nutt
Design Consultation by Laura Shinn

Six complete sweet to sensual romances from six multi-talented authors in settings that are sure to warm your heart. There's a story for everyone. Let magic of the holiday season take you away where romance awaits.

Included in this Romance Collection:

A Time to Give by Linda Swift
The small roadside restaurant where Ellen works is busy with travelers on Christmas Eve. She is counting on a bonus and tips to help pay for her boyfriend's special gift. Bruce needs a typewriter for college class work and Ellen has saved for months to surprise him. A mother and two children stop in while their car is repaired next door. Ellen learns they have a long drive ahead in a worsening snowstorm with little money and no gifts for the little ones. If Ellen helps them, she can't afford the gift for Bruce. Christmas is a time to give, but how can she choose who has the greater need?

A Christmas Wedding by Celia Yeary
Kailey Lovelace, maid of honor in her brother's Christmas wedding, hopes the best man Alex Dunn won't bolt when he sees she is six feet tall and has frizzy blond hair. At the airport, she almost loses her breath when she learns he's even taller and looks like a dream. If only he likes her enough for the week of the wedding to go smoothly.
Alex Dunn, recently discharged from the Army, can't believe his good luck when he meets his partner for the wedding. Kailey is just the right height and gorgeous, as well. He looks forward to a pleasant week in Texas.
What could possibly go wrong?

One Foggy Christmas by Barbara Miller
Lady Jane Faraday is conflicted about traveling to Summerhill for the Christmas holiday since the heir to the estate, and the man who was supposed to marry her, has died. But she has other worries than her guilt over not marrying Henry St. Giles. Stephen, the younger son and the one she loves, is still fighting the war in the Peninsula. If only he had written to her she would know where she stands with his affections. She'd wait for him if he'd say the word, but she isn't sure he's still alive.

Stephen St. Giles receives leave to return home since his beloved brother Henry is dead and the war is nearly over, but what of Jane? She has answered none of his letters. Is she now his brother's widow or did she wed someone else? And why has he heard nothing from his mother? As he trudges the last miles toward home through the fog, he feels as confused and uncertain as his misty surroundings.

Jack and the Christmas Journey by Teresa K. Cypher

Tildie Janson lost her husband, Harp, three years ago, and the only joy in her life is Jack, her husband's dog. Without him she'd be lost. With Christmas around the corner, her friends step in to help her move on by badgering her into taking steps toward celebrating the holiday. They mean well, but she wishes they'd leave her alone. On one of their planned outings, a chance encounter, with a man from her past, forces her to face life again, but the prospect scares her and she retreats. She can't let go. However, Fate-or maybe a touch of Christmas magic sends Jack on a journey that changes everything.

Return Engagement by M. C. Scout

Tanner Armitage has been overseas for nearly a year serving his country and can't wait to come home to surprise the love of his life.

An Army brat, Brynn Josephs looks forward to when he gets leave to come home though she's sure it won't be this year.

Christmas is in the air but can he successfully pull off a return engagement?

Third Time's the Charm by Gerald Costlow

Fourth in the Modern Day Sherritt Witch series.

Trudy Macalester is a young, single schoolteacher living with her newly remarried father. She discovers her new stepmother is a witch when she stumbles upon a book of spells. When Trudy reads from the book, she accidentally summons a charming rogue bent on seduction; a man nobody but she can see or hear.

All she wanted was a man who will hang around for longer than a couple of dates. It's going to be a Christmas to remember for poor Trudy.

TABLE OF CONTENTS

Thank you to all the readers and fans who
show their support for our anthologies.

Thank you to the authors for penning
such heartwarming tales.

A Time to Give

Linda Swift

Dedication:
*For Bob with thanks for all your
support and technical help.*

CHAPTER ONE

Millersville, Alabama 1975

Ellen quickly stacked heavy white plates and put them in a red plastic tub. With one deft motion, she transferred four partly filled water glasses from table to tub and collected the crumpled red-checked napkins. More slowly, she removed thick cups and saucers, saving one where the man sat until last. Theirs had been a big order, country ham and hash browns, and she'd refilled coffee cups twice. She brought the two boys more cocoa, so surely – *no, nothing.*

Ellen sighed. It wouldn't have mattered so much if this weren't the last day. Here on the Interstate she was used to people not leaving tips. It seemed as though most of them felt it wasn't necessary, no matter how good the service, since they were only passing through. But Ellen gave good service just the same, because it made her feel good. Her grandmother taught her when she was a little girl that *any job worth doing was worth doing well.*

Wiping the table, Ellen thought of her grandmother and sighed again. Today would have been her birthday. Ellen had always bought her a birthday present, even though it was also Christmas Eve.

As she set clean silverware and stiffly folded napkins on the bare table, Ellen glanced out the window. Even at midmorning, it was as dark as evening. The sky was dull gray and the red neon sign saying *Roadside Restaurant* blinked invitingly near Interstate 24.

Wheeling the loaded cart carefully between empty tables, Ellen smiled at the man sitting alone at one of them. "More coffee, sir?"

"Please," he answered, returning her smile.

The breakfast crowd was mostly gone now and it would be about an hour until the tables began to fill for lunch. Ellen poured steaming brown liquid, and then tore the check from her pad. "Will that be all, sir?"

"I believe so."

"Thank you. And have a Merry Christmas."

"The same to you. Oh, by the way..."

Ellen turned back to the table, holding the coffeepot.

"Do you know where I might do some Christmas shopping...which wouldn't be too far away from the Interstate?"

Ellen smiled apologetically. "Millersville isn't a very large town. There are only a couple of really nice stores. There's one jewelry – but maybe you aren't looking for–" She stopped, then felt her face getting red as she thought of her own ring-less hand.

The man smiled. "No, I'm not looking for a diamond. I gave her that quite a while ago. I was thinking of a velvet robe and slippers, and maybe a sweater."

"Oh, then you'll want to go to Blume's or the Village Shop. They're both on the court square, about five blocks past the Shell Station, straight down Court Street." She motioned toward the window where they could just see the gas pumps to the left.

CHAPTER TWO

Ellen slipped her order pad back into her checked apron pocket. She felt the coins inside and tried to estimate the amount. Heading toward the kitchen, she hesitated as the front door opened and six people entered. A cold blast of air followed before the last man in closed the door.

"Whew, I thought it was too cold to snow," the white-haired man said.

Ellen led them toward a large round table in the center of the room. "Will this be okay?" she asked, smiling.

"Fine." The older lady smiled back at her and sat down.

As Ellen went to get menus, she looked toward the window again. A few large flakes of snow drifted down, almost as if a slow-motion camera caught them and slowed their descent.

"Maybe we'll have a white Christmas after all," the pretty red-haired woman said.

"And that would be fine, Angela, if we were home. But I don't relish driving three hundred miles in a snowstorm."

"Relax, Papa. John is a good driver. He gets plenty of practice with ice and snow in our Vermont winters." She smiled at the handsome man with a black mustache who sat beside her.

"Just the same, I'd feel better if we had stayed—"

"Now, Henry..." The white-haired lady laid a hand gently on the old man's arm. "We've been over it all before. This may be Sister's last Christmas. And with that wheelchair, it would have been so difficult for her to travel."

"Besides, where's your spirit of adventure, Pop?" the man wearing glasses, who had hints of red in his sandy-colored hair, asked with a grin.

"It got mislaid somewhere, Jim, like most everything else does these days," the older man answered.

"I think the waitress would like us to order." The plump blonde woman spoke for the first time. She looked at Ellen. "I'll have coffee and two donuts."

"Just coffee for me," her husband said.

"I'd like some hot tea, wouldn't you, Henry?" the older lady asked.

"Yes, I guess so, Sarah. With some lemon," he added.

"I'll have hot tea also," the red-haired woman told Ellen. "With cream and sugar, please." She looked at her husband. "Are you hungry, darling?"

"Starved." His eyes wrinkled at the corners as he smiled. "But if no one else is eating, we don't have to waste time waiting while I order."

"We can wait," she answered. "We'll be there by late afternoon, even with another stop."

"Not if the roads get bad," the old man spoke again. "We need to get there before dark. That road to the farm is mighty slippery in bad weather."

"You should have had some of Mom's country ham this morning, David," the younger man said with a grin.

"Not at six o'clock in the morning, Jim," David answered. "Eating that early is against my religion. I'll have a waffle and coffee," he said to Ellen.

As Ellen walked toward the kitchen, the white-haired lady's voice followed her. "Jim and Carol are used to getting up early. He's had to be at the plant by seven for twenty-five years and..."

Ellen sighed. Just tea, coffee, two donuts, and a waffle. She couldn't count on a big tip from that.

She placed a small plate with two glazed donuts in front of the blonde woman. She set cups of tea before the old man, woman, and their daughter, being careful to remember who got lemon, cream, and sugar. Then she went back for the coffee pot.

"Yes, you college professors have got it made..." the man with glasses was saying as Ellen poured the coffee.

"Except when it comes to salary," the black-haired man answered. "What do you engineers do to earn so much money?"

"Well, for one thing, we go to work at seven o'clock," the man called Jim said with a wry grin.

"Your waffle will be ready in just a few minutes, sir," Ellen said as she poured the last cup of coffee.

Replacing the half-full pot on the burner, Ellen said to the woman pouring the waffle batter, "I'll be in the restroom a minute, Bertie. Would you watch the front for me?"

"Sure, Ellen. Take your time. I can carry this out when it's ready."

Ellen closed the door, pushed the button on the chrome knob. Quickly she emptied her pocket onto the green ceramic lavatory. Twenty-five, thirty-five, eighty-five, uh, a dollar, ten. Eight dollars and seventy cents in all. And she had been here since six. Of course, Mister Rogers had helped during the busiest time as he always did.

Marlene would come in at eleven. The lunch crowd never ordered as much or tipped as well as the supper crowd. She would be leaving at three. There was no way she could have eight more dollars by then. And she would need at least that much to add to the Christmas bonus she knew she would get at the end of the day when she got her check.

Mister Rogers had already hung the stockings on the tree before she got here this morning, just like he did last year. Ellen was counting on the twenty-five dollar bonus to have enough to buy the typewriter. *What if it was less than last year?*

The cost of food had gone up so much lately, and Mister Rogers tried to keep his menu prices very nearly the same as last year. She knew he wasn't making much profit. And his wife had been sick since summer.

Ellen had gone to Young's Discount Store and priced the electric portable models in September, right after Bruce told her about making a D-minus on his history paper because it wasn't typed. There was no way he could afford to pay a dollar a page to have his papers done. They'd talked about renting a typewriter and Ellen doing them for him, but that was ten dollars a month.

Bruce said he couldn't spare that much either. It had been a struggle for him to go to the community college, but he told her he'd always wanted to be a teacher. And somehow, Ellen knew he was going to make it.

Young's least expensive portable had been $129.95. With tax, the total came to $136.45. Ellen had it figured to the penny. And she had saved ten dollars back out of every check since October. Ten from today's check and her Christmas bonus would have made just enough. But she hadn't counted on the water pipes freezing and having to pay a plumber.

That happened yesterday, and she stayed up late figuring out a way to squeeze another fifteen dollars from her already tight budget. Still, the only way she was going to have enough money was counting her tips. But it looked like she'd cut it too short. Hurriedly, Ellen gathered up the coins and went back to the kitchen.

CHAPTER THREE

Carrying a full coffee pot, she returned to the center table. Bertie must have refilled their cups when she carried the waffle out and made a fresh pot. Just the same, she would ask them again.

"More coffee or tea?"

"You're too late, young lady. We've already had refills," the old man said, but his wink told her he was not accusing her of being negligent.

"The waffle was delicious," the black-haired man said, and added, "May I have our check now, please?"

"Yes, sir." Ellen hastily totaled the check, then went toward the register as they began putting coats on and preparing to leave.

"Sarah, have you seen my gloves? I had them on when—"

"They're right here, Papa. On the floor. They must have fallen out of your overcoat pocket." His daughter bent to pick them up, as her brother helped him with his heavy tweed coat.

The daughter's husband held the fur-trimmed coat the white-haired lady wore. "Thank you, David," she said.

"I'll get this," the one called Jim said, as he laid a ten dollar bill on the counter.

"I've got the check here. Let me get—"

"No," the man with glasses took the check, "you're driving. I'll take care of refreshments."

"Thank you, sir. Merry Christmas," Ellen said as she handed him change.

"The same to you, honey."

Ellen watched how gently the young couples helped the old people out. It must be nice to have a mother and father. Or a brother. All she could remember having was her grandmother.

Her parents died in a car wreck when she was three. They said her mother had been pregnant then. Her parents had been coming home from a New Year's Eve party and met a truck head-on. It had been snowing – like today. That was about all her grandmother ever told her about the accident in the sixteen years since it happened.

She always thought about it a lot at Christmas time...especially since she had been working part-time these last few years here by the Interstate. And now, she would be missing Grandmother at Christmas too. She died last March, and Ellen had come to work full time for Mister Rogers after graduation.

She glanced at the clock as she cleaned the table. Ten-thirty. Mister Rogers should be back soon. He always stayed at the register through the lunch hour so she and Marlene could take care of the tables faster.

As she lifted the waffle plate, Ellen saw the two crumpled dollar bills. She gave a grateful sigh. That made $10.70. Suddenly, she remembered the table by the window. She had started after the cart when the group came in, but then forgotten all about cleaning it. She pushed the cart toward the window now and hastily swept the dishes into the tub. Dried egg would be hard for Bertie to wash and she never liked to...

There, under the plate, lay a crisp flat bill.

Ellen closed her eyes, drew in her breath, and slowly exhaled as she wiped the table. $11.70. She might make it after all. Did she dare hope? No, she wouldn't think about it. For it was better not to count on anything. Then she wouldn't feel so bad at being disappointed.

Ellen looked out the window. Snowing harder now, the ground was nearly white. Just then, she saw a woman carrying a little girl and holding a small boy's hand, almost running toward the restaurant. Evidently they left their car at the Shell Station, for they cut across the snow-covered ground instead of coming in from the paved parking area. Ellen waited to show them to a table before she took the cart to the kitchen.

The little boy came in first, and stamped the snow off his ragged tennis shoes. *No kind of shoes to be wearing in a snowstorm,* Ellen thought. The woman set the child down and brushed the snowflakes off her pale yellow curls. Ellen saw she wore tennis shoes too.

"Ooooh, it's good and warm in here, Mommy," the boy said loudly. Ellen saw that both children were wearing only sweaters.

The woman smiled at him. "It sure is, David. Now wait a minute. The lady will have to tell us where to sit."

"Oh, look at the Christmas tree, Mommy! I want us to sit by the Christmas tree. Can we?"

"We'll have to ask the lady—"

"Good morning." Ellen stepped forward, menus in hand. "Will over here be okay?" She motioned to a table against the inside wall, right next to the tree. Her eyes met the woman's and they smiled at each other.

"This will be fine, thanks."

The woman appeared thin, and not as tall as Ellen. She might have been pretty if she'd had on a little make-up and had her hair styled differently. It was long and its color reminded Ellen of autumn cornstalks. She wore it pulled tightly away from her face and tied with a dark scarf. When she sat down, Ellen noticed she wore open sandals.

They must have come quite a way, Ellen thought, *or else she doesn't know how to dress for snow.*

Ellen turned the Christmas carols up a little louder. Then she placed a menu in front of the woman and another at the little boy's place, although she was pretty sure he couldn't read. "Would you like me to get the baby a high chair?"

"She's three," the little boy said. "She's not a baby."

"Just the same, we'd like the high chair, thanks." The woman's eyes met Ellen's again, and this time her smile was apologetic.

As Ellen adjusted the tiny seat onto the chair, the little girl stood transfixed in front of the tree. "Pretty Christmas tree, Mommy," she said in an awed voice.

Ellen looked at the tree, seeing it for a moment through the child's eyes. Standing on one of the tables, the top almost reached the ceiling. A real Scotch pine, it was sprayed with artificial snow and covered with red velvet bows. Interspersed among its thick branches, candy canes dangled invitingly.

"Hey, who are the stockings for?" the little boy asked, pointing toward one of the five red felt stockings which hung from the lowest branches.

"Well, one of them is mine," Ellen said.

"Which one?"

"David—"

"This one over here. The one that says *Ellen* on it." Mrs. Rogers made the stockings last year and she had cut and sewn white felt letters that spelled all their names.

"My name is David. And my sister's name is Teresa. Does any of them stockings have David and Teresa on them?" he asked hopefully.

"David, you're asking too many—"

"I'm afraid not, David," Ellen answered him. "But I'm sure Santa Claus will come to see you tonight."

"But we won't be home. Can he find us, Mommy?"

"I don't know, David." The woman opened the menu. "Do you have oatmeal?"

"Yes. It isn't listed, but we serve it. It's the same as the dry cereal."

"Then bring her oatmeal. And he'll have a scrambled egg."

"Would you like milk or cocoa for them?"

"I want cocoa," David said, "please, Mommy."

"Okay, David. And bring her a small glass of milk."

"Would he like cinnamon toast or plain?"

"Is it the same price?"

"Yes."

"I want cinnamon," David said.

"I want cinman," Teresa repeated, as she came to the table now, suddenly more interested in food than the tree.

"And what will you have?" Ellen asked the woman.

"Just coffee, black."

Ellen buttered six slices of bread. Only two should have gone with the order, but she thought the little girl would probably eat some and she knew the woman must be hungry too. She had learned to tell the ones who didn't order because they couldn't afford to and she knew Mister Rogers would approve of what she was doing. Ellen carried the toast, milk, and cocoa to the table.

"I'm hungry. We didn't have no breakfast," David said, taking a piece of the cinnamon toast before she could set the plate down.

"I'll bet you got up early and started on this trip."

"Uh, huh," he answered, as he chewed, "all the way from Florida."

"Wow!" Ellen said. She looked at the woman as she poured her coffee. "I guess you're all tired."

"It hasn't been too bad," she said. "We left at four, but David and Teresa slept most of the way."

"'Til the fuel pump busted," David said.

"My, you know a lot about cars," Ellen told him. "Are you getting a new one put on now?"

"No, my mommy didn't have enough money, so she told him to fix the old one."

"I'd better see if your egg is ready," Ellen said and turned quickly away, hoping to save the woman further embarrassment. *Diane*, her name was – at least, that was the name appliqued on the denim tote bag laid on the vacant chair.

Ellen set the bowl of oatmeal in front of the little girl. "It's hot, Teresa. Better let your mother taste it first. And here is your scrambled egg, David. Do you want more cocoa?"

"Yes."

"Yes, please," his mother said softly.

As Ellen brought the refilled cup, she asked, "Do you have very far to go?"

"East St. Louis."

Ellen looked toward the window. "It's getting pretty bad for driving, isn't it?"

"I'm going to try and make it before dark. If they can fix the pump...and if it holds."

Ellen shook her head. "That's a lot of ifs."

"Will Santa Claus find us at Grandmama's house?" David asked.

"Maybe he will, David. Of course, he didn't know we were going." She looked at Ellen. "My husband worked construction at the Naval base at Pensacola. He got laid off. There wasn't any work. Last week he went with some fruit pickers to Texas. Our rent was due and there wasn't any word from him." She shrugged. "So I'm going home to my folks 'til we can get on our feet again."

"Will Grandmama Wiley have a Christmas tree?" David asked.

"I don't know," his mother answered, and looked at Ellen again. "My brother is still at home, but he's fifteen. And my sister is back home to have her baby since her husband has joined the Navy. So Mama is going to have us all home, and only two bedrooms."

"Will we have a stocking like Ellen's on Grandmama's Christmas tree?" David wanted to know.

"I don't think so. Grandmama doesn't know you're coming."

"I want a stocking," Teresa said.

"I want a race car set," David told Ellen. "That's what I asked Santa Claus to bring me."

"Santa bring me a baby doll," Teresa added.

"Well, I hope he brings you just what you want." Ellen smiled at them, then at their mother. "Would you like more coffee?"

"Yes, thank you. I'll need it to stay awake."

After she poured the coffee, Ellen went into the kitchen for a while. She thought maybe the woman would eat the toast and leftover oatmeal if she wasn't around. The children had satisfied their appetites while the two women talked, and they sat under the tree now, talking and giggling softly, their upturned faces glowing in the twinkling red lights. And when the stereo played *Santa Claus is Coming to Town* they sang the words too.

CHAPTER FOUR

Just before Marlene came in, Lieutenant Haley stopped for his usual country ham sandwich and thermos of coffee. Ellen never bothered to take him a menu anymore.

"Good morning, Lieutenant Haley." She poured the cup of steaming liquid. "The time slipped by me today. I'll have your sandwich ready in just a minute. And then I'll fix your thermos." She took the empty thermos jug from the table.

"Good girl." He emptied two sugar packets into the cup and stirred it slowly. "I'll have to get on the road without any refills today. They're already beginning to slip and slide all over the place. And Lord knows, there's plenty of folks out there."

"Everybody is going home for Christmas, I guess."

"About half of 'em will probably end up behind old Joe Dawson's tow truck. He'll make enough to buy a fleet of 'em before the new year. Or maybe a mink coat for his wife for Christmas." He chuckled to himself.

"Is that a real gun?"

"It sure is, fella." Lieutenant Haley looked at David and smiled. "What is ole Santa going to bring you?"

"I hope he brings me a race car set. But he may not can find me."

"Why? Are you running away from home?" Lieutenant Haley asked with mock seriousness.

"No, but we're going to my Grandmama Wiley's house and she don't know it yet."

Ellen placed the sandwich on the table. "And his grandmother lives in East St. Louis. Is it snowing up that way?"

"Worse than here, they say. Illinois and Missouri are getting hit pretty heavy."

"How about up through West Kentucky and Southern Illinois?" David's mother asked.

"Haven't heard exactly. Be glad to check it out for you on the radio when I go back to the car, ma'am."

"Would you, please?"

"Sure thing, ma'am. Wouldn't want you to head up that way and get stuck in a snowdrift and these nice kids miss old Santa Claus."

Lieutenant Haley stood up, wrapping the ham sandwich in a napkin. Ellen brought the thermos, handed it to him. "Ellen, I'm

17

going to have to eat this on the road today. I'll bring your napkin back or you can charge me for it."

"Would you like a sack?"

"No, napkin's fine. Tell Jim Rogers not to send a lawman after me for taking his personal property." He laughed.

"He wouldn't do that." Ellen took the three ones, counted out change.

Lieutenant Haley fished in his back pocket and handed her an envelope. "Oh, I almost forgot. Here's a little something for you, Ellen. Have a Merry Christmas."

"Why...thank you, Lieutenant Haley. Merry Christmas to you too."

"Lady, I'll check that weather for you now. If you'll just follow me."

Diane looked at the children, then at Ellen.

"Leave them inside here where it's warm. They'll be okay," Ellen said." Why don't you check on your car too? It will be too cold for you all to wait over at the station."

"Thanks. I guess I will then. David, you watch after your sister. You both be good now. Don't bother anything."

"Okay, Mommy," David answered. Then taking his sister's hand, he said, "Let's go sit under the Christmas tree and wish real hard for Santa Claus to find us tonight."

Ellen stacked the empty dishes. Under the little boy's plate was a quarter. She dropped it in the open top of the tote bag. Then she opened the envelope. Inside was a Christmas card, a Santa Claus with a real cotton beard. She opened it to read the message and a folded bill fell to the floor.

"Hey, you dropped something, Ellen," David's voice came from behind her.

She reached down quickly and picked it up, slowly unfolded it. *Five dollars! Wow.* She made it, with a quarter to spare. And she had four hours to go yet.

"What was it, Ellen? What was in the letter?"

"It was a Christmas present, David. From Lieutenant Haley. From the highway patrolman."

"Gee. You must have been awfully good to get so many swell presents. I hope I get some."

Ellen looked at the small boy, his face so solemn and wistful. "You will, David. I just know you will."

The door opened, bringing Mister Rogers and Marlene and snow inside.

"Merry Christmas, Ellen. How's it going?"

"Slow. Merry Christmas, Marlene. I guess everybody is rushing home too fast to stop and eat."

"Trying to beat the snow storm, most likely," Mister Rogers said. "It's getting slick out there and the temperature has dropped three degrees since I left here at nine."

David's mother came in behind them.

"Where would you like to sit?" Marlene asked her.

"I've been served, thanks. I just came to claim a couple of kids." She nodded toward the Christmas tree.

Ellen wiped the table. "What did you find out?"

"It's bad. But none of the roads are closed. I think we can make it."

"Did they fix your car?"

"Yes. They patched the pump. It's holding now, but I don't know for how long."

"Look...Mrs. – uh...Diane," Ellen stopped, took a deep breath. "Why don't you all come stay with me tonight? I live by myself since my grandmother died. It's just a little house, but there are two bedrooms. And," she finished lamely, "I've got a Christmas tree."

The woman hesitated, looking uncertain. "I...thank you, but I really couldn't. We'd better move on. We can make it by dark if we don't get stuck...and if the fuel pump holds."

"All those *ifs* again." Ellen smiled. "Look, I really do wish you would change your mind. You would be most welcome."

"I want us to stay with Ellen, Mommy. Can't we stay? I bet she's got a swell tree."

"Not as nice as this one, David, but we could decorate it after I get off from work. My grandmother always trimmed our tree with strings of popcorn. We could do that."

"Golleee...can we—"

"No, David." His mother shook her head. "Families ought to be together at Christmas. Maybe Daddy will try to get in touch with us tonight. He'd call Grandmama's house if we're not in Florida. And nobody would know where we were if we're not there."

The little boy sighed, but he didn't say anything more. The woman picked up her tote bag, took out a frayed plastic billfold. "What happened to my check? Did it get thrown away with the dirty dishes?"

Ellen hesitated, afraid of offending the woman if she said there would be no charge. She took out the yellow pad, totaled the items. "That will be $4.15"

The woman counted out change, then added four dollar bills. "Here, I think that's right."

"Thank you. Will you be starting right now?"

"As soon as the man gets the chains on. Somebody had left some a long time ago. He let me have them real cheap."

Ellen reached under the counter and brought out two red-striped candy canes. "Merry Christmas, David. Merry Christmas, Teresa." To Diane, she said, "Have a safe trip."

"Thanks." Diane smiled at her. "And thanks for the invitation." She looked down at Teresa and then untied the scarf that held her own hair and tied it around the little girl's head. "Button your sweater, David," she said as she picked up Teresa.

Ellen watched them cross the snow-covered ground toward the filling station. The door opened and two men came in. Marlene went to wait on them. Mister Rogers was outside now, sweeping snow off the steps. Ellen looked at the Christmas tree. When she looked back toward the window, the woman and her children had disappeared.

Ellen crossed to the window, leaned against the glass. She could barely make out the station attendant standing by the car. He was waving them toward the station and shaking his head. So he hadn't got all the chains on yet.

Ellen reached into her pocket. She knew she could count on at least three dollars more. Did she dare count on five? If she was sure, she could give them Lieutenant Haley's bill. She thought of the little girl standing in front of the tree. *Santa bring me a baby doll.* She took the five out of the envelope and went toward the tree.

She glanced around quickly to make sure no one was looking. Marlene had her back toward the tree, talking to the two men. Ellen took her stocking off the branch and went toward the counter. She would have to put her bonus in her purse. She would explain to Mister Rogers later. She reached into the stocking. There were five bills, like last year. Twenty-five dollars in all.

Ellen opened her purse, hesitated. *Will Santa Claus find us at Grandmama's house?* David's small thin face had been anxious as he asked the question. She shoved the bills back into the stocking and added the contents of her apron pocket.

She reached into her purse and took out nail scissors and a bottle of clear polish. Luckily, she'd planned to do her nails at lunch today. She snipped the white felt letters off the stocking. The door opened. Two couples came in.

Marlene looked around, caught her eye.

"Can you get it, Marlene?"

Marlene gave her a strange look, but she got the menus and went to the kitchen for glasses of water.

Ellen crossed to the window. It was so frosted she couldn't see the car for a minute and her heart beat furiously. Wiping a place with her hand, she could make it out now. Still empty, but the attendant was bending over a back tire. Hurriedly, she cut letters from the checked napkin. Something else she would have to explain to Mister Rogers.

She wasn't sure how to spell Teresa's name. She guessed it wouldn't matter. Teresa probably couldn't spell it either. She dabbed nail polish on the letters, stuck them unevenly on the red felt – D-A-V-I-D on one side, T-E-R-E-S-A on the other. *My mommy didn't have enough money.*

Ellen stuck her head in the kitchen. "Bertie, could you make me three ham sandwiches in a hurry? Please?"

"Okay, Ellen." Bertie's voice sounded puzzled. Ellen put cocoa and coffee in styrofoam cups and fastened the lids securely. She put them in a brown paper bag, laid the sandwiches on top. Passing the Christmas tree, she reached for a handful of candy canes and added them to the contents of the stocking. More explaining to do. Without stopping to get her coat, she ran out the front door, almost colliding with Mister Rogers.

"Be back in a minute, Mister Rogers," she called as she ran.

"What— Didn't that woman pay? Ellen...?" He stopped, stared after the running figure for a moment, then went inside and watched Ellen from the window.

Ellen was cutting it close again. The woman was already helping the children into the old green car.

"Wait a minute," Ellen called. "Please wait!"

CHAPTER FIVE

The woman turned to look.

Ellen waved the stocking. "Wait. See what Santa Claus left for David and Teresa." She arrived at the car then leaned in the open door so the children could hear her.

"I didn't know it was there. But Mister Rogers, he's my boss, said Santa Claus left it here with him. And told him to be on the lookout for a boy and girl with these names who should be coming by here. Gosh, I'm glad Mister Rogers came in before you left. I didn't know about the stocking and you almost missed Santa's message." Ellen stopped, breathless, and put the stocking in David's outstretched hands.

"Gee, it's got our names on it, Teresa. Look, here's your name on this side."

"Ooooh," was all the little girl said.

David reached inside and pulled out a handful of bills. "It's money, Mommy. Like the present Ellen got."

The woman gasped softly, then said in an uneven voice, "I guess Santa Claus knew it would be hard to travel with a baby doll and a race car set."

"Yes," Ellen added quickly, "he's left you the money so your mommy can go to the store and get just what you want when you get to your Grandmama's house."

"Wow..."

"And here are some sandwiches, so you won't have to stop for lunch." Ellen handed the sack to the woman. "Merry Christmas."

Tears spilled from the woman's dark-circled eyes. "Merry Christmas to you, Ellen. I won't ever forget this."

Ellen touched the little girl's cheek. "Bye, Teresa." She squeezed David's hand, which still clutched the red stocking. "Bye, David. Merry Christmas."

"Merry Christmas, Ellen," he answered. "We'll stop by and see you next time we're passing by."

"You do that." Ellen turned and ran back toward the restaurant. She heard the car start, but she didn't look back.

Mister Rogers held the door open for her. "Ellen, you'll catch pneumonia running around in this weather with no coat on." He brushed snow off her shoulders. "Come on back to the kitchen where it's warmer. What in the world were you doing out there?"

Ellen took a deep breath. She might as well explain now. So she told him about the woman and the little boy and girl. That part was easy. When she came to the part about the stocking, she hesitated. *What if Mister Rogers didn't understand?* Finally, she blurted out the words.

"I took my stocking off the tree, Mister Rogers. I just intended to put the five dollars in it – that Lieutenant Haley gave me – but I – left my Christmas bonus in it too. And I – cut up a napkin to make David's and Teresa's names to stick on it. I'm sorry about the bonus, Mister Rogers. And I do thank you just the same. I loved my Christmas stocking, but it wouldn't have seemed like Santa Claus left the money without the stocking—"

"Ellen," Mister Rogers patted her shoulder, "you don't have to be sorry about anything. That was a wonderful thing you did for those people. And I wish I could replace your bonus. But...well, Mrs. Rogers has had so much medical expense and, well, I just can't. You understand, don't you?"

"Of course, Mister Rogers. I wouldn't want you to. Then it would be you giving to David and Teresa instead of me." Ellen heard the door open and started for the front.

"Now you stay right here 'til your teeth stop chattering. I'll help Marlene out front."

Ellen sat down in the chair by the door where she could see the clock. Twelve-thirty. In three hours Bruce would be picking her up. He was getting laid off at Sears today.

The store had to cut back on part-time help after the holidays, and Bruce couldn't take a full schedule of classes at school and work full time too. She knew he would be depressed about that. He might even talk about quitting school. She'd counted on the typewriter to let him know he had her vote of confidence.

The typewriter. What had she done?

She could still buy it, but not before nearly the middle of next semester. And Bruce said he would have lots of papers in those spring classes.

"What are you crying for, Ellen? You ought to be happy about what you did."

"I am, Bertie." Ellen wiped a hand across her cheek. "It's just...I had saved enough to get Bruce a typewriter today...counting my bonus and tips...and now, I've spoiled all that."

"Oh, I see." Bertie remained silent a minute. "Well, I expect he will understand if you tell him what happened."

"Sure he will. And I will get it later on. But he needs the typewriter now. Why, he's practically flunking courses because of turning in papers that are handwritten. I could type them for him if he had a typewriter."

"I can see why you want it so bad. Maybe you shouldn't have given—"

"Oh, no. I'm glad I did that. You should have seen their little faces when I gave them the stocking." Ellen smiled, remembering.

CHAPTER SIX

The front door opened again. Ellen could see there was a large crowd. She went up front to help.

They were busy until after two. Then Ellen went to the kitchen to help Bertie clean up. At three, she took off her apron, folded it, and put it away. She stayed in the kitchen until Mister Rogers had given Bertie her stocking and she had gone home. Virginia was here now, preparing vegetables for the evening meal.

Ellen went out front and sat down at the table by the tree. Three-ten. She might as well work on her nails. She took out the bottle of polish and daubed half-heartedly at her long nails. Right now, she would be at Young's Discount paying for the typewriter if she hadn't... She would already have the wrapping paper and ribbon from Walgreen's, and she would wrap it here before...

Mister Rogers sat down at the table. "Getting all prettied up for Bruce?"

She nodded, blushed.

"Bertie told me about the typewriter."

"She shouldn't have done that," Ellen said in a low voice.

"I'm sorry, Ellen. I wish there was some way I could help you out on it. But I—"

"I don't expect you to help, Mister Rogers," Ellen said emphatically.

"But there is one thing," he went on. "I didn't know you could type. We have a big old typewriter at home. I've had to do all the monthly invoices myself since Mrs. Rogers got sick. It's quite a chore for me. Takes up time I need to be spending here. I could bring the typewriter down here if you would be willing to type those figures for me."

"I'd be glad to, Mister Rogers."

"I couldn't pay you any extra, Ellen. But you could do them when we're not very busy. And," he looked at her, "if you wanted to stay after hours, you would be welcome to use it for personal typing."

Ellen met his level gaze with a slow smile that lit up her whole face. "That would be enough pay, Mister Rogers. Thank you ever so much."

He stood up. "I'll have the machine here ready to go Monday morning. And if I don't see you when you go out, have a happy Christmas."

25

"I already have, Mister Rogers, thanks to you."

"Don't thank me, Ellen. You earned it."

By the time her nails were dry and she had her coat on, Bruce parked outside waiting for her. Ellen's heart beat faster as she walked toward the familiar blue Chevy.

Bruce reached across and opened the door. "Hey, beautiful, can I take you someplace?"

"Where are you going?" She played their familiar game.

"Wherever you say."

"How about my house? To a tree trimming?"

"Sounds great. Will we have enough time before six o'clock? Mom wants you to eat supper with us."

"That's nice." Ellen had hoped she would be asked. "We'll have plenty of time." She looked at Bruce's dark hair, his jaw set so determinedly, as he turned onto the highway. She knew he was thinking about the job he didn't have any more. For a moment, she wished she could give him the heavy box when they got to her house.

"Bruce, a woman came in the restaurant today with two little kids... alone... It reminded me of your mom and you and Kate, you know, the story you told me about how when your dad left you—" she stopped. Maybe she shouldn't have brought it up at all.

"Yeah." Bruce kept his eyes on the road. "It was just before Christmas. And we almost didn't have any Santa Claus that year. If the church hadn't—"

"This woman didn't have any church to help her. She was just passing through. On her way to East St. Louis." Ellen sighed. "I hope they make it."

Bruce stopped the car, opened the door. "Be careful. It's slick. The sidewalk is solid ice."

Inside, Ellen lighted the fireplace. "I thought we would pop some corn and string it for the tree."

"You better pop a little extra. I didn't have time to eat any lunch."

Ellen thought a minute. "Neither did I." She went toward the kitchen. "I'll fix us some Coke to go with it."

She changed into her red dress while Bruce finished the last string of popcorn.

"Hey, beautiful, where did you say you wanted to go?" Bruce gave her a long appreciative look.

"Wherever you take me," Ellen answered, and her words had a ring of truth to them.

Bruce kissed her then, holding the string of popcorn carefully behind her. "Hey, we had better get that on the tree before we break it."

She laughed softly as she disentangled herself. As they looped the string around the cedar branches, Ellen said, "Bruce, I don't have a present for you."

"That's okay, Ellen."

"I had the money all saved to buy you a really nice present... well, almost all saved, and then today...I gave some of it away."

Bruce looked at her and smiled. "You don't have to explain anything to me, Ellen."

"But I want to." Ellen went on, "It was the woman I told you about earlier. And the little boy and girl were so afraid Santa Claus wouldn't find them."

Bruce put his hands on her shoulders. "So you helped him, huh?"

She nodded.

"Well, I didn't buy you a present, either."

Ellen swallowed hard. She knew today was his last paycheck until he could find another job. And he had to help his mother and Kate. "But I do have something old I'd like to give you, if you want it. It belonged to my grandmother." He took the ring out of his pocket, opened her hand, and laid it in her palm. It was a wide gold band with little rubies set in intricate gold-carved flowers.

"Oh, Bruce. It's beautiful." Ellen turned the ring so that the stones glimmered in the firelight.

"Of course, I can't ask you to wear it on your hand right now. But if you would wear it on a chain around your neck until I can... Well, what I mean to say is that I want it to be your wedding band someday, if you'll marry me."

"Yes, Bruce. I'll be proud to wear your grandmother's ring. Around my neck or on my finger."

"We'll have to wait 'til I can finish school, Ellen. That will be at least two more years. Are you sure you want—"

"Oh, Bruce, it won't seem like very long."

"I don't have anything to offer you. A schoolteacher won't have much money."

"Are you trying to talk me out of saying yes?" Ellen frowned at him. "My mind is made up. Besides, we've already got this house."

"You have."

"Well, it needs a man around. To fix frozen water pipes. And keep the ice off the sidewalk."

"Then if the job's open, I'd like to apply, ma'am. I can furnish excellent references from the job I left today."

"No references needed. The job is yours."

This time Bruce wasn't holding a popcorn string when he kissed her.

Ellen closed her eyes and gave her full attention to the moment. She could tell him about the typewriter later.

There would be plenty of time.

ABOUT THE AUTHOR

Linda Swift divides her time between her native state of Kentucky and Florida. She is an award-winning author of published poetry, articles, short stories, and a TV play. Linda holds an Education Specialist Degree from Murray State University with post-graduate work from U. of Alabama and was a teacher, counselor, and psychometrist in the public schools in three states.

Linda's first two books were published by Kensington. She currently has seventeen E-books (also in print) six short stories, and three novellas (in anthologies) available at major online book retailers. Her Civil War novel, *This Time Forever*, has been adapted for a feature film titled *Clarissa's War* which will soon be available through Vimeo.

Visit her website at: http://www.lindaswift.net

Other Works by LINDA SWIFT

* * * Novels, Novellas & Poetry * * *

This Time Forever
Seasons of the Heart
A Season to Forgive
A Season of Love
A Season of Miracles
Maid of the Midlands
Mistress of Huntleigh Hall
Charlotte's Resurrection
Let Nothing You Dismay
The Twelve Days of Christmas
Take Five (Speculative Story Collection)
Full Circle
That Special Summer
Single Status
A Potpourri of Poems
Song of Every Season (Haiku)
Humanly Speaking

A Christmas Wedding

Celia Yeary

CHAPTER ONE

The arrival monitor showed all flights on time. From Denver to Austin: Flight 303, Gate 6, 12:30 pm.

Kailey Lovelace paced to the wide-expanse of glass and looked below at the departure counters. Travelers of every size and description rushed past each other, dragging luggage, pushing baby strollers, holding onto small children, making the scene vaguely resemble a horde of ants on the move. Apparently one-half the nation traveled by air to spend Christmas somewhere other than home.

She almost wished she had a flight booked, instead of waiting for an arrival.

Taking one more glance at the monitor, she strolled back to sit across from her brother and her boyfriend. Neither man looked at her. She was only good ol' Kailey, best sister in the world and so-so girlfriend. She laughed to herself with a little derision. They sure noticed some buxom, prissy young woman, though, if one happened to walk by. Neither halted his conversation but continued talking with his head swiveling until she was out of sight.

She snorted to herself. *Men.*

"Hey, Kailey," her brother Sam said. "Here's an empty seat by me now. Come over here."

Hoisting her dark blue leather bag on her shoulder, she moved to the empty chair, sat, scrunched down, and crossed her arms as well as her long legs covered in black leggings. Her boyfriend, Martin, on the other side of Sam, gazed away studying other passengers. It seemed to her he was always scouting out the females, but with him, she never knew for sure what he was doing or thinking.

Maybe, if she looked as good as those cuties prancing by, he'd look at her that way. Why did he go out with her, anyway? Why did *she* bother with him?

Sighing, she turned to her brother. "Tell me again, Sam, how tall is he?"

He shrugged. "I dunno. Tall. Like you."

She flinched. "As tall? Or taller? Oh, please don't tell me 'not as tall.'"

"Stop worrying, sis, he's a good guy. Just have a good time." Shelley met him once, and since he's to be my best man and you're the maid of honor, she told me you two would make the perfect pair."

"Yeah, I bet. When he learns his partner is a giraffe, he might back out."

"Ahh, don't be so hard on yourself. Martin likes you." He jabbed Martin with his elbow. "Don't you, buddy?"

Martin turned to look at both of them, his face bland, and his eyes blinking. "What? Did I miss something?"

Kailey wanted to hit him over the head with her bag. At least he possessed good looks, he had brains, and he was *almost* as tall as she was. And he was nice to her. When he noticed her.

Sam jumped to his feet. "There he is! He's headed for the luggage area. Let's go."

The three scrambled to their feet and pushed through the mass of people, rode down an escalator, turned a corner, and entered the huge cavernous space filled with people and a high noise level. Sam led the way with Martin hot on his heels. Kailey trailed behind, knowing she wouldn't lose them, really hoping to see this Alex Dunn before he saw her.

Please, Wedding Angel, let Alex like me enough to smile as we walk down the aisle. That's my only wish.

Since Martin didn't know Alex Dunn either, he hung back, too.

Kailey reached up with both hands and tried to smooth her frizzy blond hair. Why did the Hair Gods curse a female with thick locks that did not obey one rule of beautiful hair? Hers hung well past her shoulders, and in cold weather, it crackled with electricity that made it bush out even more. Today, she'd parted it in the middle, brushed it back, and secured the mass with a silver clasp at her nape. Just to get it away from her face turned into a battle.

Once, years ago, she had it cut short. Oh, man, what a disaster. An Anglo with a blond Afro. Not a pretty sight. She hadn't cut it since, except to trim split ends.

Since the weather had turned colder, a lightweight quilted jacket worked over the leggings and long pullover fleece top. She loved the flat-heeled brown leather boots that hugged her calves, even though she had stupidly purchased a pair of dressy high-heeled boots at the same time. When she felt particularly snarky and obstinate, she'd wear them out to a party or bar. But it was an effort to act hateful, since the attitude didn't feel right. Besides, it sometimes repelled creeps, but then sometimes, it attracted them. Go figure.

The multicolored scarf wrapped around her neck with the ends trailing in front created enough warmth for Texas weather in December. Now, she wished she hadn't worn her red coat. It made her even more conspicuous, and *that* she did not need. Sam had rushed her, though, and she grabbed the first thing she found.

She heard her brother call out over the din. "Hey, Alex! Alex Dunn!"

A young man – quite *tall* – stood next to a rotating luggage carousel, watching the baggage tumble by. He lifted his head, grinned and waved. Then, he jerked his gaze back to the carousel and began moving down the line very quickly. He stepped between two people, and with one long arm reached in and grabbed a U. S. Army duffel bag, lifting it over everyone's head.

"Sorry, ma'am, sir. I hope I didn't step on anyone."

Kailey watched the older couple look into his face and smile glowingly as if he had done them a favor.

And why not? He was gorgeous, with his short military haircut, square chin, and wide mouth with fabulous white teeth. When he walked toward her brother, she couldn't keep her gaze off his George Clooney eyes, except Alex's were blue. Her knees felt a little weak, a completely foreign feeling.

For some unknown reason, Martin had moved back to her and reached for her hand, holding it rather tightly. He never held her hand in public. He also remained even quieter than usual. Oh, yeah, he did this when he felt a little insecure.

They watched in silence as Sam rushed toward Alex and thrust out his hand. Alex kept grinning, shook his hand, and returned the hug when Sam threw his arm around his shoulders.

"Come on over here and meet my little sister," she heard Sam say, with emphasis on "little." She would definitely kill him when they got home. Would he ever stop doing that?

Then Sam laughed. Alex did not, though, but glanced at her with interest, it seemed, because he did not look away.

They made eye contact and Kailey felt, yes, she was certain, a current ran from his electric blue eyes to her ordinary brown ones. Alex walked close and held out his hand to her. She had to pull hers away from Martin's so she could return the gesture.

"How do you do, Alex?" Kailey tried to keep her tone even and pleasant as though she had just met a stranger at a boring reception. His large hand enveloped hers, and he held it very

31

gently, as though he protected a baby chick. Seconds ticked by before he let go. By then she'd almost stopped breathing.

Alex's deep, soft voice said, "Good, thanks. Kailey is it?"

"That's right."

Alex smiled ever so slightly, making one dimple appear near his mouth on the right side. He *would* have to have a dimple.

He said, "That's a pretty name. I like it. So, we're to be best man and maid of honor, are we? How about that?"

"Yes, how about that?" What else was there to say? Funny, he only looked at her eyes and mouth. Not once had he glanced at the top of her head, or her feet, or her frizzy hair. She supposed he was too polite to make a point of checking out her height or her stupid hair.

"So..."

"Well..."

Kailey laughed and so did Alex. "Now that we broke the ice, do you have all your luggage?"

Alex lifted his one bag slightly. "This is it."

Her brother interrupted. "Alex, meet Martin Sanders." Martin and Alex nodded to each other, neither seemingly very interested in the introduction. "Okay, guys, let's get out of here. Alex, we parked on the upper level. Follow me."

Alex nodded and turned to Kailey. "After you."

Since her boyfriend had ignored her and walked along with Sam, she sidestepped a little so Alex would walk beside her. As they moved along, dodging other passengers, he kept an even pace with her. Seems he intended to stay right beside her, which was perfectly fine.

"You know you'll be staying at our house, don't you? We have a nice guest room with its own bath, so I think you'll be very comfortable." She moved to the right to allow a mother pushing a stroller with a screaming child to pass. "Mom and Dad are terrific people, even if they are my parents. My only warning is that Mom will stuff you with food. Feel free to cry 'uncle' when she presses you to eat one more piece of pie."

He chuckled. "Sounds familiar. So, you live there with your parents?"

The question always made her feel like a child or an adult who wouldn't leave the nest, so she gave her standard reply. "Only temporarily. I owned a condo, had it furnished just as I wanted, everything so perfect. Then the entire complex burned to the ground four months ago. I've searched for a new place ever since, but the realtor can't find what I want."

An enormous man barreled down on them, and he didn't seem to want to detour. Alex took hold of her upper arm to pull her closer to his side. The contact made her catch her breath, the possessive way he held on, and didn't let go for another few steps.

"Thanks. I didn't even see him. I think you saved me from being bulldozed."

He did that little chuckle thing, and chills ran along her neck. *Oh, man.*

Alex glanced at her. "I think we should hurry. Sam and his friend are leaving us behind."

Without thinking, she said, "That's my boyfriend."

"Oh."

Just "oh," like Alex accepted the fact and that was that. They continued on to the escalators and rode up one flight.

"Down this way, Alex. The guys have disappeared, but I know where we parked."

Without further conversation, they walked briskly toward their parking level. When they arrived at the SUV, Sam said, "Alex, ride up front with me, buddy."

That, of course, left her to sit in back with Martin.

The heavy traffic caused slow going away from the airport, but once they reached the interstate, Sam kicked up the speed until he exited on the highway that led west out to the wooded housing area in the hills.

Kailey and Martin had nothing to say to each other, much like their usual meetings. He wasn't a big talker anyway, more of an observer, so she knew he was deep in thought about something. Martin owned a big furniture chain in Central Texas and his business catered to the high-end consumers. He socialized quite a bit, from posh cocktail parties or lavish barbecues on the lake to club hopping on Sixth Street, but he never seemed comfortable. Martin liked to think of himself as a renaissance man, but when she pressed him on the definition, he always failed to make her understand.

Kailey had nothing bad to say about him, except maybe, he wasn't a warm person. Nice, yes, and very generous, but something sorely lacked in their relationship. Like good sex, for example.

She still wondered about her brother's friendship with him, as they were so different. As far as she could understand, they only shared a love of football and tennis. The men entered as many doubles tennis matches as they could, and often brought home the trophy.

Once during the drive, Alex looked over his left shoulder and glanced at her sitting behind Sam. The eye contact lasted two seconds, max, and he resumed his position and conversation with her brother. But that fleeting moment caused a flutter in her heart, something that had never happened. One look? How does that work?

The thirty-five minute drive finally ended as Sam pulled through the curved driveway and stopped at the front door. Before any of them could step out, the wide double front doors opened and her parents walked out.

Sam jogged around to the back of the SUV and retrieved Alex's bag. Carrying it for him, he said, "Come meet Mom and Dad."

On the wide porch, Sam made all the introductions.

"Mom, Dad, meet Alex Dunn, best Army buddy a guy could ask for. Alex, my dad, Robert, and my mom, Elaine."

Everyone greeted and shook hands and smiled.

Kailey's father, ever the perfect host, spoke to Alex. "I can't believe we never met you during Sam's stint in the Army, but we're real happy you're here now. All he could talk about was his good friend, Alex. You two had quite a difficult time in the Middle East, I hear. We prayed every day and then thanked God both of you escaped harm."

"Thank you, sir. My parents said the same thing."

"Are you completely free, now, son?"

"Yes, sir. All I need to do now is buy a few more civilian clothes. These I have on are a little loose in places, and a little snug in others. But I didn't want to wear the uniform anymore."

Robert laughed. "Well, you'll have the services of a master shopper. Our Kailey, here, can show you every store in the city." He turned to Kailey and smiled. "Won't you, honey?"

Kailey tolerated every single remark her dad made, because she loved him so much. How could such a good-hearted and generous man ever irritate her? But volunteering her to help Alex shop? That was a little off sides but she replied, "Sure, Dad, whatever Alex needs, we'll be glad to help."

Inside, Alex gazed around at their beautiful, perfectly decorated spacious living area. Kailey stood silent, watching him study the wall of two-story windows overlooking vast wooded housing areas with the Austin skyline in the far distance, hazy now from the humidity in the air.

He turned to her parents. "That's as beautiful a sight as I've ever seen. I thought Texas was supposed to be dry and barren."

Everyone laughed. Kailey's mother excused herself to check the upstairs guest room, probably for the tenth time today, and her dad instructed Sam to carry Alex's bag and jacket up. Martin walked to the windows and gazed out, lost in his own thoughts, as usual. Robert excused himself and walked upstairs, too.

Kailey usually wasn't at such a loss for words, but she simply couldn't find a topic. She pulled off her jacket and laid it across the back of a small sofa.

Alex walked closer to her and smiled. He nodded toward the Christmas tree.

"That's the biggest decorated tree I've ever seen."

The enormous tree dominated a corner near the massive white rock fireplace. "Mom hires a designer to decorate it, and the rest of the room, entry hall, and front door." Greenery and dozens of red candles of varying heights filled the mantle. In fact, some kind of Christmas decoration covered every available space.

She felt uncomfortable with Martin hanging around, quietly

looking out, not participating at all. Was he angry? Jealous? Uh, no, not jealous. One thing Martin had never displayed was jealousy.

"Martin, didn't Mom buy all this furniture from your downtown store?" She glanced at Alex briefly, trying to get him to include her boyfriend. But that wasn't his job – it was hers.

Martin turned from the window with a gentle smile. "She did, and my best designer could hardly keep up with her. She knew more about furnishings and decorating than he did."

"So, you sell furniture?" Alex asked.

"Not exactly just sell. We're a contract establishment. A client meets with one of my representatives, and together they discuss and design a room. We have our clients sign a contract, one that holds *us* accountable. The customer is always right, and we want him to know that by signing with us."

Alex's face remained passive. "Hmm, I never knew."

"Few people do, unless one is in the business or he has a home or business he needs decorated and furnished with just the right touch. Fortunately, Austin provides plenty of clients for us."

The conversation made Kailey uncomfortable. She thought Martin sounded pretentious, lording his position in the community over Alex. Maybe he felt compelled to make a showing for himself, since Alex had such a commanding presence with his height and good looks.

Martin looked at his watch. "Listen, Kailey, I really must run. I still have work to do this afternoon and an engagement tonight with clients. Do you mind?"

Shaking her head, she walked near him. "No, of course, we don't mind, but we thought you were staying for dinner. Mom included you."

"Please explain to her for me."

When Martin left, Kailey closed the front door and walked back to the living area. Alex stood alone, gazing out the windows again. From the back, she studied his physique. Broad shoulders, long straight back, trim waist and long legs. He'd shoved his hands in the front pockets of his corduroy slacks that fit his backside snugly and enticingly. The military must do a great job keeping their men in shape, because Alex...*Okay, Kailey. Enough.*

Alex turned, stood very still, and looked at her across the room. No smile, nothing, just a steady gaze right into her eyes. Waiting.

Taking a deep inaudible breath, she skirted the long sofa and approached him. Keeping a little distance between them, she asked, "May I get you a drink?"

He didn't answer right away, but just kept his gaze on her face. With pleasant clarity, she realized she was looking *up* into his face. She had noticed that right away, of course, but standing this close made it all the more enjoyable. She might even decide to wear heels like the five bridesmaids would.

Few people understood how excruciating it was at times to be a six-foot tall female, taller even than her brother. Everyone expected her to play basketball, and if Alex asked her that, she'd erase every good thought about him she'd had so far.

But he didn't.

"Yes, I'd love something cold to drink. Please."

His deep rich voice made her blink. "Follow me. We'll find something in the fridge."

Kailey thought he might feel a little let down. She knew the feeling, coming and going when she attended college in Oregon. Excitement about a break, flying home, her parents rushing to greet her, coming home, and then...always a letdown when the adrenalin faded away. A little depression always swooped down on her, until she got a good night's rest and the sun came up. Then she was always ready to party.

"How about a beer?" She opened one side of the huge refrigerator and raised her eyebrows.

He grinned. "Will you have one with me? I don't like to drink alone."

She hooked her fingers around two longnecks, popped off the tops, and offered him one. Holding hers up, she said, "Welcome to Texas, Alex Dunn."

He touched his bottle to hers with a *clink*, then tipped his head back and swallowed half the contents with his eyes closed. "Ahhh, heaven. Thanks."

The sound made her laugh lightly. "I thought so," she said with a nod.

"What?"

"You're tense and a little depressed. Don't you always hate the first hour or two when you arrive in a new place, not settled, not knowing what to do or how to act? I did. When it was time to return to school, I'd be so excited to go I'd be high as a kite. Then when I arrived at my room, and it was cold and dark, I always plopped on my narrow bed and cried. I missed home and wished I could go back."

Alex gazed at her and nodded. "You hit the nail on the head. Going and coming from the Middle East caused excruciating mood swings, too. Men who looked forward to seeing their wives and families very soon fell into depression for some time. It's very difficult to explain."

"But I understand."

He leaned back on a counter and she leaned back on one opposite. They sipped their beers, studied one another but said very little.

Finally, he spoke. "You know? I worried about coming down here. Sam asked me to be his best man, and I had met Shelley once, so I thought, yeah, why not? It made me happy for him to ask. Then I began to worry and wonder where I was going and how his family would look upon a stranger, someone only their son had talked about, but they had not met."

Kailey took a sip from her bottle, lowered it and wiped the moisture off the side with one thumb, making little circles. "If it's any consolation, my parents would welcome anyone we brought home, as long as the person was our friend. They're very gregarious and social. Dad's in the financial business and his middle name is 'never met a stranger.' Mom is a social butterfly who tends to everyone's wounds and heartaches. She's a people magnet and intends everyone to be happy."

Alex smiled. "When you speak of them, love shines in your eyes."

The unexpected statement startled her, making her heart skip a beat, and a lump form in her throat. She never expected an observation like that from him.

Curling stray frizzies around one ear, she shifted a little and cleared her throat. "They're easy to love."

Both turned silent a few moments. She didn't know where to look, how to act, what to do next. His words had completely knocked her back. *Love shines in your eyes.* No man she'd ever dated said a word about her eyes. In fact, she never received compliments from males except her dad. He thought she was beautiful...but he loved her.

Alex finally spoke. "Frankly, I worried about meeting you. I'm a pretty big guy, and I could just see me paired with a petite thing who didn't come to my armpit. That's a very uncomfortable feeling, in addition to throwing a wedding photo off kilter."

She laughed. Sam interrupted them, and Kailey glanced at Alex with a wan smile.

"Hey, guys. Sorry about leaving you. Had to call Shell and she had a million things to tell me. My head's spinning. See you found the beer." He opened the fridge and grabbed one for himself. He held one up to Alex. "Another? Long time 'til dinner."

"Sure, thanks."

Their parents walked in, too. Her mother immediately moved into hostess mode.

"Y'all go sit in the sunroom. I'll bring out snacks and hors d'oeuvres. Go on now, and enjoy yourselves. Robert and I will bring everything out. Robert, turn on those Christmas lights out there."

"In case you're wondering, Mom decorates every room for Christmas," Sam said as he slumped down in a heavy brown cushioned wicker armchair and propped his feet on the matching ottoman. "That's why we have a tree out here and baubles on the palms and ferns. Have a seat, Alex."

"Looks nice. I think I'll stand a while longer, though, to get the kinks out of my legs."

Elaine entered the room carrying a large tray and Robert followed with another. "Here we are. Just help yourselves. There're the napkins. Now. More beer, anyone?"

CHAPTER TWO

Upstairs in her bedroom, Kailey began removing her boots and fleece top. The clothes were too warm for the house, especially with the fireplace going.

She could imagine Alex unpacking in his room and possibly freshening up before he and Sam talked privately. Oh, how she'd love to listen. But her brother hadn't invited her.

She found a lightweight pullover knit that came to mid-thigh. The ribbon had come loose, making her hair balloon out. When she pulled the top on, she began running her fingers through the mass of hair, trying to untangle it enough to do something else with it. She had few choices, though.

Someone tapped lightly on her door. Walking barefoot, she opened it and there stood Alex dressed in worn sweat pants, a sweatshirt and Nikes, tapping a baseball cap on his thigh.

"You, too, huh?" she said. "Those clothes were burning me up. Do you need something?"

"Well...I...Sam said to tell you he had to go to his place for a couple of hours. He said Shelley would meet him there, and they'd be back in time for dinner at seven. Said they had business to discuss."

She snorted. "Uh-huh. And he just abandoned his guest. I'll have to scold him for that."

Alex laughed. "Nah, don't do that. I only wanted to tell someone I'm going for a walk. I need some air. Do you think this is enough? Just this sweatshirt? Doesn't seem very cold here."

Laughing, she told him, "You're used to Colorado weather. Yes, that's plenty, especially if you're going walking."

"Uh...would you care to go with me?"

A happy little song played in her head.

"Of course, I would love to. I need to get out, too. Give me five minutes? I'll meet you in the foyer."

Alex had waited as he said, watching the stairs when she began the descent. He stood so still and watched every step she took. Their gazes locked, and she vaguely hoped she didn't miss a step, but she wouldn't look away unless the roof caved in. My lands, those eyes. They pierced right into her...heart. And that probably was a very foolish thing.

Before she stepped off the last one, he was there with his hand held out. Automatically, she laid hers on his palm and he curled his fingers around her entire hand, squeezing slightly. Why did he do that?

"Ready?" He spoke casually as he released her hand.

"Yes. I told Mom so she'd know where we were. She has work to do in her office, so she'll be occupied a couple of hours. Dad's watching a sports channel."

Side-by-side, they jogged down the long set of steps to the driveway. Kailey turned to the left, and without thinking began to jog. He fell into step beside her without speaking. Following the driveway down, they took a quick look both ways and moved onto the paved street lined with trees, interrupted now and then by a driveway.

On they ran, slowly, but in perfect rhythm and cadence. Kailey barely heard Alex breathe, telling her he was in excellent physical shape. She, too, breathed deeply in and out with hardly a whisper. On a downhill stretch, they naturally picked up speed, and around a long curve, they slowed, listening for approaching cars.

After fifteen minutes, they'd moved uphill more than downhill. She gestured to the right. He turned with her. Soon, they stood at the edge of a high bluff overlooking the city and far into the distance. The Colorado River meandered through the vegetation, and a high wide bridge spanned the water, creating a sight worthy of a painting.

Silently, Kailey stood close to Alex while their breathing slowed and they caught their breaths.

Alex whistled low. "What a sight. I'm amazed there're so many trees, and so thick. Looks like an ocean of forest."

"It's nice, isn't it? One of Austin's treasures. Let's sit over there on the stone bench."

He said, "I bet this is really something at night."

"Oh, it is. The skyline is beautiful, and Zilker Park will show up because of the Trail of Lights and the towering Christmas tree made of strings of lights. A popular thing is to stand in the middle of the open structure, look up, hold your arms out and spin around. It's been a fixture so long I did it as a child."

He turned to smile at her. "Sounds fun for families."

And for lovers to kiss...

Bringing her thoughts back where they belonged, she answered, "Yeah. What are your parents doing for Christmas? Will you go home after the wedding?"

Leaning his elbows on his thighs, he looked into the distance. "Uh-huh. They're in Europe right now. Mom's always wanted to go on one of those long tours of villages that really put on a show at Christmastime. She was torn between going and staying home for me, but I've already spent two weeks with them. I urged them to go ahead."

"You'll go back, then."

He turned his head toward her. "Sure. Denver is home. Besides,

I don't want to let any snow go to waste. I have a lot of skiing to catch up on."

"I've never skied. The chance was there more than once, but I didn't take advantage. It looks like great fun."

"It is, and many people become addicted to it."

She laughed lightly. "Athletics can do that to a person."

Kailey stood, raised her arms in the air, clasped her hands and twisted side to side. Lowering her arms, she said, "I'm stiffening up sitting here. Ready to go back?"

Alex stood, took her arm and turned her toward him. He didn't let go, and she breathlessly waited to see what he would do. Gazing up at him, a warm sensation flowed through her body, almost making her sway from the strange intense feeling. Did he intend to kiss her?

"Kailey...I'm real glad I told Sam I'd be his best man. And now..." He stopped, dropped his hand, and chuckled low in his throat. "Well, what I'm trying to say here is you will make the perfect maid of honor."

She could not move, except to smile up at him. "You know what makes me happy, Alex?"

Grinning, he asked, "What?"

"Now I can wear high heels like the other bridesmaids. I won't be doomed to wearing flats with my dress so I won't be taller than my partner." Trying to break the tension, she comically wiped her brow and said, "Whew!"

They laughed.

CHAPTER THREE

Early the next morning, someone knocked loudly on Kailey's door. Rolling to a sitting position, she pushed herself off the edge of the bed and padded barefoot to open it. Of course, her mother stood there, all dressed up in a nice silk suit and heels, her hair styled to the nth degree, complete make-up, and smiling as prettily as a Miss America.

She did not apologize for waking Kailey.

"Good morning, sweetheart. I wanted to remind you this is bridesmaid dresses day. You remember?"

Kailey swiped her hand down her face and yawned. "Sure, Mom, I remember. Is Alex up?"

"I'm sure I don't know, but someone had made the coffee when I got to the kitchen, so somebody got there first and had the decency to make a pot. It certainly wasn't your dad. He hasn't learned to make coffee in thirty years."

She laughed. "Mom. He doesn't *want* to learn how to make coffee. That's why he married you."

Elaine shook her head, smiled, and flapped her hand. "Yes, of course, I know that. Anyway, I don't know where our guest is. There's plenty for breakfast if you look around. Mika's coming this afternoon to make dinner for us. Sam and Shelley should be here, as well, although I can never seem to count on them lately."

Again Kailey laughed. Sometimes her mom could be as dense as the dumbest blond. Or she just wanted to pretend she didn't know they were off somewhere—Sam's place or Shelley's – indulging in some premarital fun and games.

"Okay, Mom, all's well, so you're free to go...where?"

"To visit with Shelley's mother. About the dresses. And sweetheart?"

Uh-oh, here it comes. "What?"

"Have you made an appointment with a hairdresser to see what she suggests for the wedding?"

That was her mother's way of saying Kailey's hair was too long, too out of control, too...everything. "Yes, Mom, now go. I need to run through the shower. See you downtown at two with the rest of the group."

To keep her mother from having a silent coronary, she'd made an appointment a week before with the best, most popular young hair stylist in Austin – Mario. His salon was located downtown on

Congress Avenue, among the highly expensive real estate. What had she done? She'd have to sign over her life savings not to mention her firstborn to pay for an appointment with him.

Kailey had walked into his salon, hoping to speak directly with him before she made the appointment. He was working on a client's hair. When he turned to see her standing next to him, he dropped his scissors, grabbed his throat with one hand, and stretched the other toward her.

"Oh...my....*gawd*. My *Waterloo* stands before me. Peaches, I will never...and I mean *never* be able to fix...that. Don't tell me...you made an appointment."

She'd laughed out loud at his outrageous acting, and she loved him right away. "If you can't meet the challenge, Mario, I'll just go to Quik Clips. They'll do something with my hair."

Mario had reached out and grabbed her arm. "Lovie, you'll do no such thing. That would put me right into my grave. Go make your appointment—anytime you wish. I'm all yours."

She'd made it for Tuesday, since Shelley had reserved today, Monday, for the bridesmaids' dresses.

Shelley should have done this weeks ago, but she was a blithe spirit with no sense of urgency about anything. She and Sam allowed their mothers to plan the wedding, while she happily agreed with just about everything. The cake? A five-tier white Italian cream with classic white roses cascading down the tiers. The reception? In the State Room of the Bonner Hotel downtown on the river. The band, the food, the drinks? Anything her mother and future mother-in-law chose would be just fine. She acted almost like a child at Christmas, oohing and aahing over each decision as if they'd given her a gift.

Deep down, Kailey harbored a little fear about her brother marrying such a free-spirited girl. However, Shelley had earned a degree in accounting, so she did have brains.

Looking at the time, Kailey pulled on a pair of slim jeans, her tan cowboy boots over her socks, grabbed a black long-sleeved knit pullover and forced her head and hair through the crew neck, and looked in the mirror. "Ugh."

She gathered the mass of hair at her nape and struggled to secure it in one place with a scrunchy. Wetting her hands under the faucet, she ran them over her hair from top to back, temporarily smoothing the crinkles and crackles.

In a drawer, she dug around for a long, thin multi-colored scarf to wrap around her neck. Big silver hoops through her pierced ears worked, and she was ready for breakfast with their guest. If she could find him.

Jogging down the stairs, she turned at the bottom toward the kitchen where they'd had the first beer yesterday. Had it only been less than twenty-four hours ago? No sign of Alex. She grabbed a mug of coffee and strolled to the French doors that opened onto the enormous spreading patio. Outside, she wandered in and among the deep green Mountain Laurel trees, large oaks, shrubs of every sort, and meticulously tended flowerbeds, now filled with winter ground cover.

Away from the house, flagstone walkways meandered one direction and another. She took the one on the right and continued walking slowly, enjoying the brisk sunny morning air, sipping her coffee. There among the vegetation, Alex lay on a carved bench with his knees propped up.

"Hey," she called softly.

Alex turned his head and grinned at her. He swiveled to a sitting position, scooted over, and patted the place beside him.

"Did I interrupt your meditation?"

"Meditation?" He chuckled. "No, just enjoying the quiet. A wonderful sound, the quietness of a little park-like space."

"Well said. So, tell me, Alex Dunn, why do you seek a quiet place?" She placed her empty cup on the walk while she waited for his answer.

Leaning back, he tilted his head and gazed through the openings of the trees at the bright blue winter sky. "Hmmm, well, that's not a difficult question, but it's not easy to explain either. The war, I guess."

"Too much noise?"

"Sometimes. Even when it turned quiet, you could hear it in your head, or just anticipating the blasts and explosions made you think you heard it."

Since he turned silent and looked away, she sat quietly and still, waiting for him to make the next move.

"Kailey? I don't want to throw a pall over this wedding party and all the fun and excitement that goes with it. That's all I'll say on the subject, because truthfully... I just want to forget all of it."

"I understand." She sat for a moment, and then said, "But may I ask one thing?"

He turned to her with that smile, the one with the dimple on the right side of his mouth. The one she'd love to....

"Sure. Ask away."

She took a deep breath as she looked into his face. "Did you suffer any injuries? Do you have PTSD? Is that the right term?"

Surprisingly, he lifted his left arm, curved it around her shoulder and pulled her close. "Thanks for asking. People don't want to say anything. I can't blame them. Really, they don't know what to say or not to say."

Staying very still to enjoy the warmth of his arm, she asked, "So? Will you answer my question?"

"Yeah." He gave her a quick hug and lowered his arm. "I was not wounded. I do not have a stress disorder. Lots of guys do, though, and it's tough. I had something different to deal with."

Kailey was almost afraid to ask. What else could there be?

"What's that?"

"I was a medic."

The statement startled her. She turned on the bench and bent one leg so she could face him. He shifted, laid his arm on the back of the bench, and smiled.

"A medic? Are you a doctor?"

"Yep. I'd just begun working in a hospital on the staff, but joining up seemed the right thing to do. I knew I could contribute by maybe saving lives."

There's more to this man than she'd first thought. Now, he took on a new persona, a cloak of professionalism and humanitarianism.

"How did you know my brother, then? He was in combat."

"Wasn't he a helicopter pilot?"

She nodded. "Oh, he transported wounded soldiers, yes, he did. I knew that very well. Guess I didn't make the connection. I thought he took the wounded to a ship or plane so they could go home."

"No, to a field hospital in dangerous territory. Your brother should receive a medal for his bravery. He is one tough guy, let me assure you of that. All those pilots were, and they saved a lot of men."

Kailey placed her hand on his shoulder. "And you and the other medics did, too."

When she lowered her hand, he looked away for a few seconds.

"Not all. Not enough."

"And that haunts you, doesn't it?"

Alex moved his arm from the bench back and curled his hand around her neck. He leaned close, and...stopped.

He chuckled very low and shook his head. "That was a near miss, Kailey Lovelace. I nearly kissed you."

She, with her hideous hair, thin nose, full lips, and eyes too big for her face had stopped breathing. Every inch of her six-foot body ached and prickled from wanting that kiss. *Yes, Alex Dunn, I suppose that was a near miss.*

She flipped one side of her hair, raised her chin, and said, "Wow. I thought I was a goner for sure."

Alex threw back his head and laughed with her. When he stopped, he gazed at her, taking in all her features. He opened his mouth a couple of times to speak but didn't. Finally, he took a deep breath. "What about Sam? He seems all right. Is he?"

Glad to change the subject, Kailey thought for a minute. "I suppose. We never saw any difference in him. Do you think he's in denial?"

"No, I don't. I think he's okay."

"I hope so, but he's the kind who laughs everything away. You know, always the happy-go-lucky one in the crowd. Knows and loves everybody. He might also be the sort to hide his real feelings."

"But he also might be the kind who really can move on." Changing the subject, he asked, "So, what're you doing today?"

She grimaced, making him laugh. "Bridesmaid's dress. Oh, how I dread it."

He held up one hand. "I cannot identify. Sorry."

"Well, don't get too comfortable. Your turn is coming tomorrow."

He jerked his head toward her. "What do you mean?"

"Tuxedos, buddy boy."

With that, she stood and laughed at the expression on his face. "Let's find some breakfast and more coffee. What do you say?"

"Terrific."

Side-by-side they strolled back to the house, she in her boots and he in his Nikes.

After they'd eaten omelets and jalapeño tortillas with melted cheese inside, Kailey asked what he would like to do. "I have about four hours before the appointment downtown to find my dress. So, how can I help you?"

"You tell me," he said with his eyes twinkling and that dimple winking at her.

Oh, she needed to be careful around the man. He was just too good, too...everything.

"Okay. How about shopping in the mall? The big one? You said you needed clothes. I can shop for hours on end, but given we have four hours, a couple will give us time to find everything you need."

He grinned. "Let's go shopping."

In two hours, Alex carried three shopping bags. He'd found jeans, tees, sweaters, a couple of jackets, and a few dress clothes.

"Let's have lunch, Kailey. I'm starved."

They chose the upper level Food Court, loaded their trays, and found a table for two by the railing, away from the crowd. Alex began talking.

"I can't say shopping is fun, but you made it enjoyable. Thanks again. Want a piece of my pizza?"

"I'll trade for one of my tacos. How's that?"

"Great."

After he'd devoured most of his food, he wiped his mouth and asked, "I didn't ask what kind of work you do."

Kailey sipped her Coke before answering. "You're not going to believe this, but I'm a nurse."

Her statement made him sit back and study her, and a slow grin spread across his face. "I knew we were fated. To be friends."

Pushing her tray back, she wiped her fingers, sipped the drink again, and nodded. "Seems so, doesn't it? To be friends."

"What kind of nurse? Floor nurse? Specialized?"

"Pediatric. I work in the new children's hospital that just opened a couple of years ago."

"Kids, huh? Now, that has to be tough."

She shrugged. "Sometimes. Most of the time it's a joy, to see a little one who was sick or hurt get well, and go home with his family. That's the rewarding part, especially when the entire family hovers around the child – parents, siblings, grandparents, uncle and aunts. Some don't make it, and though I try not to cry over every one, I haven't learned that trick yet."

Twirling his cup for a few moments, he finally said in a soft voice, "I wouldn't have thought anything else about you. I knew you'd cry over the lost ones. Kailey, you're a special woman, with a lot to offer...the world."

Well, he didn't say beautiful, but special would do...coming from him.

Leaning forward with his arms crossed on the table, he said, "May I confide in you?"

Why did such a simple statement thrill her? Telling something in confidence seemed intimate, like a gift.

"Yes, Alex, I'd love that. I can keep a secret."

"I know. Want to know what I'm planning on doing?"

"I can't wait to find out."

Alex smiled a little sheepishly, unfolded his arms, and reached across the table with one palm up. He didn't say anything, but she knew he wanted her to place her hand there. How could she resist? When she did, he slowly curled his fingers around hers, gazing in almost a seductive manner, at least it seemed that way to her. This simple act threw her heart out of whack and it beat too hard against her chest.

"I'm researching one of the international doctors' organizations. They cross borders with their medical teams to set up temporary hospitals in places where the citizens simply cannot get any kind of help. What do you think?"

Tears flooded her eyes and she couldn't speak for a moment. "That's absolutely wonderful, Alex. Do you know the details?"

He squeezed her hand before letting go and sitting back. "I'm glad I told you. We already have a connection, you know. Our medical careers. But I don't have details yet. I'll have to decide how much time to commit to the organization – two weeks, two months, or one or two years. There are many choices and details."

Wiping the corners of her eyes, she said, "Oh, I envy you. I'd love to do that, leave home for a while, do something worthwhile while I'm young and unattached."

"You can." He leaned forward again and clasped his hands on the table. "But it would be the most difficult thing in the world you'd ever do. I know a little about it from working as an Army medic. It's grueling and horrid much of the time. But down deep, I love it and thank God he gave me the opportunity to help."

Kailey wanted to sit here and talk the afternoon away, but she had to select her stupid bridesmaid's dress. "You know? I have to go. I cannot miss that bridesmaids' meeting at the shop. It's downtown and I have to go home and grab shoes and...I don't know what else. Can we talk about this later? I have a lot of questions."

Alex stood and came to her side of the table. He pulled out her chair and when she stood, he did not back up. He leaned close. "You better believe it."

CHAPTER FOUR

Driving home from the bridal shop, all Kailey could think about was Alex. The session at the shop had been hilarious, bringing the entire group of bridesmaids closer. She even liked her dress. Bless Shelley for allowing her to have the one she wanted. Now, though, she wanted to be with him.

Dinner would be at seven, and everyone should be present. By the time she drove up the driveway, it was after five. She had to shower, wash her hair – that was always interesting – and dress. She wondered what Alex had done the remainder of the afternoon when she'd dropped him at the house.

Inside, she wandered to the kitchen where she heard noise. Mika stood over the stove, singing some horrible off-key tune, stirring something that looked like sweet dark chocolate.

"Hey, Mika," she called as she opened the refrigerator. "What's cooking?"

"You, little lady, can wait until dinner to find out. Get your drink and scoot. Your mama is upstairs resting and reading a romance novel. Wish I had time to read a love story. My time is cooking, cooking, going home, cooking..."

"Okay, okay, I get the point. You have a horrible life with that hunk of a husband who built you that beautiful house, and your kids who never make less than an A. So pathetic."

She grabbed a canned soda and kissed Mika on the cheek. "See you later, sweetheart."

Mika waved her hand without turning. "Yeah, yeah, yeah."

Laughing, Kailey jogged up the winding staircase to her room. The hallway was very quiet. Where was everyone? She pulled her long tee over her head as she walked to the closet. Sipping the soda, she pulled the scrunchy from her hair, and began to run her fingers through the thick mass. Mmmm, what to wear to dinner? Something a little dressy, for this would be for the entire family plus Alex. Her mother would expect everyone to dress suitably for the formal family dining room.

After a shower with peach scented soap and shampooing with one that was supposed to soften hair and make it more manageable, she dried and wrapped the towel around it. She twisted another towel around her torso.

Someone knocked on her door. Probably her mother wanted to make certain she would dress properly. But no, the caller was Alex.

She cracked the door and stood behind it, peeking around the edge. "You know I'm indecent."

He laughed. "Isn't that what a Victorian female said to her gentleman caller?"

Laughing, too, she said, "Well, you can't come in, I don't care how debonair and dashing you are."

He stood very still, barely smiling. What did that little gesture mean? She'd seen it now four or five times, the way he seemed to freeze and study her, pausing before he spoke.

"Am I, then? Dashing?"

"Mmm, I suppose. Do you know what it means?"

"No, do you?"

She shook her head and they laughed again. Alex possessed such an easy manner, unwound, cool...nice. Why she did always use 'nice', the most boring adjective in the English language, when she wanted to say 'stupendous?'

"Do you need something? I'll be dressed in about thirty minutes."

"I'll be around." Whistling, he walked away with his hands in his pockets, and jogged down the stairs.

When she closed the door, Kailey leaned back on it and closed her eyes. Her heart fluttered again, that almost wild feeling of wanting to do something outrageous, something out of the ordinary, maybe throw herself on his body, and...*That's enough right there, Kailey Lovelace. You're going bonkers over an almost total stranger.*

When dressed, she took one last glance in the mirror, wishing so much she could change herself in some manner. At least she'd grown up without any serious character flaws or psychological problems, even though boys called her string bean, or scarecrow, or something inane like 'Michael Jordan.' By the time she was ten, she towered over every boy in school by at least a foot. In high school, only Jack Newsom and Larry Browning stood taller than she.

An hour before dinner, Kailey walked downstairs. The deep blue silk skirt that hugged her hips and brushed her ankles, paired with a cream silk tunic with long sleeves, felt just right for the evening with the family...and guest. She wore black flats with jewels across the toes. But the hair. What else could she do? The curly frizzy mass drove her to distraction. Tonight, she'd given up and just let it float out wherever it wanted to go. Maybe no one would notice.

Right.

Sam and Shelley had arrived. Kailey heard them talking and laughing with Alex in the living area. She walked in and smiled at the scene. A big fire burned and crackled, every candle glowed, and the Christmas tree sparkled liked diamonds. Only Alex noticed her entrance.

He lowered his foot from the fireplace hearth and his elbow from the mantel as he turned to watch her. Walking around the curved white leather sofa, she approached the group.

"See you found the wassail."

Sam and Shelley turned and said their usual greetings. Alex said, "We did, and it's very good. I'm no wassail expert, but I'd say this is perfect."

Kailey grinned. "Mika makes it, and she claims it's an ancient secret Chinese recipe."

Sam frowned. "Did the Chinese drink wassail?"

The other three laughed and Sam sheepishly grinned.

Kailey shook her head trying to contain her mirth. "Okay, it's just another one of Mika's jokes. She thinks she's so funny."

Robert and Elaine walked in, smiling, greeting, holding out their hands in welcome. "Don't you all look *handsome.* Don't they, Robert?"

Always agreeing with his wife in public, he nodded. "I don't think anyone would find more good-looking young people anywhere."

Mika walked in with a large silver tray with canapés of various kinds. "Ha! More ancient secret Chinese recipes for you. You talk too loud and I hear every word you say. Now, don't spill anything on the carpet. I just had it cleaned a week ago. You need more wassail, the bowl is in the sun room on the serving bar. Dinner in forty-five minutes." She placed the tray on the large round coffee table, turned, and walked away.

Kailey wanted to laugh at Alex's expression, but she didn't. He kept darting his gaze around, looking at everyone else, but since no one paid any attention to Mika's scolding, he seemed to relax.

Her mother switched to hostess mode. "Sit, sit, everyone. You needn't stand. Shelley, tell us how the bridesmaids' meeting went."

That was all it took. Shelley picked up the thread and ran with it, rattling on for fifteen minutes about the dresses her friends would wear. "And wait until you see Kailey in hers. Oh, Kailey, you looked like, oh, that actress, you know...the tall one with the curly hair... Oh, what is her name?"

Kailey crossed her legs and swung one foot. "Angelina Jolie?" No. "Kate Hudson?" No. "Cameron Diaz?"

Finally, Kailey tired of playing the game with Shelley, because the girl would continue as long as it took to decide which actress she thought about.

Shelley shrugged her shoulders. "Oh, well, can't think of the right one."

Sam laughed. "Sometimes I wonder how your mind works."

Shelley froze and stared at Sam. "What does that mean?"

He straightened in his chair and flitted his gaze around, realizing he'd spoken when he should have slapped his hand over his mouth. "Oh, nothing, pumpkin."

"*Pumpkin?* You've started doing that, too."

"What?" Sam looked clearly bewildered.

"Calling me cutsey names that sound...*fat.*"

"No, no, honey, I don't mean that at all." He glanced around the room but no one jumped to his defense.

She stood and placed her hands on her hips. "Then what do you mean, Sam? I sincerely want to know."

Shelley's chin began to wobble, and Kailey looked at her mother. She mouthed, *Do something.*

Elaine jumped to her feet. "Oh, Robert. Look at that fire. Is that log about to roll onto the hearth?"

Everyone's attention turned to the fireplace. Robert rose slowly and strolled over, picked up the poker, and jabbed at the burning wood. "Is that better, Elaine?"

"Yes, thank you, darling. Now. Who needs more wassail? And Kailey, sweetheart, will you pass around the canapé tray?"

CHAPTER FIVE

The house had settled into an uneasy quiet. Kailey sat on the edge of her bed with her head in her hands. *What in the world had happened at dinner?*

Shelley had turned the dinner into a fiasco, a family uproar Kailey had never witnessed in their home. First Shelley had asked the questions before dinner, and everyone thought the hard feelings and tension had faded away. But when the group assembled and sat at the table, Shelley had started in on another perceived insult from Sam, disrupting his conversation and everyone else's with inappropriate comments.

Once, Elaine had quieted everyone and turned to Shelley, asking her if she needed an aspirin or something. The question was meant to urge Shelley to calm down so the family could continue their dinner in peace; instead, it caused the girl to become more agitated and upset.

Looking at the clock, Kailey knew she couldn't sleep at ten-thirty. Not with her stomach roiling around and her nerves jumping. Without thinking, she got up and left her room to walk to Alex's. When she knocked, he opened the door immediately.

"Hi." His gorgeous face was a little solemn. Poor guy. She bet he wondered what in the world he'd gotten into.

Kailey smiled with a little apology. "I can't sleep. Would you like to go outside in the garden? All you'll need is a jacket."

"Give me a minute."

Outside, they walked in silence around the winding pathway in almost total darkness. Small lampposts stood here and there, but the amount of light was intentionally low. They continued to walk quietly until the path seemed to end.

"Now what?" Alex had his hands stuffed in the side pockets of the athletic jacket.

"Now, we wander through the wilderness. Follow me."

With the faint light from the gibbous moon, she led him on a beaten dirt path that led down through thick vegetation. At last, she came to her destination – a small pavilion, resembling a gazebo.

"Here we are. My parents built this little hide-away for themselves when we were little. They forbade us to come down here, saying it was their private space. It always made me a little angry that Mom and Dad had a place they wouldn't allow Sam or me. We'd sneaked down here anyway, though, but always during the daytime. It became a place for us to play knights and princesses, or pretend we were some characters from Star Wars."

Alex looked around and turned to her, standing very close. He removed his hands from his pockets and took hers, holding them down to the side. "Good for them, that they wanted to be alone, just the two of them. They have a good marriage, don't they?"

Kailey nodded and looked into his face. "They do. If they ever argued or had hard feelings, they did it in private." She laughed a little. "Probably came down here to make up."

"So, what happened tonight, Kailey? Was that unusual for Sam and Shelley to become so embroiled in a heated argument in front of family?"

She sighed. "I have no idea what happened. I did speak with Mom a few minutes, and she waved it off as pre-wedding jitters. It makes sense, I guess, except that Shelley has always been so carefree and amiable. Very easy-going. Whatever happened, though, I know my brother, and he did not have a clue about what she was doing."

"Surely they'll make up and it'll all be over. Right?"

Kailey smiled to herself. The upset bothered Alex more than her. "I think they will. At least they left together."

"But wasn't that because they arrived in one car?"

She couldn't help but laugh. "Alex, stop worrying so much. They'll work it out."

He shrugged. "Okay. So what's on the schedule tomorrow?"

"Let's sit over here on the bench." He followed her and they sat very close. She crossed her legs, and clasped her hands in her lap. Probably, they shouldn't be touching. Each time he reached out to her, she thought her heart would either stop beating or flutter so fast it would fly out of her chest. "All right, tomorrow. Here's the plan. You will go with Alex to find the right size tuxedo. He knows where to go and which tuxes Shelley chose for you guys. Me? I have a date with Mario."

He jerked his head toward her. "Who's Mario?"

She laughed at the expression on his face, sort of shocked, a little tense. "He's the guru who will work a miracle on my hideous unruly hair and turn me into a gorgeous maid of honor."

"While I get fitted for a tux?"

"Yes, and then the entire family is gathering at the country club for dinner around six. And Alex? Martin will be there."

CHAPTER SIX

On the drive to the hair appointment, Kailey remembered the talk she and Alex had last night. He didn't say anything when she told him Martin would be at dinner, but he frowned a little. That was the first sign of any displeasure she'd seen on his face.

Kailey pulled her small luxury sedan into the parking garage. As she walked to the shop, she wondered what on earth Mario could do to her that she hadn't already tried. But he did have a stellar reputation, even with the visiting Hollywood crowd in town while making some movie. About a block away, she saw Martin walking toward her, his arm around a petite blond, whispering in her ear while she laughed. He had not noticed her yet.

When they were only a few feet apart, Martin saw her and came to a halt. "Kailey," he said in a flat voice, as though might be speaking to a lamppost.

She stopped, too, and nodded, "Martin. How are you?" What else could she say? Now, she knew why he'd been almost ignoring her existence for weeks. He had a girlfriend.

"I'm fine, Kailey." He turned to the young woman and whispered to her.

The intimate gesture irked Kailey. "You can speak up, Martin. Just tell her who I am, and tell me who she is, and we'll get on with our lives." Her own voice stunned her. She'd never spoken so coldly and sarcastically to any human being, but it just came out, anyway.

He moved a step toward her with his hands in his pockets, just as cool as you please. "A friend. She's a very close friend."

"Wonderful. Are you going to tell me the truth or beat around the bush all day?"

"Okay, Kailey, we've been going out and –"

She held up her hand. "Stop. Don't say another word. Just answer one question. Why haven't you told me instead of going behind my back?"

He blew out a breath and shrugged. "The wedding. Remember I'm an usher. I'm on my way to be fitted for the tux now. In fact, I'm late. After the wedding, you would expect me to escort you at the reception and dinner and dance, so I waited to tell you so you wouldn't be hurt. I felt it was my obligation."

"Obligation. News flash, Martin." She took a second to glance at the young woman. "You'll excuse us, won't you?" When the girlfriend stepped away and looked in a shop window, Kailey turned back to Martin. "I apologize. Really, I do. It's just startling, is all. Something I didn't expect. I'm ashamed of acting so hateful, but Martin, the fact is I'm relieved. Our relationship has dwindled down to practically nothing, but honestly, I'm fine with it."

"I'm sorry, Kailey. We met and just clicked. I should have told you right off, but the wedding..."

"I understand. Just be happy. Gotta go. Hair appointment."

Breathing deeply and slowly, in and out, Kailey continued to Mario's. When she entered the shop, loud rock music nearly knocked her off her feet. The place was almost like a nightclub, with lavender and rose lighting in corners where small tables waited for patrons to sit until their appointments. Magazines of every kind were available, and wifi for computers or whatever the client needed. Waitresses came and went, taking orders for mixed drinks or wine while they waited.

When Mario saw her, he dropped his scissors on the counter and rushed to her with his hands outstretched. "Peaches, *darling*. I couldn't wait for your arrival." He took her hand and pulled her to a small private area behind a gold and maroon screen. "Now, sit." A girl appeared with a tray in her hand. Mario looked at Kailey. "What will you have, my precious?"

Kailey laughed. She couldn't help it. Such extravagance and blatant charade made her giddy. Mario was a show in himself. She just hoped he knew what to do with her hair. He'd have to be a magician to pull it off. There he sat in his skin-tight black leather pants, black tooled leather cowboy boots, and muscle shirt made of gold fabric. His multi-hued hair reached his shoulders.

"A wine spritzer. Go easy on the wine, please."

Mario turned to face her. "All right, sweet pea. Let's look at you. Hmmm." He stood and circled her chair, humming under his breath, lifting a strand of hair, studying it, smelling it, and rubbing it between his fingers. "How tall are you, dear?"

"An even six-feet."

"Maaah-valous. Just absolutely superb."

Mario sat as the wait girl arrived with Kailey's drink. While she sipped, he observed her. He didn't make her nervous, in fact, he mesmerized her in a way. How could anyone be so enthralled and involved with...hair?

He spoke. "Tell me your hair care routine."

She took a deep breath, knowing whatever she said would be wrong. "I shampoo twice a week with a scented soap, a mild moisturizing one. I apply a thick conditioner while in the shower, leave it in for a minute, then rinse. I towel dry, and then wonder what I should do next. I do use the hair dryer, then brush..."

Mario placed his hand on his throat and closed his eyes, shaking his head. He looked frozen while he held his breath. Finally, he released it and opened his eyes.

"Now, listen to me. Never, and I mean *never* use a brush on your hair. Invest in a thick comb. It's also wise not to use a hair dryer unless it's a diffuser and you know how to use it. I'll show you later. And you should not shampoo your hair much—maybe once a month."

"Really? But all that junk builds up."

"Even so, that's the rule. Curly hair is generally dry, vulnerable to humidity, and the cuticles soak up moisture, creating the frizz."

"Oh. Sounds like I've been causing the problem myself."

"Not completely, but you've not done yourself a favor. Now, follow me. First, we will wash with a clarifying shampoo. Then I will work my magic."

Three hours later, Kailey walked out of the shop somewhat poorer, but ecstatic with her new look and instructions on how to care for her hair.

She stopped in front of a shop window and looked at her reflection. Mario had cut her hair in layers and left it long, gave it a few highlights, and told her what to do. She had it memorized. *Use shampoo no more than once a month to clarify and start over; otherwise, wash with a deep leave-in conditioner. While the hair is wet, apply a serum containing silicone, coating every curl. Let it dry naturally, scrunching often until dry, possibly using a diffuser very lightly. If you want to leave it wet and dry on its own, use a head band and pull the hair back. The band will flatten the crown.*

Four-thirty. She had an hour and a half to return home, shower, change, and make it to the country club for dinner at six. She'd have to step on it.

When she pulled into the driveway, she noticed everyone seemed to be gone. Thinking about her own tasks and timetable, she entered and jogged up the stairs to her room. Not a sound in the entire house. As she began removing clothing, she called her mother.

"Mom? Where is everyone? I'm home changing and it's as quiet as a tomb."

"Well, darling, your dad and I are downtown buying little gifts."

"Little gifts? For whom?" She moved to the closet and began pulling out articles of clothing, tossing them toward her bed.

She heard her mother sigh. "For the bridesmaids' presents from Shelley. You see, dear, she's far too distraught to do it, and we didn't want her mother to know, so we volunteered."

She hopped on one foot and then the other removing the flats she'd worn to Mario's. "What are you talking about?"

"Kailey, I'll fill you in later. You will be on time for dinner, won't you?"

She heard resignation in her mother's voice. What now? "Yes, of course. Where's Alex?"

"He'll be at dinner, don't worry."

"Okay, just curious where he is. Is he with Sam?"

"No. Sam is trying to talk with Shelley...you know, darling, just please dress and get to the country club."

Kailey felt cold fingers of anxiety crawling through her stomach. Sam, Shelley, Alex. All three missing in action. What was going on?

Just before six, she pulled into the club's valet parking, stepped out, gave the keys to the attendant, and rushed through the front doors. She instructed the hostess of her destination, and the young woman led her to the blue room next to the cascading pool. The table was set, complete with flowers, and there sat her parents all alone.

Her father stood and approached Kailey. Taking her arm, he told her how lovely she looked and led her to sit beside her mother.

"Kailey, sweetheart, your *hair is gorgeous*. I have never seen it look so wonderful. The handiwork of Mario?"

Kailey managed a little chuckle. "Yes, isn't it grand? You like it? He even taught me how to care for it properly. I've done the wrong thing my entire life. Practically cost me half my 401K, too."

Elaine leaned over and kissed her on her cheek. "Worth every penny, my darling daughter. You are so precious to us."

"Mom, please. What's going on? This is turning out to be quite an ordeal."

"You're telling me. Actually, I really don't know. Your dad and I are on the outside, in a way. Shelley's mother is trying to deal with her, but she's at a loss, too. Shelley seems to balk about everything, when she seemed so carefree and happy before."

"She loves Sam, don't you think?"

"I do, but the girl has become irrational. Have you talked with Sam? He's going crazy trying to figure out what's wrong."

Kailey blew out a breath and studied the cascading water outside the glass. So beautiful, so soothing and peaceful. If only this wedding would go away.

"There's more." Her mother was speaking to her.

"What?"

"Alex might be late. Robert, you were the one who talked to him. Can you explain?"

Her dad had been sitting, calmly drinking a bourbon and water, listening to the interchange. Now, he shrugged. "Not much to tell. He asked to borrow a car so he could go to the airport and pick up a friend."

Kailey's stomach jerked. *A friend? Why would one of Alex's friends be coming to Austin, knowing he would be involved in a wedding?*

More calmly than she felt, she asked her dad to continue. But he had little to say.

"That's all."

"*Dad*. Surely there's more to tell. How did Alex act? Happy? Excited? What?"

He reached over and patted her hand. "Sweetheart, honestly,

that's all I know. He was at the house when we were and got a call. He moved to another room to talk, and when he returned, he apologized and asked if he could impose on us further and borrow a car. I will note that he did look a little upset."

Her mother added, "Well, more like bewildered when I saw him. Don't you think, Robert?"

Nodding, he agreed. "Yes, maybe so. Surprised or bewildered. He assured us he'd be at the dinner, though, if not a little late."

Kailey slumped back in her chair. "Now, here we are, it's half past six, and no one is coming to dinner. Okay, I'll just lay *everything* out on the table. It's about Martin."

After Kailey's explanation of the encounter with Martin, she added that he would still be one of the ushers.

Elaine remarked. "I hope you're not upset, darling. We never thought he was right for you, anyway."

"Me, too. Our relationship never went anywhere, but I didn't expect him to go behind my back. Obviously, he wanted someone shorter."

"Oh, sweetheart, that's not true. People don't fall in love based on height."

She lifted one shoulder. "I'm not so sure."

At seven, an hour late, Sam walked in alone, slouched down in the chair next to their dad, and poured out his heart about Shelley's behavior.

"She says everyone is pushing her, that she has no idea what's going on, and really doesn't care. Mom, Dad, if something doesn't change in the next couple of days, she'll call off the wedding. I know she will."

Elaine gasped. Robert growled in his throat.

Kailey spoke directly to her brother. "Where is she right now?"

"At her place, watching movies, eating popcorn and chocolate bars, painting her toenails, sitting around in old warm-ups. She won't even talk much, except to assure me of her love. And I believe her. I think she really does care for me and wants to marry me. But...there's something going on I can't figure out, and you can't pull anything out of her. Her parents have spent hours with her, making one attempt after the other, but she just smiles a little and continues her little stall tactics."

Sam paused and looked around. "Where're Alex and Martin?"

Kailey thought she'd scream by the time they repeated all the explanations. "Mom, can we cancel dinner?"

"No, we can't. Robert, would you summon the waiter? We have to eat dinner somewhere."

Halfway through their dreary meal, Alex walked in. Kailey's heart began beating hard against her ribs.

Robert and Sam stood and shook hands with him. He wasn't smiling, either, just like the rest of them. She saw trouble written all over his face.

Alex scooted in between Sam and Kailey and glanced around at everyone. "I'll explain the best I can. A friend decided to come down and visit, hoping I'd be happy about it and we could go to the Bahamas after I finished my wedding responsibilities. We discussed this at the hotel, and I said I'd return in a few hours to discuss it further. That's all there is to it."

Kailey ground her back teeth. *Men.* They always saw situations so simply, thinking a gloss-over would suffice. *Details. She wanted details.* But he would not say anything else, leaving her feeling uneasy. He never said "he" or "she." That was deliberate, and she'd bet anything the friend was a woman.

At the end of the meal, just before they stood, a pretty woman, maybe thirty years old, dressed stylishly and smiling, walked through the entrance to the blue room and straight to their table.

"There you are, Alex. You should have given me better directions. Fortunately, my cab driver knew exactly which country club I meant. May I sit down?"

The men stood while Alex seated her in his chair next to Kailey. Since he had given up his place, Sam moved across the table so Alex could sit there. Now, the visitor—or *party-crasher*—separated Kailey and Alex.

Kailey's temper began to rise. Knowing in her heart she had no hold on Alex, the thought of a complete stranger coming between them, literally and figuratively, still made her blood heat.

Would this wreck the wedding even more? Martin thought he would be her escort for the dinner and dance, but now she wouldn't allow that for a minute. And he'd better not bring that little petite thing to the wedding, either. He had no right.

Logically, Alex should now be her escort; in fact, he should have been all along. Now, *he* had a stranger tagging along, too.

She had a mind to join Shelley, eat popcorn and chocolate bars, and watch movies. *I wonder what kind of movies she has.*

The devil made her do it. She rose from her chair and asked for attention. "If you all will excuse me, I think I'm becoming ill." She waved her hand in the air. "But carry on. The party doesn't need to end just because I'm leaving. Mom, Dad, I'll see you later."

With her parents and Sam protesting, she picked up her small bag, retrieved her jacket, turned and walked away. Before she could leave the building, Alex was on her heels. He followed outside, and before she could summon the valet to bring her car around, he reached out and grabbed her arm, turning her to face him. Right there in the parking lane.

She jerked her arm, although his touch did make her almost swoon. *Swoon?* "Let go of me. What do you think you're doing?"

A car honked. Alex waved at the driver while he propelled Kailey around a corner into an alcove with a bench and potted plants. A man sat there smoking a cigarette.

Alex spoke politely. "Do you mind, sir? We need a little privacy, here."

Casually, the older gentleman stubbed out his cigarette, stood and walked away.

Alone, Alex turned Kailey so he could anchor her by holding both her arms. Not many men could have held her since she was often taller, but Alex stood over her by six inches, plus he was muscled and very strong.

Alex moved his face closer to hers. In a low voice, he spoke, his warm breath drifting into her nostrils. "Kailey, *please* listen to me."

Silently and passively, she gazed into his gorgeous eyes.

"Are you in love with Martin?"

She shook her head. "No. We're not even a couple anymore. He's had another girlfriend all along."

"So, you're a free woman."

Kailey almost stopped breathing but managed to whisper, "Yes."

He lowered his head and kissed her, very softly, then more firmly. He moved one arm to circle her shoulders, and the other to her waist, hugging her close to his lean body, staying with the kiss.

Kailey wouldn't have moved even if the building exploded. This is what she'd wanted, what she thought about from the minute she met him at the airport. Foolish? Maybe. *Probably.* But she couldn't help herself.

Still, there was that other woman.

Pulling away slightly, Kailey said in a normal voice, "Please let go of me."

He released her but did not step back. So she did, just a tiny step.

"I need to go home, Alex. You have a car and you know where the house is if you need your room. Maybe I'll see you tomorrow."

"No, wait, please. Kailey, damn it, I don't know exactly how to say this, but...I'm very interested in you. Right from the beginning, I just fell for you without even considering anything else in the world. It was as though I'd been waiting, and then, you were right there in front of me. Now, with this kiss, I can't let you go. Do you understand?"

Lying, she said, "No, I do not understand. You have that other girlfriend in there, and you should go back. You're responsible for her, since you invited her here."

He raked one hand through his short hair. "That's just it. I didn't invite her. She's a...pest. From home. It's hard to explain, but she...follows me."

She held up a hand. "No, don't explain. I have to go. Will you please step aside?"

He did, and she walked as calmly as she could on shaking legs to the valet and gave him the keys. While she waited for her car, Alex walked near and just stood there until she got in and drove away. At the end of the drive before she turned onto the street, she looked back and saw the woman standing beside him.

Without understanding what possessed her, Kailey drove straight to Shelley's condo. At the door, she repeatedly rang the bell until the door opened.

Shelley wore old gray sweats, the shirt too large because it was probably one of Sam's. Her hair was unkempt, as though she'd been in bed and hadn't combed or brushed it. She was barefoot with freshly painted toenails—bright red. She still wore her engagement ring.

That's a good sign.

"Kailey! What're you doing here?"

Kailey shrugged and grinned. "Running away?"

Shelley laughed and pulled her in the room. Hugging her hard, she told Kailey she really needed company. "I'm hiding out, girlfriend. That's the same as running away, isn't it?"

Kailey stopped her and held on to her hand. "Shelley, honey, can you tell me what's wrong? We need to fix this. Sam is going crazy."

"Not now, Kailey. Now, listen. For the moment, you and I will just do whatever we want to. No wedding, no white dress, no bridesmaids, no showers or bachelorette party. No elaborate reception, no dinner, no dance. Ohhhh, Kailey, my darling friend. I want you for a sister so much, but I cannot explain any of this. Will you *please,* just please let's have a little fun?"

Kailey took Shelley's face between her palms. "You got it, sister. Let's party."

"Take off your wrap, your shoes, whatever else you want, because I have movies and all the trimmings. How about a glass of wine?"

"Oh, my, yes."

"And who did your gorgeous hair? Tell me everything."

After three hours, Kailey lay prone on the plush carpet, and Shelley lay face up on the sofa with her arm across her eyes. Kailey stirred, stood, and turned all the lights on low.

Shelley had poured out her heart in-between bowls of popcorn, wine, and chocolate. Both of them had overdosed on such rich indulgences.

The doorbell rang...and rang and rang. Kailey stumbled to the door and peeked through the security peephole. *Alex. And Sam.*

With a little adrenalin perking her up, she opened the door, standing there in her lacy black bra and a pair of too short sweat pants that came to mid-calf. She pointed a finger at both men and said, "If you laugh, you can just turn around and go home."

Sam groaned and covered his eyes. "Sheesh, sis, put on some clothes."

She glanced at Alex. He stood with his hands in his coat pockets, grinning, looking from her eyes to her breasts, and back to her eyes. Funny, she wasn't embarrassed. *I'd have on less if I were in my swim suit.* And she liked the little thrill that ran through her.

Leaving the door open, she turned away, waving her hand at them. She looked around the room, under the table, behind the sofa, when finally she found the sweatshirt – one of Sam's, too – behind a door. Pulling it over her head, she walked as straight as she could to the sofa, shoved Shelley's feet to the side, and sat down.

"Sit up, Shelley. The guys want to talk." She glared at both of them. "Well, sit, both of you. I'll get a crick in my neck looking up. Hey, Shell, wake up. Look who's here."

Shelley slowly moved to a sitting position and barely glanced at Sam and Alex. They'd taken the chairs facing the sofa. Alex still had that stupid little grin–it used to be intriguing, now it was stu... no it wasn't. Who was she trying to fool? He still displayed that dimple, the one she couldn't take her eyes off when he did that little mysterious smile thing.

Sam leaned forward, propped his arms on his thighs, and linked his fingers. "Shelley, what the *hell* are you doing? You've got to tell me. I'm going crazy, here."

Snuggling down in the corner of the sofa with her legs bent under her, she twirled one lock of hair, turning her head this way and that way, studying her fiancé. "Well, I guess I don't like all these wedding preparations. It makes me nervous, sort of sick feeling, if you really want to know. Oh, I think a dance sounds really good, but I don't want any of this falderal going on just so we can marry. Everyone around me got very carried away with this and that, especially my mother. Then your mother got in on it, and pretty soon, I just got lost."

"Honey, why didn't you say something earlier? We could have done something different."

Shaking her head and rolling her lips inward, she picked at the chipped pink polish on her nails. She straightened her legs and turned to Kailey. "Oh, would you do my nails? Look how tacky they are."

Kailey moved closer and linked her arm through Shelley's. "Listen. Forget about the nails for now. We'll get them done, though. That's a promise. What do you want to do? Tell Sam and put him out of his misery."

Speaking to Kailey instead of her fiancé, she said softly, "I really want to marry Sam, but I'd rather do it my way. Neither of us had any say in anything. In fact, we didn't even discuss it." Glancing at Sam, she asked, "Did we?"

Sam stood, walked to her, and squatted down. Placing his hands on her knees. "No, we didn't, sweetheart, but we can't call off the wedding. We've – they've –spent too much time and money. I don't know what else to do except get through it."

Leaning close, she kissed Sam without touching him. "Let's go to Las Vegas and get married. Kailey and Alex could go with us."

He shook his head. Kailey could tell he was stunned and a little distressed. Going to Las Vegas was no choice at all.

Kailey spoke. "Shelley, going to Las Vegas doesn't take care of the problem of all the preparations – our dresses, the cake, a band, a dinner...flowers..." Her voice trailed off. What else could she say?

Alex remained silent throughout the discussion. Finally he cleared his throat and spoke up. "May I make a suggestion?"

They turned to him and all three nodded. He stood and paced back and forth a few times before he stopped and spoke.

"Just hear me out. Shelley, if I understand you, your main objection is that you had no control over your own wedding. Correct?"

She sat up straight and nodded, keeping her gaze on him.

"This is Tuesday night, or rather, very early Wednesday morning. What else is there to do as to wedding preparations?"

Shelley lifted her shoulders and let them fall. "I have no idea."

"Kailey?"

"Not much. Wedding rehearsal is Friday at seven. We might party a little afterward, because the wedding isn't until four Saturday afternoon."

Alex blew out a breath. "Here's a plan. Shelley, if you and Sam got married in Las Vegas, how would you feel about still going through the ceremony, dinner, and dance? You know, so you won't disappoint everyone. That way, you'll take control of your own wedding. Get married where and how you want."

Silence hung in the air. Shelly stared at Alex, he became nervous and raised his eyebrows at Kailey, Sam kept blinking and looking back and forth from Alex to Shelley, and Kailey felt giggles coming on. She tried to hold them in, but a bark of laughter erupted from her, and she began to laugh. The idea was so ludicrous, yet so right, the thought made her giddy.

Shelley stood. "Listen, everyone. I have made a decision."

The three froze and listened to her.

"Sam, do you want to marry me as much as I want to marry you?"

He stood and nodded.

"Then, here's the plan. The four of us dress right now, someone get on the internet and get four seats booked to Vegas – whatever airline you can get is fine– and we get to the airport. We don't need extra clothes; we don't need a room. Just go out there, find one of those cute little chapels, and do it."

Now, all three stood and clustered around Shelley.

Sam shouted, "Shell, this is crazy!"

Kailey placed her hand on her brother's arm, hoping to calm him down. "This is not crazy. Just decide if you agree, and if so, do your part."

Sam stared at his fiancée, and then began to laugh. He threw back his head and guffawed, making all of them join him. "We're all crazy."

While Sam got on the internet to find an available flight in the next few hours, Alex sat in a chair and propped his feet on an ottoman, waiting.

Kailey and Shelley ran to the bedroom, dressed, brushed their teeth, shared make-up, and re-arranged their hair.

Shelley stopped and gasped. "I have to tell my parents."

Kailey told her, "Me, too, but let's wait. When we have the flight booked and we're at the airport, we'll call and explain."

Continuing throwing a few items into a large handbag, Shelley said, "Okay. That'll work."

She whirled around and circled her arms around Kailey. "Thank you. I didn't know it, but this is what I want."

"But promise me, Shell, when we're back home you have to go through every event, including the ceremony at the church."

"Oh, I will. I don't want anyone to know we're actually married except us four, though. Not even our parents. Just tell them it's a pre-wedding party. We have to have a secret pact."

CHAPTER SEVEN

Kailey sighed and looked at her watch. It took four-and-a-half hours from Shelley's place to boarding the plane. They were lucky to get a flight.

Sam and Shelley moved all the way to the back of the plane so they'd have a wall behind them. . Kailey didn't even want to know what was going on.

Kailey and Alex snagged an aisle seat halfway back. She didn't mind where she sat, as long as she was near him. Usually, she wanted an aisle seat, too. A tall person had more difficulty moving across to the window. There never seemed to be enough leg room.

She blew out a breath. "I can't believe we're doing this."

Alex leaned close and spoke very softly so his voice wouldn't carry. "I'm glad you wanted to go. Now I'll have you all to myself for a few hours."

His nearness created some sort of breathless feeling in her chest and throat. Slight goose bumps ran along her arms, and her hands trembled. Swallowing hard, she also spoke in a low voice.

"Who is the woman, Alex? Anyone important?"

His face was so close she could see the tiny flecks of silver in the blue eyes. "I'd like to just say 'no one,' but I want you to understand. It's important to me that you believe I would never invite anyone to this wedding. She's from far back as college when we dated a few times. Now, she pops up in all kinds of places, thinking I'll be glad to see or hear from her. I had to block her e-mails while I was in Afghanistan."

"Is she a little...off?"

"No, not really. Just self-centered, at least that's my opinion. She's apparently never been told no her entire life. She just won't allow anyone to deny her."

"So, are you free now?"

He grinned. "As a bird. She finally became angry when I told her I was in love. Screamed that she never wanted to see me again."

"I see."

"Let's not talk about her anymore. It's taking time away from us."

Us. Kailey's heart did that little flip, the one she had to pay attention to, the one that would probably lead her right into trouble. She and Alex barely knew each other, and he already talked about love. No man had ever loved her – not even lied and said it. The perfect man sat beside her, but they'd met only three days ago – not enough to really know each other.

Her heart had never been broken, but that meant nothing. It could happen with someone like Alex Dunn, though, if she didn't keep her head.

Alex smiled at her and squeezed her hand. "We're lucky to be on this plane, don't you think? I thought security would never let us through. If Shelley hadn't started crying, we might still be there."

The thought made Kailey laugh lightly. "I never thought about that list of things they look for, like people traveling with no luggage or anything. Probably the fact we had return tickets for the next day – right after midnight – made them feel better. Wow, I've never been questioned so much. It makes me a little more sympathetic toward people who are arrested. Once or twice, I wasn't sure what my name was."

Alex pushed up the armrest between them, leaned his shoulder to touch hers, and captured her hand. The warmth from his skin flowed right through to her heart. Taking advantage of the short time they had before buckling seat belts, she pressed into his shoulder, too. He gazed at her, studying her eyes, then her lips. Not once did he look at her hair.

She whispered, "Do you like my hair?"

He whispered back, "It's very pretty, and don't worry. I noticed. It's just that I liked it before, too."

Pulling her head back a little, she smiled at him. "You did? How could you? It was a mess. Has been my entire life."

"How could I? Kailey, I notice and love everything about you."

He kept his gaze on her eyes for a few moments, then moved to her mouth, and back to her eyes. She blinked several times and had an urge to lick her lips. She didn't, though, thinking how he might take the gesture, maybe that she'd done it on purpose to entice him.

The intense moment stretched out until the steward came on the intercom with instructions on how to buckle your seat belt, survive a crash, and float in an ocean. As if there was an ocean between Austin, Texas and Las Vegas, Nevada.

By eight in the morning, they'd landed and left the airport in a taxi, bound for the Strip. Alex sat up front with the driver and asked him, "Can you take us to The Little Blue Chapel? I have the address if you need it."

Before they left Shelley's condo, she'd done a quick internet search for wedding chapels in Las Vegas – the perfect one. She and Sam decided to marry around five in the evening, so they wanted to locate the chapel and make arrangements. The cab driver said he knew where everything was in Vegas. After thirty minutes of heavy traffic, they arrived.

Against Sam's protests, Alex paid the cab fare. Sam and Shelley got out first, with Kailey following. The four of them stood on the sidewalk and gazed at the small chapel.

Shelley clasped her hands under her chin. "Ohhh, it's so beautiful. Don't you think so, Sam? I just love it."

Sam seemed speechless, and he allowed Shelley to pull him along to the front door. In the small foyer, a set of double doors blocked their entrance to the actual chapel. A door to the side opened, and a man dressed in a tuxedo told them, "Come in! Come right through here to the office. How can we help you?"

Kailey and Alex waited outside in the courtyard. They sat down on a wooden slatted bench under a tree to get out of the sun. Alex scrunched down, stretched out his legs, and linked his hands across his stomach.

"This is such a pretty little place. I thought all the chapels out here were those cheesy Elvis places. This one is like a miniature cathedral."

Alex's answer was, "How long do you think they'll take? I'm hungry."

Kailey agreed she was, too. "I wonder if they'll have to get a license somewhere. Do you know how these places operate?"

"Not a clue, but it sounds logical that they'd need a license. Don't they already have one in Texas?"

"They do, but I don't think it would suffice for Nevada."

The door opened and Sam and Shelley rushed out. She said, "We need a taxi. The license bureau is downtown. Also, we need fifty-five dollars cash for the license, and neither of us has that much. We should find an ATM machine on the way."

Alex rose, walked to the street, and hailed a cab.

CHAPTER EIGHT

Las Vegas and every wedding chapel never shut down, and the Marriage License Bureau didn't either. In a short time, Sam and Shelley had the license in hand. The four of them stood on the steps of the building.

Sam looked at his watch. "We gained some time. It's only nine-thirty, so we have seven and a half hours to kill. I say we have breakfast before I crater on the sidewalk."

Instead of hailing a cab, they walked around a little and ran across a local café that served breakfast twenty-four hours a day. Kailey thought the place might have been there since the gold rush days. Inside, the tables and chairs were the old chrome and green Formica kind, with ceilings fans blowing cigarette smoke around, and cracked linoleum on the floor.

Shelley wrinkled her nose. "I don't know about this place."

Sam told her, "It's busy, Shell. That means they serve good food. Or do you want some glitzy place on the strip? If you do, we can grab a cab back down there and find something."

Kailey glanced at Alex and grimaced. He chuckled under his breath but kept quiet.

Shelley turned to Kailey. "What do you think? Is this too...*local?* Y'all want to go back to the strip?"

Kailey peeked at Alex and he gave an imperceptible shrug. "Well, I think it would be fun to soak up some local flavor. We have hours yet to visit the Strip. I'm game. Alex?"

"Yeah, sure. Looks fine to me."

A waitress approached with four red plastic coated menus, printed on the front and back. "You guys made up your minds yet?" She laughed and without waiting for an answer, led them to a booth along the wall.

After an enormous breakfast, the four of them sipped the last drops of coffee.

Sam placed his arm around Shelley's shoulders and hugged her close. "That was one of the best meals I've ever had. Good idea you had there, sweetheart."

She looked at him. "It wasn't my idea. Was it?"

Back on the sidewalk, they conferred and decided to find the big shopping mall on the strip. Shelley decided she wanted a new dress and shoes and a make-up session in a department store for the wedding. Kailey thought the idea was necessary, since Shelly wore faded jeans and an old sweater, even though it was cashmere. She might buy a new outfit, too. The guys decided to wear what they had on since they were more presentable. Shelley though, urged Sam to buy a new shirt and tie if Shelley could find something suitable.

Around two in the afternoon, Kailey thought she'd drop from exhaustion. Sam and Shelley, though, were so keyed up from the new clothes and the approaching wedding, they wanted to go off alone and to play the slots and find just the right restaurant for their after-wedding celebration.

They all agreed to meet at four in front of Caesar's Palace, just inside the main door off the Strip.

Kailey sighed. At last she and Alex were alone. "What do you want to do?"

They stood outside the Venetian, thinking they'd go in, but Alex leaned against a wall, out of the way of people streaming past. "What would I like to do? Kiss you senseless, Kailey Lovelace. That's what."

Shaking her head and laughing lightly, she placed her shopping bag on the sidewalk and leaned against the wall beside him. "What would that accomplish?"

"Probably more than we could handle right now. Or maybe only more than I could handle. I'm not sure about your feelings."

"My feelings? For you?"

"Yup."

Looking sideways at him, trying not to appear coy, she asked, "How do you know if I have any or not?"

"The way you look at me."

"*Humph.* How do I look at you?"

"Want to know the truth?"

Kailey repositioned herself to prop one foot against the wall. "That sounds ominous. But yeah, I'd like to know the truth."

"You study me like you want to see inside my brain, find out what kind of man I am."

Lowering her foot, she faced him. "I do want to know that. Right now, though, I'm wondering if I understand myself."

"What do you mean?"

"This doesn't seem like the place to discuss something serious."

"Give me a hint."

She sighed before speaking. "I've never been an impulsive sort. But with you, I might not be thinking clearly."

"I said the word 'love' too soon, didn't I?"

Nodding, she murmured, "Hmmm-mm, but it didn't really distress me."

"Maybe it was inappropriate of me, but you bring on unfamiliar feelings. It's hard to explain, but when I think about leaving here and going home, I hyperventilate a little, fearful I won't see you again. Or maybe you won't care if you don't."

"Alex, it may be a little early in our relationship to become entangled so much." She sighed and gazed away at the hordes of people walking one direction, and others going the opposite. Passing each other, changing places, hoping for something new, something different. "I'm really tired. I'm used to missing sleep when I work long hours, but not this much. We need to find someplace to sit. We don't have long before we meet at four."

"Okay. Maybe you're right." He looked around, up and down the street. "Let's go in here. Maybe they'll have a lounge with a band. We could have an early beer or a soft drink."

"Lemonade. That's what I need. A big icy glass of lemonade. That's a good idea."

The place was enormous inside, but they followed signs and found the perfect place. A nice band played different kinds of music, and a female vocalist sounded good and best of all, they found a small dark booth against the wall. She stashed her shopping bag in the seat and slid in.

Alex moved in beside her and sat close. After they ordered, he relaxed against the back of the seat and turned so he could see her. A little smile escaped her, but he remained solemn and studied her.

"You're making me nervous." In reality, he made a lump form in her throat, and something like love squeezed her heart. *Oh, what is he doing to me?* A combination of emotions roiled around in her chest – appreciation of his good nature, desire for his arms around her, and fear of falling for him so fast with nothing to hold on to. It was like freefalling, floating out in space, not knowing where she was exactly, not what she was doing, not knowing where she would land.

The worst thing that could happen did. Tears gathered in her eyes, and she couldn't look away fast enough to avoid his seeing them.

"Ahhh, Kailey, honey." He circled his arm around her and pulled her closer. Placing his hand on the side of her head, he gently pushed her head to his shoulder. "You're tired, I know, but I don't understand these tears."

"I don't either, Alex. It's that entanglement thing, I guess."

They sat in silence. The loud music and talk and laughter receded into the background, away from their space, cocooning them in a private world. Kailey would never forget this moment.

CHAPTER NINE

At four o'clock, Kailey and Alex arrived at the meeting place and waited for Sam and Shelley. The two lovers rushed up, breathless, each of them talking at the same time.

"You tell, Shelley," Sam said.

"We won a jackpot of *three thousand dollars*. In a dollar slot machine. We pooled our money and counted out twenty-three dollars, and we went for it. The machine kept taking our money, and we were down to six dollars, when the next hit was magic! Those silver sevens rolled by – then one, two, three jackpot signs lined up. That gave us thousands of dollars!"

Kailey laughed and hugged Shelley, having fun along with her brother and her future sister-in-law. Forty minutes in the future, to be exact. "That's grand! Congratulations. I think this is a sign of good luck on your wedding day."

Shelley stopped and took Kailey's hands. "Oh, we do, too. It's so eerie that you said the same thing."

"What will you do with the money?"

Sam laughed and shook his head. "Shelley gave a hundred dollars each to the three attendants who arrived with the cash. And then we located the cocktail waitress who brought us our beer. Because the young woman acted so nice, we gave her a hundred dollars, too. Then out on the street, she handed a hundred dollars to five different people who looked like homeless people."

Kailey glanced sideways at Alex and grinned. She bet he thought the same thing she did. "Drunks." But Shelley had a generous heart and a giving spirit, so if it made her happy, that was the important thing.

Sam looked at his watch. "Look, y'all, we have less than an hour to get to the chapel, get dressed, and get married."

CHAPTER TEN

After the successful wedding, and the scrumptious feast at a plush restaurant at Caesar's Palace, Sam and Shelley shocked Kailey and Alex. At nine p.m., the four of them stood outside the restaurant, and Sam said he had an announcement.

"Shell and I have a room here at Caesar's. We're not going home until Friday morning."

Kailey thought her heart would stop. "What? *No, no, no.* Sam, you cannot do this. The rehearsal is Friday evening at seven. If you have a layover or delay, you won't make it. Please, don't do this."

Shelley said, "But we want to."

"Okay, now you're being selfish. Both of you. Sam, I thought you had better sense. You know this is not smart."

"You're saying my husband has no sense? That is not fair, Kailey. Not at all. We'll make it, don't you worry. We just want this time by ourselves."

"Shelley, you'll be alone on your *honeymoon.*"

"*This* will be our honeymoon. That trip will be...just a vacation. Well, and more honeymoon."

Kailey placed her hands on her hips and turned in a tight circle. "I cannot believe this. If I thought for a minute you'd pull something this stupid and childish, I would never have gone along with it. Think how your parents will feel."

"If you tell them in the right way, Kailey, they won't be upset. You're diplomatic. Think how to say it."

Holding both hands up, Kailey said. "Oh, no, you don't. I will not tell them. Sam, you get on the phone right now and call both our parents and hers. I will not be the fall guy."

"*All right.* I'll call Mom and Dad and ask them to tell Shelley's parents."

Kailey grabbed his arm with both hands and held on. "No! Absolutely not, Sam. Do not, and I repeat, do not put this off on Mom and Dad, either. Think how you're acting, Sam. My lord, you've gone *crazy.* If you treat our parents like this, I will never forgive you. If they forgive you, fine, but I won't. I'll hold it against you as long as I live. And Sam, Mom will..."

"Okay, *okay.* Stop, dammit. I'll call our parents, and Shelley will call hers." He turned to his new wife. "And don't argue, Shell. You have to call your parents right now."

Shelley's chin wobbled, and tears began to stream down her face. "You're yelling at me. You're *mad* at me."

He hugged her tightly and said, "No, honey, I'm only upset because Kailey is. Will you call your parents?"

She snuffed and sniffled and said, "Yeah, I guess so."

Kailey turned to Alex. "Let's get to the airport. I'd rather sit there than kill another hour or two out here. All right?"

Alex nodded, looking worried, but he walked away with her, leaving the newlyweds on the sidewalk.

CHAPTER ELEVEN

The plane left on time and Kailey and Alex landed in Austin by dawn. They hadn't talked much on the way home. Both dozed, even though the woman in the window seat really wanted to carry on a conversation. On the drive to Kailey's home, Alex seemed relaxed, but he remained silent. She glanced at him a couple of times, not daring to take her eyes off the heavy traffic for long.

"Alex, is something bothering you?"

Turning his head toward her, he laughed. "What a trip this has been so far. No, nothing serious is bothering me. I'm just trying to sort it all out. I don't understand Sam or Shelley's attitude about their parents. Wasn't all that a little over the top selfish?"

"Definitely. And it wasn't fair to us, either. Shelley has acted out of character since you arrived. I don't mean you had anything to do with it; it's just that she's always been sweet and cooperative. A little passive, really."

"Does Sam make all the decisions?"

"Basically, yes."

"What kind of work does she do? I'm just wondering how she performs in a work atmosphere."

"That's the odd part. She's a CPA, very bright, has a great position with a big firm here in Austin, and makes a good salary. As flighty as she is at times, you'd think she'd be a flop there. Not true, though. She's top-notch."

"Interesting. It might be because she's in charge of her own little space. She seems to need that control sometimes. Like getting married in Las Vegas."

Kailey pulled into the driveway of her home, killed the engine, and sat for a moment staring out the windshield.

"What're you thinking, Kailey?"

"That if they don't make it to the rehearsal, how distraught the parents will be. Come on. Let's go in. I need a shower, then I'll make breakfast for us. There should be coffee in the kitchen. All right?"

"Sure. I need a shower, too, and clean clothes."

An hour later, they met in the kitchen. Her parents had gotten up, dressed, and joined them. Elaine spoke to Kailey while they finished last cups of coffee.

"Sweetheart, can you remotely explain this whole fiasco to me? I was very surprised the four of you would fly off to Las Vegas."

"I'm sorry, Mom. And Dad, you, too. Honestly, I don't know what came over me."

Alex cleared his throat. "Kailey, may I explain?"

She looked at him and shrugged, wondering what he had to say.

"Elaine, Robert, I apologize. The idea to go to Vegas was my idea. It seemed right at the time, and we all got caught up in it. I feel really bad about it all, and that it distressed you."

Kailey shook her head. "No, Mom, he's not to blame. One thing led to another, and he just clarified what Shelly was trying to say and couldn't. She felt shut out of the wedding preparations, and maybe a little controlled. We learned she doesn't do well in some circumstances unless she is in charge. . That's why we went, and I believe that's why they stayed longer. So Shelley could make the decisions. ."

Elaine sat back and placed her hand at her throat. "I'm speechless. Her mother and I thought we were doing the right thing, and Shelley always hugged and thanked us so sweetly. I never would have guessed anything was wrong."

"I honestly don't think Shelley knew anything was wrong either, until she began thinking about it. Well, it's over, they're married, even though they thought they could keep it secret, and now we'll just hope they make it for the rehearsal."

"Oh, we do, too."

Pushing her chair back and standing, she said, "I'm going to sleep for a few hours. Alex? Do you need a nap, too?"

"Believe I do."

As they walked upstairs to go to their respective rooms, Kailey stopped Alex. "Would you like to go out tonight? We could have dinner down on Sixth Street, maybe find a bar with a good band."

"That would be great. What time and how should I dress?"

CHAPTER TWELVE

The sun had barely peeked over the trees, when Kailey awoke, yawned, and stretched. Last evening had been so much fun, as she and Alex roamed Sixth Street with all the other young adults, having dinner, partying, dancing, and strolling beside Lady Bird Lake.

Late that night, she'd taken him to Zilker Park where the Trail of Lights delighted young and old alike. They'd watched the children inside the Tree of Lights twirl with their heads thrown back and their arms outstretched, making themselves dizzy. She remembered from her childhood how the lights seemed to swirl around her in red, blue, and green circles.

Kailey had struggled with the desire for Alex's kisses and hugs, but she did everything possible, within the bounds of politeness, to make sure he knew she did not seek that from him. The thoughts of falling for him frightened her. In addition, she wanted to proceed with caution. She barely knew the man.

This was Friday, rehearsal day, and no one had heard from Sam and Shelley. Once again, she became angry at them for ignoring the feelings of family, especially causing distress and even tears from Shelley's mother. Elaine had gone to visit her, trying to console and assure her they'd be back in time for the rehearsal.

Today, though, the December air crackled with crispness and the bright Texas sun shone on a clean, sparkling world. She would make the best of the day, intending on entertaining Alex as much as she could.

They met in the breakfast room. Dressed in jogging pants and a silk long-sleeved pullover, she drank coffee, ate a boiled egg and English muffin with marmalade while reading the morning news.

"Morning," he said as he reached for a cup and poured his coffee.

She smiled to herself at his short hair smashed on one side and sticking up slightly in back. He hadn't shaved, either, and the shadow of dark growth made her stomach clench and her palms perspire.

Alex sat across from her and propped his elbows on the table, sipping, looking over the rim of the cup, studying her. When he placed the cup on the table, he leaned back and sighed. He never took his eyes off her.

"What're you staring at, Alex Dunn?" She asked the question in a soft, teasing voice. Oh, lands, he was so wonderfully beautiful, so male, so athletic, strong and sure.

"I'm looking at you, Kailey Lovelace."

Silence, while her diaphragm seemed to contract, closing off her breath. She felt paralyzed, mesmerized, and maybe a little love struck. *I'm looking at you.* Such a simple phrase, it was, and yet it held bright promise and possibilities beyond her imagination. Were their feelings moving along too fast? Had their emotions intensified from the close proximity they'd lived in since Sunday? Maybe, or maybe not.

Kailey knew one thing, though. Staring at each other across the breakfast table when he still had that bedroom look did not help matters.

CHAPTER THIRTEEN

Kailey had gone jogging with Alex soon after breakfast, and then she attempted to remove herself from his vicinity as much as was polite. She was, after all, the primary host for him, since her brother only thought about himself and Shelley, essentially cutting everyone off so they could be alone. One day when she weren't so furious with Sam, she'd make him understand just how rude he'd been to his Army buddy who flew all the way from Denver to act as his best man.

At seven that evening, the wedding party assembled in the sanctuary of the large, beautiful church.

The reverend stood on the top step of the chancel and asked, "Now, do we have everyone present?"

Kailey stayed quiet and let Shelley's mother explain.

"No, Reverend Evans, the...bride and groom are missing. They have been...detained. No, they've been...delayed. Just carry on."

"Well, all right. They really should be here, but we must move on. Your coordinator is Mrs. Whitlock, and I'll turn the proceedings over to her."

Mrs. Whitlock stepped up and clapped her hands like a schoolmarm. Kailey thought she looked like one of those nineteenth century spinster teachers with her hair in a bun and wire-framed glasses, but apparently she was married, and knew what she was doing.

"Let me give you an overview. We'll start in the middle. That is I will line all of you up exactly where you will stand during the actual ceremony, exactly as the audience will see you. First, where are my maid of honor and best man? Oh, there you are. You two will act the part of the bride and groom."

Kailey chanced a glance at Alex next to her, but he was already looking at her, grinning, with that enticing dimple winking at her.

After fifteen minutes of frustrating "stand here," "ladies, hold your hands as though you're holding your bouquet," and "No, no, don't fold your arms, gentlemen," the wedding party stood in perfect alignment.

Reverend Evans stood in his place, holding a small Bible, with Alex and Kailey standing before him. She held her hands as though she carried a bridal bouquet, and Alex stood straight and tall as though he waited for inspection from his platoon leader. His square chin level with the floor, the curve of his neck holding his head in perfect alignment, and his broad muscled shoulders encased in the blue oxford cloth of his shirt brought an ache to her heart and lump to her throat. He was so appealing.

Mrs. Whitlock stepped forward. "Oh, lovely, just beautiful. Now, our officiate the Reverend Evans will go through the wedding vows, but he'll use only the headings. We don't want to spoil the big day and hear the actual words."

The coordinator directed Kailey and Alex from behind on their proper responses, both verbally and physically. The reverend recited the beginning, the charge, the speaking of the vows, the prayer, the blessing, and the presentation of the newly married couple, pausing between each so Kailey and Alex acted appropriately.

A fleeting thought passed through Kailey's mind that this was useless because the bride and groom weren't here to watch how they should act. However, she became engrossed in the ebb and flow of the ceremony, so solemn and sacred, yet so joyous, that she imagined she truly was the bride and her groom stood beside her, repeating the correct vows, binding their hearts and souls in the sight of God forever.

"Amen. Now this is where the groom kisses the bride. However, it is not necessary for our stand-ins to perform the act."

The statement startled Kailey, bringing her out of her dreamy state, causing her cheeks to flare with embarrassment. The uncomfortable feeling increased when the bridesmaids and groomsmen began to softly chant, "Kiss her, kiss her, kiss her."

Mrs. Whitlock frowned at the young adults. They became very quiet and still, but not because of her admonition.

As directed, Kailey had turned toward Alex. He brought his arms around her waist, brought her flush with his tall warm body, and placed his open mouth on hers, kissing softly and gently, until her knees almost buckled.

Everyone applauded and laughed, except of course, Mrs. Whitlock...and Shelley's parents. They hadn't looked happy throughout the entire rehearsal.

"Ladies and gentlemen, we'll now practice the recessional, and last, we'll practice the processional, now that you know where to stand."

CHAPTER FOURTEEN

With the sun barely up, Kailey lay in her bed and stared at the ceiling. She'd replayed that scene a thousand times in her head. *Kiss her, kiss her.* And did he ever. She recalled it as an earth-shattering episode, and somehow she knew life would never be the same.

The week had sped by. One more day to entertain and act the host to Alex. When in the world would Sam and Shelley ever come home? They *had* to sometime today, because the actual planned wedding would occur at four o'clock– nine hours from now. If they weren't here, both families would be the talk of Austin for a long time.

Again, she met Alex in the kitchen, and this time both her parents were there, plus Mika. In a way, she wished to be alone with him, but she also knew that was unwise. What could they do for a few short hours? She would need at least a couple of hours to shampoo, arrange her hair properly, and dress. Also, the wedding party should be at the church at least one hour early.

Her father stood and greeted Alex. "Have a seat, son. Mika will get you a plate. Just tell her what you want."

Mika walked over with a spoon in one hand and the other hand on her hip. "You would like coffee, first? How about pancakes and bacon and eggs? Or juice first."

Alex paused and glanced at Kailey. "Are you going to sit?"

She said, "When I get my coffee. Here, Mika. Let me get Alex's cup and you get our plates. Just fill them up."

When they had cups of coffee and filled plates, Kailey turned to her parents. "Have you heard from Sam yet?"

Her mother shook her head as she wiped her mouth. "No, we have not. We're becoming quite distressed about all this. I cannot for the life of me understand what they were thinking. Is there a possibility they won't make it at all? Please tell me that won't happen."

Kailey shrugged and sipped her coffee. "At this point, I don't have a clue what they're up to. I can only hope they make it on time."

"So, darling," her mother said, "what will you and Alex do this morning?"

"We haven't discussed it. We'll think of something after breakfast." She gazed sideways toward him, but he was so busy eating Mika's superb breakfast she thought he wasn't listening.

When they finished and all the chitchat had diminished, Kailey walked upstairs to brush her teeth. Alex followed, but before she entered her room, she turned to him.

"Hey, I have an idea. Want to play a little one-on-one? It's cool out, just right for a game."

He sort of blinked and pulled back his chin. "You know how?"

The question caught her off-guard, because the entire world took one look at her and believed she played basketball. She opened her mouth, closed it, and while she wanted to say, "Of course," she didn't.

"Something wrong? Did I say the wrong thing?"

A smile curved her mouth slightly as she gazed at him. "That was the sweetest thing anyone could say to me. Did you know that?"

"Sweet? What do you mean? Girls don't usually play one-on-one. I was just surprised."

"You're the first man I've ever met or gone out with who didn't ask if I played basketball. It never occurred to you, did it? Or if it did, for some reason you didn't voice it."

"No, I didn't think of it, but I'll ask now since you do know the game."

"Not basketball. I ran track. Long-distance, anything other than a sprint or short race. I'm too tall and leggy to race the shorter girls who have thick calf and thigh muscles. So, do you want to play?"

He flashed that special grin that made the dimple appear. The one that he used when he was truly happy and delighted. "Yep, sure do." Chills skittered down her back.

"Okay, meet me out back in ten minutes."

Behind the patio, her dad had built a small court with one basket, just large enough to shoot hoops and play one-on-one. He had taught her to play, because Sam was always too busy with his own tennis games or girlfriends. As handsome as he was, the girls flocked to him his entire life.

She wore silk shorts with the slit on the side, her Nikes, and a tank top. He emerged dressed similarly.

"It's pretty chilly out here. Sure you have enough clothes on?"

She laughed. "I'll warm up very quickly. So, want to do that first? Warm-up?"

"Sure."

For a few minutes, each stretched leg muscles, did knee bends, raised their arms and twisted from side to side.

"Ready?" she asked.

"Ready. How about scoring? One point for normal shots and two for shots beyond the three-point line. I see someone had the court painted."

"That was Dad. Sam plays tennis. Okay, that scoring is good. How about a fifteen-point game?"

"Yep, that's good. How about make-it-or-take-it possession?"

"Done. And the clearing point is...oh, in that corner."

"Agreed. Want to shoot for first?"

"Yes, and since you're the guest, you're up."

The game began. Kailey got the ball first, dribbled, ran behind him, feinted, turned and made a two-point-shot.

"Whoo-eee, lady! You'd better watch out now. I do not give females any quarter."

"Yeah, right. Show me, big guy."

She trotted to the start point, began dribbling toward him as he tried to block her, made one turn and scored again.

Kailey laughed as she ran to the start point again. "Are you asleep? You'd better wake up and start playing pretty soon, or I'll skunk you."

"Ha-ha-ha! Just wait. I've only been observing to know how hard to go on you."

She dribbled the ball in a circle all around him. "So, hotshot, when are you going to figure that out? We can't play all day, you know."

In a sudden move, he slapped the ball from her dribble, turned and made a two-pointer teardrop.

"Sweeet, Alex Dunn."

She crouched on her toes, moving back and forth, arms spread, watching as he jogged to the start point. He slapped the ball from one hand to the other. He stood with his long muscled legs spread, with the calves in square bunches of muscles, even at ease. When he began to move, the muscles rippled up and down.

A smattering of light hair covered his calves and forearms. As he turned and twisted, the tank top with large arm openings revealed part of his chest, and the sight made her yearn to see it all. His electric blue eyes twinkled and shone like stars when he laughed, and he laughed with abandon often. Alex truly enjoyed himself.

After an hour, Kailey called time out. "Stop. Oh, man, I am beat. Okay, I give up. I admit I am not up to your physical level. Let's sit on the porch steps."

"Sure, thing." He looped his sweaty arm around her shoulders, and walked her to the step. "Oh, sorry. I got sweat all over you. Let me get some of it off." He placed his hand under her hair and swiped down her neck and back, very slowly, creating shivers down her back. Then he turned her to face him, and with both hands, swept down her arms. When he reached her hands, he took her fingertips and held them lightly.

They stood facing the other, and Kailey experienced that weak feeling. The eyes caused the sensation. No, his entire body caused it. With little encouragement, she could tumble right into his arms.

In an attempt to change the mood, she plopped down on the steps, stretching her legs out in front. Alex did the same, leaning back and bracing himself with his hands.

"That was great, Kailey. I've never played one-on-one with a girl."

Laughing, she said, and I've never played with anyone as good as you. Did you play in the Army?"

"Yeah, that was one diversion, but we played more volleyball so more guys could participate. Our games were vicious. It sure did take our minds off our jobs, though."

The patio door opened and Sam stepped out. "Hi, you two. We're back. Betcha thought we weren't going to make it."

Kailey stood and hugged him. "Sam Lovelace, I am going to kill you for what you've done to Mom and Dad. I hope you've apologized."

Hugging her back, he said, "I've been properly contrite. If I could explain this whole thing to you, I would, but I can't."

"Well, now you don't know what to do in the wedding. You'll make mistakes."

With his fist, he bumped under her chin. "That's another thing, sis. It doesn't matter. Everything will be just fine."

CHAPTER FIFTEEN

At two forty-five, someone knocked on her door. She took one quick peek in the mirror. Amazing. Mario had not only created the perfect style, he had taught her how to care for her hair in a simple manner. By directions from Shelley, she had pulled the left side of her hair back and secured it with a small silver clasp. At the church, the attendants would get a small white rose posey to place there. Her dress would not be pink like the bridesmaids', but a silvery rose, very pale and enchanting. She loved the satin that clung to the curves of her body and fell in a soft flare to the floor. Best of all, she wore her silver backless heels, just as all the other bridesmaids would.

She opened the door to Alex. Once again, he took her breath away with his gorgeous body and slight smile. So sexy and so...*male.* She knew without a doubt that he was one of the good guys, one that would always look after others, rarely thinking of himself, and probably never realizing how handsome he was. This man was one in a million.

The black tuxedo he wore enhanced everything about him, making his eyes brighter blue and his mouth more appealing, and his entire body so very special, tall and straight and sure.

"Hi." To say that one word almost choked her, for her throat had closed and her insides trembled.

"Hi, yourself. Can I come in, Kailey?"

He was so solemn, so quiet and still. Very serious.

"Yes." She stepped back to allow him entrance.

Inside her room, he leaned back against the door and stared at her with those beautiful eyes. "You are the most beautiful woman I've ever met, Kailey. Will you listen while I try to say something?"

She cocked her head to the side. "Well, yes, of course. Is something wrong?"

He pulled away from the door and took her arms, pulling her very close. "No, something's very right. I've fallen in love with you. There won't be another woman in the world for me. I'd like to know how you feel."

Stunned, she stared at him. Yes, he'd mentioned the word love in passing during this week, but this declaration was formal, sincere, from the heart.

His warm clean scent surrounded her, wrapping her in a soft

cocoon of exciting new feelings. *Yes, I do love you too, but I'm frightened.* Placing her palm on his cheek, she whispered, "Alex, I do love you. The day you stepped off that plane was a momentous occasion I knew would change my life. But..."

Holding just a little tighter, he kissed her softly. "I knew you'd have reservations. I'm not asking for any kind of commitment, only a statement about my feelings. There's no need for me to pretend otherwise, and I wanted you to know."

"Can we talk later? Before you go home?"

"I planned on it. For now, I'd like you to think about flying to Colorado the day after Christmas. That would be Tuesday. Can you do that? We can ski for an entire week. I used to work as a ski instructor during my college days, and the owners of the lodge insist I stay with them each time I show up. I'll reserve one of the best rooms for you. Think you might do that?"

The thought made her heart sing. Smiling, she said, "I'd absolutely love to. And what about your idea of joining an international medical team?"

"That's another topic to discuss for you. I'm holding my breath here, because I want to hear a yes so badly. Will you consider joining me? I've decided on one year."

One year alone with him with no family or familiar surroundings. That should be plenty of time to become very well acquainted.

"This sounds perfect for me. I still have two weeks away from the hospital, and I'll give them notice when we learn when and where we'll go. We can stay together, can't we?"

His eyes twinkled. "One of the suggestions is to have a 'partner'. Someone you feel close to, maybe bunk with."

She laughed. "Aha, now I understand the real plan."

"Just joking. Men bunk with men, women bunk with women."

She stuck out her bottom lip. "Ahhhhh, dang."

Alex smiled so beguilingly, she threw her arms around him and initiated the kiss. Her exuberance excited him, because he picked her up without breaking the kiss, twirled her around, and finally set her on her feet. With his arms around her lower back, securing her body to his, he whispered.

"I propose we set a wedding date about one year from now. How does that sound?"

"Perfect. We'll have a Christmas wedding, and we'll do it our way."

"It's a deal."

They sealed the promise with another kiss that lasted several minutes.

Her mother knocked and called through the door. "Come on you two. We don't have much time to get to the church."

"Okay, Mom."

She looked at Alex and smiled into his eyes. "I feel as though we've already had a Christmas wedding."

"You know? When I came down here to act as best man, I just hoped I'd have the perfect maid of honor to fit my height. Instead, I found the girl of my dreams, the perfect bride."

The End

ABOUT THE AUTHOR

Celia Yeary, a native Texan, former science teacher, graduate of Texas Tech University and Texas State University, is mother of two, grandmother of three boys, and wife of a wonderful, supportive Texan.

Celia and her husband enjoy traveling, and both are involved in their church, the community, and the university. Central Texas has been her home since 1974.

She has published numerous novels and novellas, and articles for a local magazine, Texas Co-op Power.

Visit Celia's website: http://celiayeary.com/

Romance and a little bit of Texas blog:
http://celiayeary.blogspot.com

Celia Yeary: Amazon page:
 http://www.amazon.com/s/ref=nb_sb_noss_1?url=search-alias%3Dstripbooks&field-keywords=celia+yeary

Stories by Celia appearing in Victory Tales Anthologies:
Addie and the Gunslinger
Along Came Will

Other books by Celia:
Kathleen: Trinity Hill Brides-Book 1
Lorelei: Trinity Hill Brides-Book 2
Annalisa: Trinity Hill Brides-Book 3
Beyond the Blue Mountains

One Foggy Christmas

Barbara Miller

Dedication:
*For my Greensburg Writers Group, who make
sense of my Regency stories.*

CHAPTER ONE

Christmas Eve, 1813, Somersetshire, England

When she heard the carriage slow down, Lady Jane Faraday assumed they were coming to a village. Her parents were both dozing on the opposite seat. She lifted the flap on the carriage window and noted the menacing fog along with the freezing draft of damp air that made her next breath show in a cold puff. Still there were lit shop windows, people with packages scurrying out of the way of the carriage. The breeze brought with it the scent of roasted goose and fresh baked bread. All things that should cheer her. She was trying to feel more optimistic about Christmas than she had last year, but how could she be happy after Henry's death? And there was still no word from Henry's brother Stephen in the Peninsula. She loved Stephen, but he had not written, so perhaps he did not return that affection. She had been only sixteen when he left.

She pulled her black wool cloak tighter about her and clasped her cold hands together inside her ermine muff. The bricks under their feet had long ago lost their warmth, so she wiggled her toes in her half boots to keep some circulation. She didn't mind the cold, but this beastly fog made her feel uncertain of the next step, let alone the next mile.

Past the village, the team picked up speed again though they could not canter at their usual pace. She wondered how the coachman could keep going when she saw nothing but vague shadows passing for buildings and dim lights that must be windows into candlelit rooms where people enjoyed the warmth of their hearth. It was as though the coach was floating through the clouds and might fall to earth. They had left home a good four hours ago. It did not seem at all like Christmas Eve without snow.

Last Christmas, she wanted the weather to prevent their arrival at Summerhill, the estate of her parents' good friends, the St. Giles. She had feared Henry might be compelled to ask for her hand. Even this year it would be an uncomfortable Christmas with Henry dead only two months from a riding accident. Henry loved horses. How terrible to die that way, though she did not know the exact manner of his death. She never knew what to say to people when a death was untimely. When was death ever timely?

A selfish thought crept into her mind like a tendril of fog. Henry's demise let her off the hook. No one could possibly now expect her to become engaged, though she wished he had not died to save her from that fate. It was his brother Stephen she loved. With no word from Stephen in many months, it seemed his father had given him up for dead in Spain, though Jane still hoped. Henry had been his parents' conduit for news of Stephen and now that was ended.

How strange. No matter how much you planned and prepared, events conspired to take you by surprise for good or ill. About Henry she was confused. She had kept him at arm's length for the four years he had courted her, and he had not made the task difficult. Almost as though he knew about her and Stephen. She'd been prepared to hold Henry off forever in spite of pressure from her parents. Now she felt guilty as though she could have prevented his death by marrying him.

Before they left the house today, she'd overheard her mother speaking to her father when they thought she wasn't listening. Her mother hinted Henry had killed himself. She hoped it was not for love of her since Henry well knew she did not return that affection. She prayed she had not misinterpreted Henry's feelings. Thinking back and rehashing every moment, his courtship had seemed like a show he'd put on for the benefit of their parents. She had never feared him making a proposal, only the broad hints dropped by her parents after every visit.

Her mother jolted awake and that made her father open his eyes. "I think the fog is clearing," her mother said. She pursed her lips and pulled her bonnet tighter about her brown curls.

Her father removed his hat and peeked out. Some flakes of snow settled on his graying hair. "Because it's getting colder. Perhaps we should stop at an inn."

"Nonsense, we can't be more than a stone's throw from Summerhill." Her mother leaned back and folded her gloved hands in her lap. "We shall keep going."

"We could be driven into a ditch," her father insisted.

Her mother always assumed the best would happen, but her father the worst. Jane cleared her throat. "The horses could be injured."

Her father just looked at her to let her know he had thought of that and was not willing to countermand her mother to avoid the risk. He always did what Mother wanted.

The match between her and Henry had been talked of for years by her mother and Lord Summerhill. She could not comprehend her mother's eagerness to reach Summerhill when a match between the families could no longer be. Plus they were still in mourning so a ten-day holiday seemed indelicate. She sighed. Jane had endured four years of uncertainly; she could stand anything for ten days.

CHAPTER TWO

Lieutenant Stephen St. Giles paused to get his bearings. He had often been on foot in the wilds of Spain and Portugal and managed to return to camp but never in such a beastly fog. It would be embarrassing to lose his way within striking distance of his ancestral home, but this mist was deceptive. Landmarks he thought he recognized proved to be something else, not a cottage but a sheepfold, not a path but a stream, hence the wet boots which were now freezing his feet. He blew out a breath and watched he droplets condense in the wet air. His dark green rifleman's uniform glistened with beads of moisture.

He supposed the area had changed much in the four years he had been in the rifle corp. Even trees grew up. But the road should not have moved. Every landmark seemed to betray his memory. If not for the death of Henry he might not have come back.

His departure from home had been wrought with despair and guilt, brought on by his father pushing him away as though he wished to disown him. He could not understand his father's behavior, but he must have offended him in some way that was lost to him. The fog was a good metaphor for his last months at Summerhill, fraught with confusion and misdirection.

His time in Spain gave him back his confidence. Putting his skills to use, Stephen had felt valued for his marksmanship, his willingness to take risks, to out think the enemy. He'd had friends there. The news of Henry's death had been bitter, especially conveyed in a letter from the family solicitor rather than a parent. The death notice had contained no details. Stephen had asked for leave and his captain insisted he return to England.

Though he had heard of his brother's death from Mr. Chadwick, their neighbor and solicitor, he'd had no word about it from home. In a way that was not odd, since only Henry wrote to him. What could Stephen have done to alienate both his parents?

After he'd fallen in a ditch a while back, he should have stayed at the coaching inn with the other passengers waiting for the fog to lift, but the possibility of getting home by Christmas Eve had tempted him to imprudence. He must speak to his mother. And would Jane be there with her parents? Did he dare hope? He considered the possibility that Henry had married her, but had not wanted to tell him.

He might have to swallow his pride, if he saw any inhabited dwelling at all, and ask the way. He stopped to catch his breath and looked around him in a circle for any inviting light or even a rooftop. The only peaks he saw could have been the tops of pine trees. Better off staying on the rutted track. He trudged forward, feeling the road as best he could with his feet and trying to recall if any of it seemed familiar. However, he had never walked. He'd always been riding or driving a carriage. He had done plenty of marching these last four years, so even if he were going in the wrong direction or in circles he kept warm by moving quickly.

He thought about Henry and how much he owed him. His brother had tried to keep their father from forcing him to take a position in the army. His brother had meant well, but he was thankful he had not been sent to the university as Henry suggested with the church as his goal. He could not see himself filling that role. In the army his marksmanship had made a difference. The war was won or nearly so. It was after they had crossed the Pyrenees and won that desperate battle at St. Pierre in France that Chadwick's letter caught up with him and won him the leave he had not asked for in years. He dreaded seeing his father again, and Summerhill would never be the same without Henry. At least his mother would welcome him.

With six years separating them in age, he'd been a child to Henry when he'd left. Now that he was twenty-two he would have savored Henry's companionship.

He'd had a good life in the army, but he had given something up, his youth. The mystery of his expulsion from Summerhill still haunted him. What if he was not welcome? He'd gotten precious few letters from Henry, none from his mother and father. He wondered if any of his missives had reached his mother. She might think him dead. It might have been better if he had waited at the inn and sent a messenger to announce his arrival.

Stephen suddenly saw a gate emerge from the brutal fog and recognized the stone work on either side of the wrought iron. It belonged to the churchyard and was adorned by a pine wreath and red bow, a welcome mark of the season. Now he knew where he was and not more than half an hour from home. But something stopped him.

He swung the gate open and walked though the mist to the St. Giles plots. There was fresh earth in one spot, cementing the tragedy into reality in his mind. He was too late for Henry, possibly too late for his mother and probably too late for Jane. He should have thought of all this before he agreed to the army as his escape.

CHAPTER THREE

Too late Jane discovered they were not the only guests at Summerhill. Lady Agatha and her son, Bertram, had taken up residence here and seemed all agog to further their acquaintance with her. She recalled the lord's sister and her unpromising son from holidays before, and had not liked the outspoken mother then either.

Amid the flurry of greetings Bertram gripped her arm and led her to the empty drawing room. "I must speak to you," he said. The room was chilly so standing in front of the fireplace did her no good. Bertrand stood taller than she recalled and he'd grown into his St. Giles' dark looks, making him somewhat handsomer. Without letting her catch her breath, he went down on one knee and grasped her right hand. "Will you marry me?"

"No, absolutely not. Let go of me."

Bertram sprang to his feet like a young colt. "I see. I should have spoken to your father first."

Jane retreated to the door. "No, don't you dare speak to him, and never mention this again."

She turned and fled upstairs to the guest room she usually occupied during her visits to find that her valise had been delivered there. She pulled off her bonnet and muff, and tossed them on the bed. She had been trapped again and guessed her mother expected her to align herself with Bertram Syn, the new heir. He had proposed to her as if it had been an unpleasant task he wanted behind him as soon as possible. What nerve. She tried to calm herself as she washed her face and traded her wool traveling dress for a gown of gray silk. She also unearthed a wool shawl to hide the gooseflesh on her arms.

The door to her room was thrust open by her mother without the courtesy of a knock. "Are you ready to go down?" Her mother wore a dress of amber silk, a bit too festive for mourning, but Jane kept her opinion to herself.

"Mother, did you know?" Jane draped the grey wool shawl about her shoulders against the chilliness of the house. It was not warm and festooned with greenery as it had been in holidays past, but cold and uninviting.

"Know what?" Her mother's round face held an expression of innocence.

"That they would be here."

"Of course. How could you have forgotten Lady Agatha is a widow? I'm sure it's only natural that Bertram's uncle shows some partiality toward him. For all we know he is the heir."

"He is not. Stephen yet lives." Jane stomped her foot and wondered what everyone would think if she did not go down for dinner.

"I know what you would like to believe, but you can't make it so by wishing it."

"If Stephen is alive, you would have no objection to me marrying him?"

"Of course not, but the war is nearly over and there has been no word. If he were alive, we would have heard. Always a dutiful boy, he would have written his mother."

"Yes, I suppose he would have." Jane was satisfied to get her mother's agreement that Stephen would be the preferred suitor. In her heart she believed he would return.

"So be polite." Her mother tweaked one of Jane's long brown curls and smiled. "There's no rush. Indeed it would seem odd for you to switch your affections from Henry to Bertram overnight." Her mother stepped into the hall and motioned for her to follow.

"You know I had no romantic feelings for Henry."

"Good then. You are not grieving for him."

Jane gasped. "Of course I am. He was a childhood friend."

"You must marry someone."

Jane followed her mother into the hall and made for the stairs. "No, I shall find employment rather than marry without love."

"Don't be ridiculous. What can you do?"

"I can teach."

"You wouldn't dare embarrass us with such a notion."

She was going to be twenty-one in a few months, so would have the power to decide her own future. Most girls her age were married but she did not care. She could refuse Bertram if he asked again and apply for a position at a girl's school. Anything would be better than living a lie.

CHAPTER FOUR

The fog was lifting but the snow fell now in clumps and soaked through the dark wool of Stephen's uniform. He had seldom seen such a storm even in the mountains in Spain. With a sigh of relief, he slung his pack and rifle off his shoulder and clapped the knocker on the front door of Summerhill. He still had a key but did not want to take anyone by surprise. He stomped his feet to try to get some feeling back.

The door cracked open. "Not today," old Foster said and moved to push the door closed.

"But—"

"Go 'round to the kitchen." Foster did close the door on him then.

The butler had not recognized him with his watery old eyes. What a joke. Laughing, Stephen hefted his pack again and walked to the back entrance. The maid that opened the door shook her head and began to push it shut. Stephen said the cook's name and the girl said, "Cook is busy. The family is at dinner."

Stephen was stunned. He could open the door and push past her, but what sort of impression would that make? Truth to tell, he had not wanted to arrive unshaven and damp. He turned his frozen steps toward the stable block and eased the door at the end of the aisle between the stalls open. He smelled the sweet scent of hay and heard the horses munching contentedly before he felt the warmth of their bodies. He pulled the door shut quietly, and walking down the row of stalls, was pleased to see both his hunters in their same boxes. They knew him and blew into his hand, whickering to him.

"Who goes there? What are you doing to those horses?"

"Getting a welcome home, Bossley." Stephen saw the stooped old man holding a lantern up and squinting.

"Mister Stephen? I say, how did you get here in this ghastly fog?"

"I walked." Stephen came toward him and was surprised by a warm hug. Old Bossley smelled of hay and sweet feed. The embrace brought back memories. Bossley had taught him to ride, and he spent long hours with the man trying to perfect his skills. Bossley had been a kind and patient teacher though Stephen was not as apt a pupil as Henry.

"Forgive me, sir," Bossley said, seemingly embarrassed at his exuberant welcome. "I was overcome. Let's get you up to the house."

"I have been turned away from both the front door and the back. They must think me a deserter begging for bread."

Bossley stepped back to regard him. "You do look a bit ragged."

"Any chance of some hot water?"

"Aye and a razor. You can shave and wash up in my room while I heat some soup and tea in the grooms' common room."

"Bossley, not a word to anyone that I am back."

"It will be a surprise to some of them. Not a word. It would ease your mother's mind if you could let her know. I could carry a note to the house."

So his mother was alive and apparently well. Stephen blew out a sigh of relief. "I'll think about it. Where are all the lads?"

"Gone off home for the holiday," he grumbled, "leaving me to look after the teams and hunters. His lordship doesn't have to pay them if he gives them the holiday off."

Stephen was not surprised by his father's behavior. The man had never cared if others struggled to survive. Stephen pulled a coin from his pocket and pressed it into the old man's hand. "Here's a sovereign for being faithful and letting me in when no one else would."

"It does my heart good to see you here and well. Your brother said you was wounded."

"Last year. Glad Henry did get some of my letters."

"I do miss him. Wash up and shave, then tell me all."

* * * * *

An hour later Stephen had his feet on the stove in the groom's room telling tales of his adventures and feeling more at home than he ever had in the house those last years before he left. This was how it had been on campaign. This was his life now, not sleeping in a feather bed being waited on. Not hanging garlands of greenery and singing wassail songs in the orchard. If things did not go well here, he still had the army, but before he decided anything, he needed to find out about his mother and Jane.

Bossley refilled his tankard with ale and pursed his lips. "Much as I enjoy your company, you do have to tell them you are back."

Stephen sighed. "Perhaps tomorrow. I shall sleep in the loft tonight and it will be a better bed than I have had for many a day."

"You can have my bed for all that, but why keep your presence a secret?"

"With Henry gone there is no joy left here for me. I can't help feeling somehow guilty about his death."

Bossley looked away. "I'm sure I don't know what you're talking about."

"How did he die? You can tell me."

"Kitchen gossip. It ought not to be spoken about by anyone."

"Did someone shoot him?"

"Nothing like that. He took a jump wrong on Belarus, a new horse he'd purchased. The horse stumbled and fell, and Henry was thrown. Your brother hit his head."

"He was such a careful rider." Stephen was puzzling over this when the door to the stable creaked open and soft steps came down the row of stalls. Then the sound of someone weeping caused the men to stare at each other. Stephen's feet hit the floor and he put down his mug of ale. When he pushed open the grooms' door and stepped into the alley between the stalls, he saw a girl stroking one of the horses. He approached the small figure as she threw back the hood of her cloak and long brown ringlets trailed down her back. It was Jane.

"Why so many tears on Christmas Eve?" Stephen whispered as he approached.

"Oh," she gasped in surprise, "I thought I was alone. I'm sorry." She wiped her eyes with her gloved hands before turning toward him.

"Who has hurt you?" He almost touched her but didn't know if he had the right.

"I know that voice," she said as if trying to recall how, then a small sound escaped her lips as recognition sunk in. "Stephen!" She rushed into his arms and hugged him as though their lives depended on it. "I did not know you would be here." She pulled back to look at him. "It's truly you, not a ghost?"

"It is really me. You have not changed a bit."

"You have. You seem taller."

Bossley appeared between the rows of stalls with a lantern. "'Tis because he lost so much weight. We'll have him fit in no time."

"He's right." She stepped back to look at him in the light. "You are thin, but you're home." A sudden frown stole the relief from her face. "Do you have to go back?"

"I'm on leave, but the army is marching through France. The war can't last much longer and I will be mustered out or put on half pay."

"Home for good." She grasped his arm and stroked his cheek then stepped back as though she realized her imprudent behavior.

"I hope so. Unless my father really has disowned me."

"Don't joke. He may have done as you suggest. Bertram is here with his mother and he is acting like the heir. Or rather your aunt is acting like her son is the heir."

"Bertram, my foolish cousin? So that's why you were crying."

"Yes. He forced himself on me and very clumsily, I must say. It makes me want to weep."

"So you are not married?"

"Of course not. I promised you I would wait."

Stephen breathed a sigh of relief and let his hand rest on her waist under the cloak. "I recall saying you were too young to make that decision, but since you have waited, what do you want to do now?"

"Punch Bertram in the nose."

"Well that too, but I meant with the rest of our lives. No vows were spoken between us. You were only sixteen, too young to make such a decision, but if your father is agreeable..."

"Yes, yes I would marry you. I will marry only you."

"I am happy you waited for me." He stroked her face with his rough hand and thought again about how much she had stayed the same and how much he had changed.

"With difficulty. They tried to marry me to Henry."

"I know about your parents' plans, but Henry never wrote anything about the future. Henry said he wanted to wait, not marry until it proved the right decision, and he had not felt it would be anytime soon."

"He might have told me, so I would not have worried about how they were throwing us together. He was very attentive but never made any advances."

"Could he have suspected my inclination?" Stephen asked. "I inquired about you in every letter."

"And I asked about you every time I saw him. Don't you see? He was saving me for you."

He sighed and pulled her to rest against his chest. "It's the kind of thing Henry would do."

"Not to interrupt," Bossley croaked, "but I think you both should go to the house And Miss Faraday should go before they mount a search."

Jane sighed and let go of Stephen. "It takes forever for them to have tea. I am safe from discovery. They will think I was fatigued from the trip and have gone to bed. We brought no servants with us so no one will even miss me."

"Still, it is cold out here. Get on with the both of you. Mister Stephen, I'll bring your pack up to the house tomorrow."

Stephen took her arm and the lantern and walked her across the stable yard to the back steps. He put his hand on the latch. "Locked for the night."

"Oh, I had not thought of that."

He smiled and set the lantern down. "Before we go in, there is one thing I want to do."

She stared up at him, her breath making mist in the cold air. He leaned and kissed her, sharing his warmth with her. They stood like that for many minutes even after the kiss ended, embracing each other.

"I don't know what my prospects are, but I will speak to your father."

"No matter what he says I will marry no one but you. Now, shall I knock?"

"No need. I have a key."

After seeing Jane to her room, Stephen went down the hall to his quarters. He lit a branch of candles, then put the lantern out. He drew the dust covers off the furniture and stretched out on the bed. So much had changed in the last half hour. Jane loved him, had always loved him, and been faithful with no prospect of marriage. Whatever else the morning had in store he could count on that. Still he puzzled over Henry and why he apparently had shielded Jane from marriage with him or anyone else.

Henry had written but never hinted at his plans. Perhaps he had been unsure of Stephen's feelings. No letter ever reached him from his father or mother. When he thought back over their lives here, his father had been cold to him only those last few years. Probably why Henry had taken him under his wing. His mother had not shown a preference between her sons. He would never broach such a subject with his father but his mother he could ask. Stephen found a nightshirt in the drawer, and took off his uniform coat. For the first time in months he would sleep in a bed.

Before he could change, his door cracked open and his mother slipped inside and ran to him. She was in a dark robe and slippers, her golden hair braided for the night. He could see silver threads in it but she still looked incredibly beautiful.

"Jane told you," he said.

His mother hugged him tightly.

"She did not think I should spend Christmas Eve without having my only wish fulfilled. Jane came to say goodnight and broke the news. She is a caring girl."

"I arrived late and did not want to disturb anyone. I found her in the stable."

"She loves you and has held out against marriage to Henry or anyone else."

"I am sorry I was not here for you when Henry died."

Between her tears she kissed his face and finally let him seat her on his bed while he took the straight chair.

"You are here now. That is what matters. I don't sleep much anymore, but I will sleep tonight knowing you are safe. Christmas has been empty without you."

"Then I'm glad Jane told you. I did not want to shock you."

"It is your father who will be shocked. He has had you dead and buried these many months."

"He changed so much before I left, as though he wanted to be rid of me. Was it something I did?"

"No, that wasn't it." She looked away as though the truth proved too gruesome to relate.

"Why then? I confess after being turned away by old Foster at the front door and the larder girl at the back, I began to think I wasn't wanted."

"I may as well tell you." She gave a profound sigh. "He doubts you are his son."

The statement caught Stephen like a physical blow. He jerked in the chair and it creaked. "But that's ridiculous."

"I know. I loved only him. That all seems dead to me now. The marriage that once seemed perfect crumbled before my eyes. I gave him two sons, and suddenly he decided he didn't want to own one of them." Her tears were flowing freely now and Stephen came to sit beside her and hold her. "It's your blue eyes and gold hair, like mine used to be, that he holds against you."

"And you had to face this all alone," he said.

"Henry knew and stood up for me. It's the thing they argued about the most."

"Good old Henry. How bitter for you. How hard for you to have to face his loss without me."

"Your father's temper worsened after Henry's death. I think it overset his reason. No one was as shocked as I when he invited the Faradays here as usual. I'm not sure how he will behave once he sees you are alive."

"I wrote to you every week. I never knew if you were receiving the letters or not."

She dropped her arms and stared at him. "I didn't receive your letters. So you received none of mine?"

"None."

"Henry heard from you on a regular basis and shared with me until... Then it ended."

"I wrote every chance I could. They can't all have been lost."

She looked up at him and tears began to flow again. "Your father must have thrown your letters to me away, and the ones I put on the hall table to go to you. I should have sent a servant to the village with them."

Stephen held her as she wept. His father had accused his mother of infidelity, which proved a horrific accusation for a woman to bear, then cut her off from him.

"You are home now and very authoritative looking. Perhaps you can convince him he was wrong."

"I haven't changed that much, have I?"

"Yes, your face is creased with care, your skin is burnt by the sun. Your hair looks much like mine did when I was younger, but he never accepted you favored my looks. Perhaps, he simply doesn't remember."

"I'll make him believe you." Stephen was not quite sure how he would accomplish this, but he had to convince his father that his mother had not betrayed him.

CHAPTER FIVE

Christmas Day

Jane woke before dawn as she always did on Christmas. When she glanced out the window the fog of the night before lingered in the yard and grounds, leaving the house surrounded by a milk-white sea where hillocks and trees were islands peeking through the surface. Then Stephen emerged from the whiteness and strode toward the house. He no longer wore his dark green uniform, but a black suit that hung on him in places but fit tightly across the shoulders, emphasizing how he had changed. Still she would know his sure stride anywhere.

He looked up, and seeing her at the window, waved. The sun broke through for a second and glinted off his blond hair. He was so handsome he took her breath away, and he loved *her*. That's all that mattered. She did not wait for the house maid to attend her but slipped into her grey wool dress and ran down the stairs. Her sense of anticipation for the day was reawakened. Stephen was waiting for her at the door into the breakfast parlor.

"Have you been up long?" she asked as she rushed into his arms. He gave her a kiss that felt warm and passionate without being possessive before he glanced around the hall. It was sweet how he cared for her reputation when they were not properly betrothed. She cared not a whit who saw them.

"I've been awake for an hour. I helped old Bossley with the horses." He opened the door to the breakfast parlor and they entered. He chose a corner chair and seated her at the table so they could converse quietly.

"Do the others know you've returned?" she asked.

Stephen laughed. "Only the upstairs maid, whom I startled. She promised to have the kitchen staff make up tea and toast right away."

"That means all the staff know by now. You still might surprise your father and the rest of the guests." Jane looked forward to witnessing the expression on all their faces when they realized Stephen was alive.

"Lucky me."

Two servers rushed in, the maid with a tea tray and old Foster with a rack of toast and dish of bacon. "So good to have you home, sir. I have informed all the staff," Foster said.

"Thank you, Foster. It's good to be back even under such sad circumstances."

Foster stiffened at the sound of his voice, then left.

Stephen chuckled. "Apparently he finally made the connection to the rumpled traveler on the doorstep, the one he turned away."

Jane smiled. "You won't tell on him."

"No, it is so easy to get along with servants if you simply don't say anything, but that does not work with family. I should have talked to my parents a long time ago."

Stephen served Jane breakfast while she poured the tea. It was as though they were already married. Jane recalled on Christmases past there had been greenery on the windowsills and adorning the mantel, both Stephen and Henry's doing. Then Stephen had left for the service, leaving Henry to decorate at Christmastime, but now he was gone, and Lady Summerhill had not bothered this year. Stephen's mother had suffered far more than she these past four years.

She watched Stephen eat slowly and methodically as though the food came at a great price and must be savored. "Do you mind so much that I told your mother?" she asked.

"Of course not. It was the right thing to do."

"The times I have talked to her over the years, your mother expressed much sadness that you did not write. She had to live off the words you sent to Henry."

He put down his fork and looked at her. "Mother and I figured out why she never received my letter telling her I was on my way home or apparently any of my other letters. When Henry retrieved the post and brought it to the table he'd already opened his letters, but Father went through the rest of the mail."

"Surely he would not withhold news from you when he knew how desperate your mother was about your welfare."

"I don't like to think he would, but there seems no other explanation."

His mother came in smiling then, wearing a dark blue silk dress. She kissed his cheek, and then took a seat on the other side of Stephen. "Don't stand on ceremony, Jane. Please pour me some tea."

Jane was startled into obeying. "Why does Lord Summerhill treat Bertram with so much favor?"

"I—I cannot say." Lady Summerhill glanced toward Stephen.

He smiled and patted his mother's hand. "I have negotiated a marriage with this young lady, so she is soon to be in my confidence."

"Even if my father objects, I will marry no one but Stephen," Jane added.

Lady Summerhill breathed a sigh of relief. "Then you may as well know. My husband does not think Stephen is his son."

Jane choked on a sip of tea and took a moment to recover. "That's absurd."

"My reaction exactly," his mother said.

"And mine." Stephen pushed his plate aside.

Jane thought over the implications of her hostess's revelation. "Will he take any action?"

Lady Summerhill smiled bitterly. "You mean other than sending Stephen off to be killed?"

"Let it rest, Mother. We don't know what he intended. At least I am back. I'm sorry I was not here when you lost Henry."

His mother stared into her teacup. "It was not your fault."

The door opened and Jane's father entered, but stopped at the sight of Stephen. "You are?" he asked.

"Stephen." Her beloved rose and stepped forward to shake her father's hand. Her father seemed stunned but held his hand out anyway.

"He has not changed that much, Father."

"I have been gone a long time," Stephen said. "I'm not surprised you do not recognize me."

Jane's mother pushed into the room and regarded Stephen with surprise and then calculation.

"Mother, Stephen is home from the war. Surely *you* remember him."

"Of course, but I must say, this is a surprise."

"To all of us," Lady Summerhill said.

Her mother seated herself across from Stephen and Jane poured her some tea. Her father stalked along the sideboard, putting bacon and toast on his plate. Jane was glad at least her mother welcomed Stephen, though she suspected her motives.

"Yes, I must have been a sight with my beard and ragged uniform. I took refuge in the stable until I cleaned up." Stephen sat back down and turned to his mother. "I see my hunters are still here. I thank you for keeping them."

"It was Henry's doing. He knew you would want them when you came back. Your father spoke of selling them, but Henry said you had put them in his charge and would not permit it. They had a terrible row about it."

* * * * *

The door swung open and Lord Summerhill stood in the opening.

Stephen made deliberate eye contact with his father and saw the old man's eyes widen in surprise. Cousin Bertram, who appeared much taller from the last time he'd seen him, peered over his father's shoulder. Stephen wondered where Aunt Agatha was but recalled she liked to sleep in late.

Suddenly the room felt crowded.

"I say, Stephen. Good to have you back." Bertram pushed in and clapped him on the shoulder. "So very good." His cousin went straight to the food and loaded a plate. He was not as pudgy as he used to be and hardly seemed like an interloper. In fact Stephen got an impression of relief from Bertram.

"So you're back." Lord Summerhill pronounced the words like a reprimand. With his dark brows and grim mouth it was hard to say what he meant by the phrase.

"As I promised in my last letter to Mother, which she did not receive."

His father pursed his lips and looked toward the sideboard. "I didn't think a mere rifleman could get leave, even for a funeral. But of course you did not arrive in time."

Stephen noticed his mother cringe at the word funeral. "An officer can request leave, when not in the thick of battle. I received Mr. Chadwick's letter at St. Pierre on this side of the Pyrenees. It was already a month old. Once the battle was ours, my second lieutenant was happy to take over for me. Since we are pushing the French back to Paris, my service is not required."

"So you mean to stay?" His father's eyebrows arched in surprise.

Stephen thought it an odd response even for a parent who was so alienated from him. "I'm not sure."

"Of course he's going to stay," his mother said, and laid a hand on Stephen's. "Where else would he go?"

"I'm sure Father and I will have a chance to discuss my future after breakfast, now that I have a future."

* * * * *

Though Jane enjoyed the meal more now that things seemed to be going in the right direction, she did not like the scowl on Lord Summerhill's face. She had to do her bit to make sure their marriage would be accepted as the best course. She did not want them pushing her onto Bertram even if he might inherit from his uncle.

When Stephen left the table with his father, she took her mother into the vacant morning room. No fire burned in the hearth and she drew her shawl about her for warmth. "This changes everything."

"Yes, clever girl," her mother said. "You have already found favor with Stephen. Can you contrive to engage his interest?" Her mother paced and rubbed her hands together.

Jane stifled an impatient sigh, but knew it was useless to speak to her mother of true love. "I am doing my best. Recall, I was not yet seventeen when he left, but now he sees me as a woman. What would Father say to such a match?"

"He will agree, of course. I will see to it." She rubbed her bottom lip.

"Then I am content."

"Jane, you need to let Bertram down easy."

"What? Oh, I will." She was surprised her mother had so much sensibility, but in her opinion Bertram needed no consolation.

* * * * *

Though Stephen had followed his father into the estate office, when the man had beckoned, there appeared no urgency on his parent's part. Lord Summerhill dealt with two supplicants and a letter before turning to Stephen who stood in front of the cold fireplace. He rested his arm along the mantle and regarded his parent as though the delay was of no concern.

He had faced the French guns and snipers, had been pursued by cavalry and laughed in their faces. Toward the end, he had taken far too many chances and had been wounded in the shoulder because of such foolishness. If his father had expected him to throw his life away, he had almost done so.

Lord Summerhill looked up. "You come back here and expect everything will be as it was."

"No, nothing will ever be the same again with Henry gone."

"You never cared about Henry," his father accused.

"Of course I cared. He was my brother, and he stood up for me and, kept you from showing your contempt for me. I will miss him for that and for his good humor and other kindnesses."

"You'll get the title, of course," he said as if Stephen had not spoken. "However, the estate is not entailed, you know. I can leave it as I wish."

"Of course. I think you should do as you wish. I want only one thing from you."

His father's brows drew together in confusion, probably unable to guess what could be more to the point than the title and estate. "What is that?"

"That you apologize to Mother for your unjust accusation."

"How dare you." His father flew to his feet and leaned forward, his fists on the desk. "May I point out: you are not in a position to be an authority on your birth."

"Apparently, neither are you. She has told me about your unfounded suspicion, which finally must have been your reason to send me away. That's when it all started, trying to get rid of me."

"I will not apologize."

"I believe she speaks the truth. I am your son. Why don't you believe her?"

Lord Summerhill shook his head. "It's true you don't look like me or Henry. Bertram is more in my likeness than you are."

"I look more like Mother, as she looked in her youth. If you continue to persecute her, I'll ask her to live with Jane and me – wherever we go."

"You and Jane Faraday? So that's how it is. You know she has only 500 a year."

"We have not discussed her income. In fact I have yet to speak to her father."

"Then you are hardly in a position to dictate terms to me. You wouldn't even accept the cavalry regiment I negotiated for you."

"I had two very good reasons for not accepting."

"What are they?"

"I am a much better shot than a rider, hence the rifle corps. Also I did not want to take our horses into the maul of war. I hear I have Henry to thank for the care of mine. Jane and I can leave on those if no other option comes our way."

His father stared at him in amazement as though digesting these statements proved a difficult task. Stephen thought it a good moment to leave him and seek his beloved.

CHAPTER SIX

Jane thought she had managed her mother well. With her on the side of marriage to Stephen, her father would have to capitulate. She realized she was thinking of their situation as a war campaign, probably because she had read so much about strategy in books and the newspapers.

She found her former suitor in the library hiding behind a newspaper.

"Bertram, I must speak to you."

Bertram jumped to his feet with a stunned look on his face. "Well yes, I was meaning to seek you out." He cleared his throat and tugged at his cravat. "This changes everything, you know."

Since it looked like Bertram was about to disavow his desire for her, she decided to let him have the moment. "Does it?"

"Stephen is back. There is no need for me here now, and I..."

"Yes?" She tried not to enjoy his discomfort. Clearly pursuing her had not been his idea. Perhaps it was why he had been so inept at it.

"I wish to withdraw my offer of marriage," he said with a rush as he moved around the chair as if the barrier would draw home his point.

"You have not spoken to my father, so no blame will be attached to your withdrawal. No one knows of it except the two of us, or of my refusal."

"Well thank God you did not agree. If you had, we would be in a pickle."

"Quite right. I understand and accept your withdrawal."

"That was a near miss, wasn't it?" He wiped his brow with his handkerchief.

Jane laughed and then Bertram joined in.

"Yes, a very near miss," she agreed.

Jane left him and strode into the gallery that connected the main house to the east wing where Bertram and his mother now had rooms. She wanted to see the row of portraits of the St. Giles heirs, hoping to see a resemblance between them and Stephen, but they were all dark-haired. Stephen's portrait had not yet been taken since he'd been away on his 21st birthday. Henry was the most comely of the St. Giles' heirs with softer black hair and a generous mouth.

Near his portrait was one of Lady Summerhill and – Stephen? But that could not be. This was painted when she was much younger and Stephen would have been a child or not yet conceived. Besides, he had told her there was no likeness of him.

Booted steps arrested her examination of the portrait. When she saw Stephen she ran to him and put her arms around his neck.

"Have you spoken to Father?" she asked.

"Yes and he seems in favor of our marriage, even though I am unsure of my prospects."

"That is because I convinced Mother it is a good idea."

He kissed her cheek. "I see you have been scouting the flank."

"I actually know what that means," Jane said. "Yes, it is good to know who is with you or against you."

"We could not talk settlements since I've no idea of my worth. Besides my pay, which I have saved, I have two horses and nothing much else so far as I know."

Jane smiled at him. "I have been saving my pin money. We can rent a cottage and open a small school. I can teach literature, history and watercolor; you can teach geography, French and Spanish."

He laughed. "Sounds peaceful."

"This portrait, who is it?" She pulled him across the hall and pointed at the likeness. "He looks so much like you."

"That is Felix, my mother's brother. He died soon after this portrait had been done."

"But he looks just like you or you like him. Doesn't that prove you favor your mother's side of the family?"

"It proves nothing except she is my mother."

"Oh, I see." She looked away from the portrait, which had been no help after all.

Stephen turned her chin toward him. "Don't despair. At least we have a plan. Your parents are on our side."

She forced herself to smile. "True. Your father is the only impediment."

"He may yet see reason. Now, they are setting the dining room table for more than are here. Do you know who is coming?"

She sighed. "The days of big Christmas celebrations are over at Summerhill, but I believe the Chadwicks and the vicar and his wife are always invited for dinner." She took his arm as he walked her to the main part of the house.

"Aunt Agatha and Cousin Bertram will round out the numbers then. We will all be thrown together for the whole day."

Jane heaved a profound sigh. "Do we have time for a walk before our confinement?"

"Yes, and there is someplace I want to share with you."

* * * * *

While Jane went for her cloak, half-boots and gloves, Stephen grabbed a large market basket from the pantry and a jug of cider.

Jane stared at these items but did not question him. He led her to the orchard where the snow of the previous night barely covered the ground. The apple and pear trees he and Henry had planted were mature now, but they were bare at this time of year, their dry leaves crunching under his boots. There were eight rows of trees plus grapevines trellised along the side of the orchard near the stable. He anointed as many of the trees as he could with the jug of cider.

"An offering?" she asked as she followed him, holding the basket.

"Something like that. I can't remember any of the Wassail songs. They've all been stamped out of my mind by war songs."

"*Here we go a wassailing among the leaves so green,*" she sang. "That's all I remember. It feels good to think of these trees blooming and being bountiful in the new year even if we will not be here to see them."

"It feels good to have a future especially with you."

"What is the basket for?"

"Come, we have a stand of holly a little ways into the wood grove. It was always my job to cut the low branches and take them to the house."

As he handed her the branches with their glossy leaves and red berries she said, "The berries against the green leaves are so vivid." She placed them gently in the basket as Stephen used his knife to cut them.

Along the lane stood a windbreak of pine trees. Stephen stopped to cut some boughs to bring back to the house with them.

When they came around behind the stable, he placed his bundle on the ground and clipped some ivy growing wild along the stone wall. "If we had more time we could go to the oak grove on the hill for mistletoe."

"We don't need it." She dropped the basket and he kissed her.

When he drew back he looked at her in amazement. "I can scarcely believe I am here and you are to be my wife. It seems like a dream."

"Believe it." She stood on her toes for another kiss, but they heard a carriage come around the house.

"We had better stop dallying and get these inside or it will be too late to decorate before dinner.

They ditched their outer garments in the back cloak room and hurried to the dining room where they decorated the epergne with holly sprigs and the mantel with ivy. Next they twined ivy along the banister in the entry hall and made a nest of pine boughs on the hall table. Then they entered the drawing room where the others were gathered and found Foster in the act of lighting the Yule log with help from the footmen. "Is that from last year?" Stephen asked.

"Yes, sir. Mr. Henry saved it."

"Wonder of wonders." Henry had saved a bit of log because he knew it would mean a lot to Stephen. He felt for a moment closer to his brother, but also sadness weighed heavy on his heart. His brother should be here, standing beside him. He felt his loss more keenly than when he'd first heard of his brother's demise. Henry's absence from the drawing room, where he belonged, made Stephen confront the permanence of this loss more vividly than the fresh grave in the churchyard.

"I'll take that, sir," Foster said of the remaining greenery he still held. "I am glad you remembered."

"Shall we go in to dinner?" his father asked as he jumped to his feet and interrupted the moment.

Chadwick hung back and on the way across the hall, he clapped Stephen on the shoulder and said, "We need to speak, but not today. Call on me tomorrow."

Stephen nodded, but wondered what the solicitor had to tell him.

The meal was not as uncomfortable as Stephen feared. There was too much food, of course, starting with a large pike, moving on to roast goose and all the requisite side dishes, and then ending with fruit and nuts. Food aplenty, and it made him remember the days his soldiers had gone to sleep hungry.

He saw that his father could still fake cordiality. It wasn't until Mr. Faraday proposed a toast to the happy couple that his father's expression turned mutinous. Lord Summerhill did not drink to Stephen and Jane, though even Bertram drained his glass. Aunt Agatha stared at her plate, which she had hardly touched.

When it was time for the ladies to leave the gentlemen to their port, Stephen rose and went into the hall to speak to his mother.

"I am to meet with Chadwick tomorrow at his home and I believe I shall have a better idea where I stand then. If Jane and I can set up household in a reasonable place, would you wish to live with us? Jane would enjoy your company as much as I would."

"That is kind of you. What are your immediate plans?"

"To return with the Faradays to London to set things in order. We cannot be married for a good four months. Mourning must be observed."

"I will come for a visit when it gets closer to the wedding," she said, tears of joy sparkling in her eyes. "This has turned out to be a joyous Christmas after all." She kissed his cheek and went in to talk to the other ladies who were exclaiming over the added greenery.

Stephen still stood in the hall, thinking how little it took to make some people happy when his father came to find him.

"What the devil do you mean by leaving the room?"

He gave a heavy sigh. "If we are to have an argument, I'd prefer it in your office rather than in front of company."

"Very well."

Stephen followed him into the cluttered room and stood in front of the cold fireplace. How many times had he been called to task for some minor offense that had not been his fault? He knew how often Henry had intervened on his behalf, and what it had cost him.

"The marriage between you and Jane is unacceptable," his father spat. "For the sake of the family honor, Jane, who was known to be engaged to Henry, must marry Bertram."

"She was never officially engaged to Henry. However, what does that matter and what has it to do with family honor?"

"I will talk Faraday out of this madness," his father continued his rant as if Stephen had not spoken. "She should marry my heir, Bertram."

"Jane is nearly twenty-one and not a commodity. In a few months she can marry whom she chooses."

"I will not have all my plans subverted by you," he blustered.

Stephen paced in front of the fireplace. "Yes, I have been a disobedient child. First, I went into a regiment of my choosing, and then I survived the war, which you thought would kill me. Unfortunately, Henry did not survive. I have been wondering how you would blame me for that."

His father glared at him. "He as good as committed suicide over worry for you."

"Nice try, but Henry loved life too much. He just wanted to live his own, not the one you designed for him. If not for Henry I would have had no letters at all."

"Henry was an obedient son except in the matter of the letters. He insisted on reading them at the table or I would have intervened."

"Are you admitting you hid my letters to Mother and destroyed hers to me?"

"It was better that everyone stopped thinking about you. Perhaps the talk would have died down."

"What talk? Henry was not in love with Jane. He would never have married her. He wanted his freedom." Stephen stopped and folded his arms with finality.

"And how was he to manage this..." his father threw up his hands. "Freedom you speak of?"

"By waiting here for you to die and all your plans with you."

His father stood slowly and leaned his hands on the desk. "How dare you?"

"I have dared worse and have the scars to prove it. Do you really think you can plan everything? You cannot control people no matter what you offer them. If you can't accept change and the decisions of others you will end up destroying the family."

"You are not even part of this family."

Stephen came to lean on the desk. "If you truly believe I am not your son, you should have had the honesty to tell me to my face?"

His father stepped back. "That would have created the scandal."

"Much like the one Mother will create when she comes to live with Jane and me? You have finally lost her. You've lost everyone. How can a king imagine himself in control when all he has left are servants?"

"I never accused your mother of infidelity." His father's gaze avoided his, shifting to the window.

"Not publicly but you said it to *her*." He did not want his anger to get the better of him, but his father must admit the wrong he had done.

"That's not what I said."

"She is innocent."

"People still talk about your appearance," his father insisted.

"So you withheld my letters from her. You sent me away to die then denied her news of me."

"You never wrote me," he countered.

It surprised Stephen to hear hurt in his father's voice. "I did once and no reply came. What would have been the point? I had no idea my offense was being born. What happened? You used to treat me like Henry."

"Unfortunately, you cannot prove you are a St. Giles." The older man turned away and thrust his hands in his pockets.

"And you cannot prove otherwise."

"You never stood up for yourself like a St. Giles."

Stephen gave him a menacing glare. "I am doing so now. I never understood the accusation."

"I couldn't make any. As I said, not without a scandal."

"Tell me, who put the thought into your head that I might not be your son?"

His father looked away again. "It's obvious you bear a resemblance only to your mother."

"Just as Henry looked only like you. One would never *know* he was Mother's child unless told so."

For the first time doubt crossed his father's face. And something else, possibly regret.

"Now tell me who planted that wicked thought." Stephen's fist came down on the desk in spite of himself.

Summerhill flinched and said, "It was Agatha who noticed you do not look like any of us."

"Except I favor Mother. And Bertram looks like Agatha, not his father. Have you thought about that at all?"

Lord Summerhill glanced up as though something was finally dawning on him. "It was merely an observation she made."

"Probably on every occasion she saw me," Stephen said, not hiding his bitterness.

"It was difficult to ignore."

"It was a veiled accusation made by a woman who had everything to gain. If she could shove me out of the way and anything happened to Henry, which it did, then Bertram was next in line. I never liked Aunt Agatha and now I don't feel badly about it." He turned on his heel and strode out of the room. His father made no move to stop him.

CHAPTER SEVEN

Stephen went to the drawing room, but the vicar and his wife had gone home after dinner rather than stay to witness a family row. Since the fog was creeping in again, the Chadwicks excused themselves. Stephen and Bertram walked them to the door. Mr. Chadwick begged Stephen once again to see him at noon on the morrow at their house since paperwork needed to be completed.

Bertram looked like a trapped mouse as they bid farewell to the company in the hallway.

"Where is your mother?" Stephen asked. "I need to talk to her."

"Closeted with Uncle. I saw her go into the office. That can't be good news for me. They'll both think I botched my pursuit of Jane's hand, but truly I am not ready for marriage. It's all turned out right with you engaged to her. Why can't they leave things alone?"

Stephen clapped him on the back. "They are plotters, Bertram. That's how we got into this mess."

"Do you know what Mother told me? That you are not his son. I never heard such a whopper in my life. Do you think she is quite sane?"

"I'm not sure, but don't let it concern you. You will always be a welcome visitor to Jane and me. Your mother is another matter."

"She does not make many friends even among family. I'm not sure why Uncle allowed us to come live here."

"About four years ago, wasn't it?"

"Yes, just before you went to the army."

Jane came into the hallway. "What shall we do? It seems sacrilegious to play billiards on this day."

"We can't walk," Bertram said. "We'd get lost in this fog which is creeping back over the grounds again."

"I could play the pianoforte for you," Jane suggested. "I brought sheet music."

Stephen smiled. "That would be a wonderful relief."

While Jane sorted her music, Stephen built up the fire in the drawing room. Bertram volunteered to turn the pages. It turned out Bertram had a respectable tenor voice. The impromptu concert pleased Lady Summerhill and the Faradays. All looked happier than they had at dinner.

Besides his aunt's gossip, there was another matter niggling at Stephen's mind. Henry was gone, but Stephen hoped it was not because of anything anyone had done. He was sure Bertram was innocent of any wrongdoing and Agatha could not have killed Henry, though she might have wished him dead. He refused to believe their father have driven Henry to kill himself. Stephen thought Henry was made of sterner stuff. His death had to be an accident.

Agatha and his father never joined them in the drawing room.

Stephen planned to help old Bossley with the stable work that afternoon. It would give him time to think about the letters. He was unnerved when Jane appeared in her cloak and half boots to help. Bossley dissuaded her from mucking stalls so she distributed grain, then sat and watched them finish the chores.

He introduced her to Bart and Ruby, his two hunters, and she smiled when he described them as their mode of escape if things got to be too much. He thought Jane would like nothing better than to ride off with him, convention be damned.

He recited the history of each horse in the stable and they stood talking to old Bossley for as long as possible to delay their return to the house

"It's a relief you've spoken to Father," Jane said.

"Yes, and after the toast I don't think he will change his mind even though we have not discussed settlements."

"Is that the only reason for delay?" she asked.

"We need time to mourn Henry."

"I agree. We can delay our happiness. I came here not knowing what to expect. I never received a single answer to any of the letters I sent you. I feared you dead until your mother mentioned Henry had heard from you."

Stephen looked at her, hoping his worry did not show.

"Don't look so downcast. I don't blame you for not having time to write me with all your duties."

He glanced aside, hoping for some distraction. "I received a letter from you, one that was posted from Hastings."

"That was when I visited my sister. But nothing else from me?"

"I fear not."

She looked puzzled and her delicate brows puckered over her expressive eyes. "Did you answer?" she asked.

"Yes. Of course." Stephen did not want her to puzzle this out but could not lie to her.

"I received nothing." Her lips had a delicious pout to them. "How many letters did you send me?"

"Four or five... dozen."

She stared at him. "I did not get a single one. That means..."

He put down the pitchfork and embraced her. "We don't know what it means."

"I would suspect Mother, but Father is the one who franks the letters. He must have thrown mine away and destroyed yours to me as well."

She spun on her heel and marched toward the door, but he caught up with her and hugged her, turning her in his arms. "Let it go."

"How could they?"

Stephen blew out a breath and shook his head. "I don't know, but we have a chance at a future now, so forget the letters."

"But it was a part of your life and mine they destroyed. Four years when we could at least have had the letters."

"We have each other now or almost."

"I'll never forgive them." Jane's gaze took a determined set that he knew he could not kiss away.

"If you knew what war was like, you would be willing to forgive a great deal more just to have a life again. Promise me you will not argue with them."

"You don't know what it's like to feel powerless, to have someone else decide your future for you and not even listen when you express an opinion."

"I think I do know. If I did not want to be a cleric, I had no other choice, but to go into the army where I had to follow orders."

A tear ran down her cheek. "Of course you had more to bear than I did, more uncertainty."

"Not more, just different."

"Holding out against all of them became so worrisome."

He gripped her elbows and pulled her into a hug. "They did not break your will after all. You held out and we are together again."

Jane sighed. "I still have the awful feeling something will go wrong."

"Do not fret. I will know more once I talk to Mr. Chadwick. Please say nothing to your parents until then."

"You are right." She dashed a hand across her eyes. "I am acting like a spoiled child. I will hold my peace, but they had better not stand in our way."

CHAPTER EIGHT

Jane changed into a green silk dress and stole a sprig of holly to clip in her hair. The songs they'd sung earlier had made her realize she missed the festivity of the season. Henry would understand their need for normalcy, and in a sense it honored the seasons of old where Henry sang beside them. They needed to celebrate his life as well as mourn his loss.

She was surprised to see Lord Summerhill and Lady Agatha at supper that evening. The atmosphere between the two appeared as frosty as the air outside. Her own parents sent each other worried glances since Summerhill's gruff attitude toward them and his lady proved difficult to ignore.

To fill the awkward silences, Bertram asked Stephen about the war and looked so expectant, Stephen told him about the battles he'd been in, careful, Jane thought, to edit out anything that might give someone a turn during the meal. He talked about the food and the wine, comparing it to the capons and pear wine they had tonight, and pointed out how blessed with plenty they seemed to be.

"And none of your doing," his father said.

Jane cleared her throat. "Stephen was one of many who fended off Napoleon's advances. We cannot minimize his role."

Lord Summerhill stared at her as though she was an ant who learned the art of speech. "What has that to say to the state of things here?"

"England is unlikely to be invaded now," Jane answered.

"It was never a possibility," Lord Summerhill said.

"I have followed the war in the papers and it was Napoleon's aim."

Her own father stared at her. "You followed the war. Why?"

Jane looked across the table at Stephen. "Because I am interested in such things."

"Young ladies should not be," her mother said.

"Nevertheless, I have read about the battles and the aftermath." Her voice dipped as though she were speaking of something forbidden.

"I still don't see why." Her father shook his head.

Stephen's sharp intake of breath drew their attention. "Oh God, you were looking for my name among the dead or wounded."

Jane shifted in her seat as all eyes fell on her. She blinked back a tear. "Yes, I was," she said. "I had feared the worst."

"But you were supposed to marry Henry," Lord Summerhill said. "He was courting you."

"We were never in love, and I believe Henry kept up the pretense of courting so I could wait for Stephen's return."

"So it was all a ruse." Faraday seemed to be in awe of his daughter.

Stephen blew out a breath. "I had no expectations."

"Neither had I," Jane reminded him. "I have had time to reflect on how Henry treated me, not as a future wife with words of love, but more like a...sister. We spoke of Stephen more than anything else."

Lady Summerhill smiled at Jane and Stephen. "Taking it on blind faith."

Her father frowned at them. "Were you carrying on a secret correspondence?"

"There was nothing secret about it. Besides, Stephen got only one of my letters and I received none of his."

She stared at her father who seemed merely puzzled, but her Mother overturned her water goblet. "Letters will be the death of us all."

Stephen shook his head as his mother calmly leaned forward and laid her napkin over the wet place.

"What promise did you make her?" Lord Summerhill demanded of Stephen.

"Nothing, Father. I could promise her nothing."

Old Foster dropped a bunch of silver in the pantry with a crash loud enough to make the ladies jump.

"Clumsy fool." Even Lord Summerhill seemed relieved to remember servants could overhear them arguing.

Stephen smiled. "He's probably just reminding us this is not the place for this discussion if there is a place for it at all." He looked around the table and no one but his mother, Jane and Bertram could meet his eyes.

"Yes," Jane agreed. "We should let the past rest and focus on the future."

* * * * *

No more was said while the final course was served, a warm fruit custard. It was with relief that Jane rose with the other ladies and went into the hall. Instead of turning toward the drawing room, she went up to her room and gave in to another bout of tears. Now she knew. Her mother had betrayed her.

She was done crying when her mother opened the door and let herself in. "You have to understand why I did it."

"Are you planning to explain? That would be a feat."

"Henry seemed perfect for you."

118

"Because he had the best prospects. Do you know why Stephen was sent away?"

Her mother shrugged. "The second son always goes into the military."

"No, Lady Agatha came to live here with Bertram that summer. She convinced her brother that Stephen was illegitimate."

"But that's absurd. I'm very sorry."

Jane looked up and saw an unusual sincerity in her mother's face. "Did you burn them?"

"What?"

"The letters."

"No I kept them."

Jane jumped off the bed. "You mean I can have the letters?"

"I do not keep such things on my person. They're at home. All is settled, isn't it?" her mother asked.

"As far as Stephen and I are concerned."

"He'll have the title at least."

"Mother, if he was impoverished and had nothing but the two horses in the stable, I would marry him anyway."

"Admirable, but let's hope this isn't the case."

Jane groaned but her mother had already swept out of the room.

CHAPTER NINE

Lord Summerhill had abandoned his male guests as soon as the port was served, letting them all breathe easier.

Bertram looked across the table at Stephen. "The newspaper reports the Battles of the Nive were closer run than you let on, particularly St. Pierre."

Stephen thought his cousin did not sound like such a fool after all and answered his comment.

"The French are more desperate fighting on home turf. They know they will lose. There should be no more action until spring. They will retreat and fortify somewhere in France and we will beat them again. Next year the war will be over."

"You won't go back then?"

"I doubt it."

"Will you stay here?" Faraday asked.

"Not in this climate. I might move to London. I'll know more after I speak with Chadwick tomorrow. Perhaps then we can discuss the future."

Lord Faraday smiled and leaned back in his chair. "I look forward to it."

Bertram sat up straight. "I say, could I run up to London with you?"

Stephen smiled at him. "Your company would be most welcome, Bertram."

"It's a bit too frosty here for me, and I don't mean the weather."

Stephen laughed and suggested they join the ladies in front of the fire. That turned out to be only Mrs. Faraday and Jane. The servants had done wonders with the rest of the greenery, making a wreath of the leftover pine boughs for the front window, arranging ivy along the mantle and tying the remaining stems of holly to the base of the candelabra. The red berries and glossy green leaves glowed in the golden light.

Finally his mother came in smiling, and he looked expectantly at her. "Your father wants to see you."

"Again?"

"Please be nice. He has apologized to me."

Stephen was tired of confronting his father but entered the room anyway with a blank face. If he wanted peace for Christmas he could ill afford to judge the man.

"Please don't loom over me," his father said. "Just sit down."

He sat in the chair across the desk from his parent and sighed.

"After talking to my sister and your mother again, I realize I should have confided my true concerns to your mother. I mentioned what Agatha had said to me, but I didn't say I believed it. I simply did not want it repeated everywhere."

"I don't follow." Stephen was used to his father worming out of his mistakes and getting away with it. He did not believe his mother merely mistook his father's words, but he bit his tongue on the matter. He would listen to what his father had to say and relinquish judgment until all was said. He recalled his mother's smile and decided to listen to the small voice that warned him to let it go.

"I never wanted you to die." There was anguish in his voice and the desperation of someone who has been misunderstood. "I just wanted you away from Agatha and her poisonous tongue."

His words finally sunk in and Stephen heard the meaning behind them. "Ah, that's why you let them move in here. She couldn't gossip about the family in the household the way she could have in London."

"You were ever a quick lad."

Stephen thought of all the times he'd been called a dunderhead by his father, but merely sighed. "Things did not turn out as you expected."

"No, as soon as you were gone, she thrust her chick under my nose as if Bertram could be a replacement for one of my own. Henry and I argued about it on more than one occasion. We argued the day he rode off and fell over a jump. After Henry died, Agatha redoubled her efforts.

So it had not been suicide, but might have been prevented if Henry had not been angered. He looked at his father who seemed to be waiting for a blow. What would be the point? Heated words would not bring Henry back. "If all you say is true, why the frosty welcome then?"

"Agatha renewed her campaign and threatened to spread her lie if I welcomed you home."

Stephen shook his head. "I'm glad the French did not have her on their side."

His father did not laugh at the joke. "I made a terrible mistake and I think Henry died for it."

This admission surprised Stephen and he weighed his response carefully, finally deciding on what he thought Henry would prefer. "His death was an accident."

"We argued about sending you away. I kept thinking he killed himself so he would not inherit Summerhill. To punish me, you see. You said yourself he didn't want the title."

"Henry had a mission. He would never have abandoned it midway." Stephen realized he cared enough about his father to disabuse him of the notion he killed his own son.

"What mission?"

"To keep Jane safe for me."

"I see." His father leaned back in his seat and the chair creaked in protest.

"I only wish Henry were here so I could thank him. Henry loved life, his own and everyone else's, too much to ever consider ending his on purpose."

His father stared at him. "After dashing the idea of university it was logical for you to go into the army."

For the first time, Stephen considered his part played in his dismissal. Perhaps his father wasn't the only one who remembered the past as they wished. "No, I wanted to fight. I just wish I had not left under a cloud."

"I am proud of you in my own way, even though I did not approve of your choice, a rifle company."

Choice? His father was an old man and would never change. Perhaps what his father perceived to be the truth was more useful to all of them than what had actually happened. Stephen was no longer sure after all this time what had been said. Surely the intentions of all of them were as blurry as a dense English fog.

"Have you nothing to say?" His father toyed with his pocket watch.

He looked into the man's dark miserable eyes and smiled. "I know this has been a difficult day for you, but would you come to tea and let everyone know we are finally at peace?"

"It will be embarrassing."

"Do you imagine you are the only one with guilt? Me, Aunt Agatha..."

"She is packing and will leave as soon as the weather permits."

"Where will she go?"

"I own a house in Manchester and the tenant's lease is up so she will reside there."

"That will inhibit any gossip," Stephen said. "I warn you Bertram plans to spend some time with me in town."

"He would be better off with you than with my sister."

"So we are of one mind." He waited for his father to say more, but when he didn't he said, "You will apologize then?"

His father rose slowly and arranged his watch fob. "I have apologized to your mother."

"This is not negotiable. You must set it right, at least in this small group. They are all aware of your claims."

"Very well." Lord Summerhill preceded Stephen out of the room, but hesitated at the door of the drawing room.

"I must tell you: Henry had a will done, years ago. He always feared for your future. He left you everything he'd inherited from his grandmother on the St. Giles side, the London house, and his income."

"Are you telling me this now for a reason?"

"It's my way of wishing you a Happy Christmas."

"I thank you, sir, for putting my mind at rest, but I would have much rather had my brother at my side."

"So would I."

CHAPTER TEN

Jane stood transfixed by the fire – the slow crumbling of ash and the flare up as some new bit of wood caught – she thought it was beautiful in spite of the destruction.

"Would you stir the logs, Bertram?" Lady Summerhill asked.

Lord Summerhill came in ahead of Stephen and took his seat. The tension seemed to have gone out of him. "As you all know I am the first one to admit when I have made a mistake." Blatantly untrue, but no one said a word to the contrary.

Stephen stared heavenward to hold in what Jane assumed was a guffaw. She felt herself pursing her own lips in sympathy as her betrothed took a seat on the sofa next to her.

"I was very wrong to cause the recent estrangement between me and my wife and to send Stephen away under a cloud of doubt. I hope that when the time comes, he will take up the management of the estate. And I am happy to welcome Jane as the future mistress here."

"I am happy to welcome her as well," Lady Summerhill said.

Stephen nodded slowly as though he was trying to decide if his father's words were adequate.

The rattle of the teacart broke the silence and Stephen felt relief at passing over a rough place so easily. Foster smiled at all of them as he helped the maid unload the platters onto the table before they left them to their tea.

"Stephen." Jane leaned close so only he could hear her, "Mother still has the letters, yours and mine. If you come to London with us you can have them."

"I will treasure them. It will be like living our lives backwards."

"You don't suppose your father kept yours to your mother," she whispered.

"I do not plan to ask him. That he has exonerated Mother, even obliquely, is enough for me."

"He seems a different person."

"Perhaps he is."

Jane gestured toward the mantle. "The room is warm and beautiful now, and all it took was a fire and some vegetation."

He looked around. "It's not the log and the greenery. The warmth comes from the people."

"When shall we wed?" she asked.

"When we have summer, flowers and fair weather. Let us plan it for the Peace Celebrations."

She sighed. "Peace, something I thought never to see with our families."

He leaned close and kissed her, which caused some throat clearing from their fathers but a cheer from Bertram.

The End

ABOUT THE AUTHOR

Barbara Miller teaches in the Writing Popular Fiction graduate program at Seton Hill University and is Reference Librarian at Mount Pleasant, PA Public Library. She has published historical and contemporary romances, mysteries, young adult books, a storybook and a paranormal novel. Two of her plays have been performed at the Pittsburgh New Works Festival.

You may email scribe@fallsbend.net or visit www.fallsbend.net

Stories by Barbara Miller appearing in Victory Tales Anthologies:
Myths, Legends, and Midnight Kisses, 2015 Collection~ *The Haven*
Be My Always, 2015 Summer Collection~ *Hometown Flame*

Favorites of Ms. Miller:
Kelly's Rules
Christmas Fete

Jack and the Christmas Journey

Teresa K. Cypher

Dedication:
*To Dave, for your unending support, but most of all,
for never going a day without reminding
me what romance is.*

CHAPTER ONE

Tildie shivered. It was December 20th, and everything was already as gray as chimney smoke. Harp would be in his glory. Oh how he'd loved winter.

The weather was about to make a change; cirrus clouds never lied. When the alarm clock went off, the sky had been clear as a bell, but in the first couple hours of daylight, high, wispy clouds drifted in. "Mare's tales," Harp used to say "Weather coming in thirty-six hours or less." He always swore he could forecast better than anyone on TV. And that was from just looking at the sky.

She hung the broom back on its hook and looked around the yard. "Jack!" A flash of black and white bounded her way, his tail whooshing in a circular wag. When she reached down to pet him, he sat in front of her, offering his paw. She shook it then patted the top of his head. "I should've just let you sweep the porch with that tail of yours, huh?"

His chocolate-brown eyes searched hers. When he did that, even three years later, she imagined he was asking her, "Where is he? When is he coming home?"

"You're such a good dog," she sweet-talked him. "You're getting too used to me being home. My vacation this week'll spoil you for sure. And then next week you'll try to follow me out the door when I leave for work."

He eyed her like he understood every word she'd said.

"One more year, buddy, and I'm retiring. Then you'll have me every day." A red ribbon flapped in a new breeze. She tucked it into the pine boughs hanging on the porch posts. One more glance at the foreboding sky and she ushered Jack inside.

The scent of fresh coffee filled the kitchen. Jack looked expectantly up at her. His toenails clicked on the hardwood floor two steps behind her as she made her way to the pantry. A few minutes later, he was eating his morning can of food, and she was taking her first sip of morning brew. The phone rang, breaking the blissful silence.

"Hello, Janson's."

"Good morning, Tildie. What're you up to today?"

"Hi, Sissy. It depends. Sounds like a loaded question to me."

"What's that supposed to mean? Never mind. Lindy, Carol, and me are going out to breakfast, and wondered if you wanted to come too?"

"I don't know. I have so much to do."

"Pffft! You don't have anything to do. C'mon. Step out for a bit. We want to get things done before the storm moves in. Christmas won't wait."

"There is a storm coming? I was just telling Jack there was some sort of weather on the way. Those cirrus clouds, Harp used to say."

"Don't change the subject. Breakfast?"

"I'll pass."

"Why?"

Tildie looked around, trying to come up with an excuse that would prevent the heckling that was sure to come. Her eyes rested on Jack licking his bowl. "I don't want to leave Jack alone. This has been hard on him. You know how he loved Harp."

When she answered, Sissy's voice was soft, but carried a touch of scolding—which sliced right through Tildie. "Jack is fine. And yes, it was hard on him, and it was hard on you. It's still hard on you. But Harp's gone, and you're here. You have to go on living."

Tildie controlled her breathing, trying to will away the crushing feeling in her chest. She didn't want pity. And she sure didn't want to be bossed around. She just wanted to be left alone.

Sissy broke the silence. "How about we stop over then? Maybe you can fix us breakfast?"

"I don't have enough eggs."

"It's settled then. We'll pick up eggs on the way. Anything else you need? Do you have bread? Preserves? And milk? Tea, too, because you know Lindy doesn't drink coffee. Who doesn't drink coffee? I always said something about her wasn't right. We'll just pick up everything we need on the way. See you in a half hour. Toodles!"

"Wait, I'm..." The phone went silent. Well, so much for heading them off. The last thing she felt like was having company.

She looked around. Nothing needed to be straightened. Maybe take Jack's bed outside and give it a good shake; that was pretty much it. Then she remembered the hand towels for the powder room, the red and green ones with poinsettias and snowflakes embroidered on them.

She hurried to dig them out of the back of the closet in the guest bedroom where they'd been buried for three years. They were too pretty to hide in a closet. Ben's mother always stitched such beautiful things. While she located the stepstool, her thoughts turned to Ben, Harp's best friend.

They grew up next door to each other. She and Ben had been buddies since they were big enough to wander into each other's yards. When they went to first grade, they'd met Harp. The rest was history. The three musketeers, or the three stooges as her dad had been fond of joking with them. Ben was the best man at her and Harp's wedding.

Then the thought followed – the same one always, about the New Year's Eve they celebrated together, and they'd all had a bit too much to drink. Her and Harp, and Ben and Charlene... And what Harp said to her just before he dozed off, hours later. Charlene left Ben within a week of that night. Tildie knew; it was her fault. And the thirty years that had since come and gone had done little to soften the sting.

She folded the towels, design out, and arranged them in a basket on the vanity. A little bit of Christmas inside the house to match the little bit outside on the porch posts.

CHAPTER TWO

She heard them before she saw them. Sissy wasn't the loudest, but she was the boss. Anyone watching and listening would figure it out in a heartbeat. One quick knock and then the door opened. "We're here!" A tornado of grocery bags, chatter, and friends blew inside.

Carol rifled through the pots and pans until she pulled two skillets out of the cupboard. Sissy set up the coffeemaker while Lindy dumped a bag of fresh fruit on the counter. "Fruit salad anyone?"

"I thought I was making breakfast for you three?"

Sissy pointed to a counter stool. "Sit. Take a break. We have a big day planned for you."

It was easier to acquiesce to Sissy's demands than it was to argue with her. Tildie learned years earlier to pick her battles. She parked herself at the counter. "What do you mean you have a big day planned for me?"

"I watched that weather channel—you know the one that has the cute weatherman in the afternoon. You know, they give the forecast twenty-four-seven? Anyway, they said we're good until day after tomorrow, early morning. Just some cold rain. So, we thought," She looked at the other two and they grinned at Tildie." We'd take you shopping and then out to lunch."

"I have no need to –"

"Did you buy cookie-making ingredients? Do you even have a tree? "Sissy made an exaggerated show of looking around her. "Because I sure don't see one anywhere. And do you have the stuff you need for your famous peanut-butter fudge? How about the gingerbread cookies?"

"I'm not making cookies. I don't do that anymore. Or fudge."

"Yes you are. And what about Christmas gifts?"

Sissy was unstoppable. "What about Jack? Doesn't he get a stocking with doggie treats? And what about us? We're your best friends. Don't we get gifts?" All three laughed at the final question.

Tildie put her head in her hands. Part of her wanted to laugh along with them, and part of her was still fighting it all. How could she laugh and be merry when Harp couldn't? In spite of that, she lifted her face and smiled. They were trying to help her out of the rut. And as much as it hurt to admit it to herself, she wanted out of that rut. But she couldn't figure out how to reconcile her feelings of needing to grieve him forever, and needing to return to the living.

"Well, I can't have you—or anyone you talk to, thinking I'm Ebenezer. And Jack does deserve to rip open a few gifts. No tree though. I can't do a tree."

Sissy grinned from ear to ear, accentuating those devilish dimples the boys had always loved. "It's a plan. Now let's get some food fixed and plot our course for the day."

An hour later, while Lindy loaded the dishwasher—all the while complaining about being stuck with cleanup duty, the other three sat sipping the last of their coffee. Sissy said, "It's agreed then. We go to the mall first. We'll stop at the pet store, and then the home store because you'll need to buy my gift there, and Soaps and Scents because Lindy and Carol love that stuff. Then lunch, groceries, and the tree-lot on the way home."

Tildie piped up, "I said, no tree."

"Oh, we're getting you a tree."

Lindy seconded it and Carol looked on, bobbing her head up and down.

Tildie bit her tongue. Waste of time arguing now. When it came down to it, she just wouldn't get a tree.

CHAPTER THREE

By the time they sat down to order food, by Tildie's estimate it was well past lunchtime. She needed to collect her thoughts and catch her breath. They chose the Brick Oven right in the mall, rather than fighting traffic on the way to one of the eateries downtown. From where they sat, they could watch passersby, and see most of the restaurant. They were chatting away, commenting on what people were wearing when a familiar face appeared among the mall walkers. *Ben.*

Carol sighed. "Man oh man, I think he looks good with gray hair."

Lindy chirped, "He'd look good with green hair, or purple hair, or even no hair."

Sissy said through a smile, "The man's still got it."

Tildie looked down at her plate – doing everything she could to avoid their conversation.

"Oh look. He's coming this way," Sissy was out of her chair before Tildie could stop her. "Ben! Oh Ben?" Her voice rose well above the patrons' chatter while her arm, waving like a turning windmill, completed the spectacle. " Hey, come sit with us."

Tildie's cheeks burned, and her smile felt stiff when she looked up and met his eyes. He stood before them, wearing his easy, lopsided grin. *God, still shades of the handsome kid he was decades ago.*

Lindy held out her hand and when Ben offered his own, she grasped it and hung on, then hung on some more. Her head was cocked off to one side—not enough to look awkward—like Jack when he's trying to understand a human word. Just enough to have that inviting, questioning, 'I'm so available' look. Then she batted her eyes at him.

Tildie bit the inside of her cheek. *The nerve of her. She actually just batted her eyes. Who does that?* Yeah. Sissy was right. You can't trust someone who doesn't drink coffee. She pulled herself out of her thoughts in time to hear Lindy say, "So, if you're free, my church is having our Christmas cantata tomorrow evening. I'd love it if you'd come. We could stop and have pie afterward."

His smile never changed, and it must have darn-near broke her heart when he said, "I'd love to, but I have plans. Thanks for thinking of me."

Thinking of him? Wow. Tildie was pretty sure Lindy thought of him often. The way she'd turned on the flirt, practically throwing herself at him. *Shameless.*

Sissy said again, "Join us? We can have an extra chair pulled over."

Tildie came back out of her thoughts. He was looking right at her. She looked away, trying to come off as casually watching the television above the bar.

He said, "It looks like you are almost done. I don't want to hold you up. I'll..."

Lindy batted her eyes again. "We can hang around. We..."

Tildie cleared her throat, giving the devil enough time to commandeer her tongue. "We do still have to get groceries, remember?"

Ben's face fell, but he recovered in a heartbeat, and his trademark grin returned to his oh-so-handsome mug. "Well, you ladies enjoy your grocery shopping."

Sissy narrowed her eyes at Tildie and added, "And Christmas tree shopping."

Ben nodded at Sissy. "You don't have your tree yet?"

All three of them groaned and pointed at Tildie. Sissy accused, "The scrooge here wasn't planning on getting one."

Tildie felt the weight of their stares. Her face was no doubt, fire-engine red. "There's really no need."

Sissy narrowed her eyes right at her. "Matilda, we all have trees," She looked back at Ben and asked, "Do you have a tree?"

"I have to. The kids and the grandkids, you know."

Awkward silence filled the air. Just before turning to walk away, Ben said, "Did you need a truck to haul the tree? I'd be glad to help."

Tildie was starting to shake her head no when Sissy-to-the-rescue answered for her. "That'd be great. Ben, you're a real peach of a man."

He pulled out a business card and said, "My cell phone number is on here. Call me when you have the tree picked out and I'll come right over. I'd be happy to haul it for you, Til."

Her childhood nickname rolling off his tongue made butterflies dance inside her. And he'd handed the card to her. *To just her.* "Thank you, Ben."

He'd no more than turned to leave when Sissy elbowed her. "Get out that mistletoe!"

"Shush! Sissy, you're embarrassing."

The three of them laughed. And in a weird twist, Tildie felt like crying, like she had just cheated on Harp.

CHAPTER FOUR

The grocery store was uneventful other than Sissy taking control of what Tildie needed, and planning her next few days for her. "Tomorrow you'll bake your gingerbread cookies. The day after, make icing and decorate them. Oh, and make your peanut butter fudge the day after that. I'll be over to help, by the way. You'll donate some to the church, again, for their snacks and coffee after the Christmas Eve service. I'll stop by and pick them up on my way, in case you back out at the last minute."

Something inside Tildie snapped. "I need to go home, right now."

"What? You haven't gotten your tree yet."

"I told you, there will be no tree! I need to go home. I just want to be left alone."

"Before you go, give me your wallet. Your Christmas fixings are in this cart, and you just might feel different come tomorrow morning."

Tildie threw her purse at Sissy and headed for the car. Tears streamed down her face while bitter cold stung her cheeks.

After loading the groceries in the trunk, Sissy sat in the driver's seat. She eyed Tildie. Her voice was stern. "You were doing great until that little mess in there."

"You still have Phillip. You can't imagine what I'm going through. Or you'd understand."

"Never said I could. But I know you have to do more than exist."

"Well excuse me! I'm sorry! I never asked to be widowed in my early sixties. Harp and I were going to travel. We had places to see. We had plans. We..."

"Plans change." She dug in her purse and handed Tildie a tissue.

There was one more scene on the way home. In the end, there was no tree, just as Tildie had said since the beginning of the emotional fiasco the day turned out to be.

They helped her carry her bags in the house, and then she nearly chased them out the door. She sat down on the floor and hugged Jack and let him lick her face. "Such a good boy you are. Such a good puppy." He danced and rubbed against her. Pulling him close, she soothed, "I love you, Jack. I don't know what I'd do without you."

Three hours later, she turned on the radio. Bing crooned about what he was dreaming of. Tildie thought about what her dreams were now. All changed, and that was the reality of it. Dreams were for people with a bright future. Dreams were for people with love in their lives. Dreams were for people with hope. She gazed into Jack's eyes, and the words filtered into her mind like someone else had spoken them, and the voice was unmistakably Harp's. "Dreams are for everyone."

Maybe they were. But she owed this to Harp—to never stop loving him. She'd always told him she'd love him forever.

She sorted out and took stock of what Sissy picked up at the store. She was in pretty good shape for making her cookies and fudge. Sissy had helped her make both at least a dozen times.

Her eyes brimmed with tears. Sissy was a good friend. Pushy and sometimes irritating, but actually the best of friends. She'd been pretty mean to her today. She would call her in the morning and see if she was still interested in coming over to bake cookies. Then she would apologize for the way she had behaved.

CHAPTER FIVE

Somehow, vanilla had not made it onto the grocery list so Tildie had to go out. So much for the idea that early morning shopping would be less hectic. The only way to describe the mall traffic was insane. She was cut off more times than she could count.

Maybe they'd seen her graying hair and figured since she was an old lady, she was an easy target. Then again, maybe 'graying' wasn't the right word to describe it, like it was still in the act of happening. Because it was pretty much a done deal. Harp had some salt, but he was still mostly pepper when he... When he died.

He was gone. And there wasn't a thing she could do about it.

She consciously worked to change her thoughts. She pictured Ben standing by their table yesterday. His hair was mostly salt, like hers. And his eyes were just as blue as when they were in grade school. He was the first boy she'd ever had a crush on. He never knew, though. She never told a soul. All these years later, it was her secret. When they were kids, he never returned any attention, at least not attention more than just being buddies. And she'd always been too afraid of being turned down to dare let him know how much she liked him.

Still, that hadn't stopped her from daydreaming about folding up a note – like a triangle-shaped football all the boys played with at the lunch table. She would have flicked it at him and it would have sailed straight through the uprights his thumbs formed. In her girlish daydreams back in the day, he always smiled when he read her words. *Do you like me? Check yes, or no.* And he always checked yes, carefully folded the note back up into the triangular shape, and flicked it back to her.

Then in junior high, Harp was the one who actually wrote a note to her. Gone was her crush on Ben. She recalled the way her heart pounded and she couldn't think straight when they went to the eighth grade dance. And he'd kissed her. That sealed it. She was forever Harp's girl.

He was gone, and she was still his girl.

The grocery store was crowded. She hurried past unsmiling people pushing carts heaped with what was supposed to bring them joy. Somehow it didn't make sense. Heading down the baking aisle, she stopped in her tracks. She realized she was whistling along with the store music, having a holly jolly Christmas. The realization did something amazing. She felt a smile creep across her lips.

She stretched, trying to reach the pure vanilla on the top shelf. A body came unsettlingly close, reaching over top of her, and snatched vanilla that was just beyond her fingertips. A familiar voice made her heart thump. "Did you need this?"

She smiled even harder when she turned and accepted the bottle. "Thanks, Ben."

"You're welcome, Til."

Oh, that lopsided grin. "Christmas dinner shopping?" She looked past him but there was no cart in sight. She would swear he was blushing when he answered.

"I already have my Christmas groceries bought. We keep it simple. I make the turkey and the stuffing, and the kids bring the sides."

"Who brings dessert?"

He shook his head. "Never gave it much thought. The kids have already eaten at the other side, and they're actually not very hungry when they arrive. I think they just show up to humor me. Or, they're afraid I'll go hungry if they don't come over. The grandkids are all sugared-out already. So I just do without. I admit, I miss the brown sugar pudding we used to have for Christmas – the one you gave Charlene the recipe for.

Tildie ignored the brown sugar pudding remark. "How is your mom? I still have the towels she made for me."

"She's slowing down some, but still does pretty good. She's eighty-nine years old now and likes where she lives. It's assisted living, but she's drifting toward needing more care. I'll stop at the nursing home and pick her up on Christmas morning. It gives the kids a chance to see her without having to add that stop to their list. She still asks about you."

His last sentence caught her off guard. "She always was a sweet lady."

"You should go see her some time. She'd like that, a lot. You could stop on Christmas day."

He looked so hopeful. She wanted to hide. Changing the subject, she said, "So, if you aren't here for dinner groceries, what'd you forget?"

He looked away, and when he looked back, the flush had returned to his cheeks. "I don't need anything. I was driving by and saw your car in the parking lot."

She swallowed hard, unsure of what to say. Panic rose in her stomach, but some little part of her felt sort of giddy.

"I was hoping that maybe you'd have lunch with me?"

"I really can't," She looked at her watch. "Sissy is meeting me at my house, actually about now. I'm late. We're baking cookies today."

He looked away, and when he returned his gaze to her, his smile wasn't quite as brilliant. "Gingerbread? God, you make the best gingerbread cookies on the planet."

"Yep. On the list."

"Then, add me to the other list, the people who would love to get a plate of your cookies?"

"Done. You're pretty close to the top of that list." She thought she might have her own lopsided grin going on. Flirting really felt good.

"Am I being too forward if I ask who's higher on the list than me? Because I'd like to know just who the competition is." He winked.

She felt her cheeks warm, and had to look away.

"I mean for cookies. You know. Um..."

Her cell phone brought the suddenly awkward moment to an end. She looked at the screen and said, "It's Sissy," then clicked to accept. "Sorry, I'm at Wagner's Market, a quick stop for vanilla. I'll be right there. You know where the spare key is. Let yourself in."

He reached over and touched her arm. "Seriously, Til, am I being too forward to ask if there is someone higher on the list than me? Seeing anyone?"

She took a deep breath, savoring the tingling in her stomach and the way her heart pounded. "Jack. He's my main man these days. My only man. I... I'm comfortable with that, Ben. I'm just not ready to let go, I..."

He squeezed her arm and said, "It's okay. I shouldn't have asked," Then as if to move the conversation another direction, he said, "You still have Jack? I like that. I remember the day I opened my door and he was standing on the porch, skinny, wet, scared. A gangly pup."

Tildie smiled. "Yep. Harp always said you didn't want to keep him because he was well past that chubby, cute, anyone-would-take-him-home stage."

Ben folded his arms across his chest. "That's me. I only want cute puppies in my life," He winked at her again, but then his smile faded. "Seriously. I'd have kept him, but Harp stopped in that day, and if you recall, he'd just retired. After a few too many beers, he confided that he was losing his sense of being needed. I really thought the dog would do him good."

"You were always such a good friend to him."

"And he to me. I really miss him."

Tildie felt the pain in Ben's words. *Time to move on.* "And I think you were right about Jack making him feel needed. For the three years the two of them buddied around together, they were nearly inseparable. Part of me thought that Jack was the kid we were never able to have."

Ben seemed without words, and only nodded in reply.

"I really have to run."

He unexpectedly pulled her close. "You know, if you need anything, I'm here."

Flustered, she nodded as she backed away. Her face felt hot, and was maybe apple red to match the temperature. She turned and started walking away, then paused, looked back to find him standing in the aisle watching her. "If you stop by tomorrow evening, I'll have that plate of cookies ready for you to pick up."

The grin was instant. "I'll see you then."

CHAPTER SIX

Jack met her at the door. He jumped up and down, and then placed his paws at her waist and gave her the sniff test. "I know, buddy. I might have hugged someone else today, huh?"

"Who!" Sissy raced around the corner from the kitchen, her eyes wide and her mouth set in motion. "Who did you see when you were out?" She gave a sidelong look and raised one eyebrow. "Tell me, Tildie. Is *getting vanilla* the new code-word for something else, huh?"

"Oh, for crying out loud, Sissy! You and your dirty mind."

"What do you mean? I didn't go there. But you must have. All I meant was maybe getting a hug, or you know, a peck on the cheek. Sheesh." She rolled her eyes and then busted out in a great, big laugh. "Seriously, who did you run into?"

"Why does it matter who it was?"

"Well, in case you haven't noticed, for the last three years you've been the queen of *don't-even-look-at-me-let-alone-dare-to-hug-me*. And though I'm looking on from the outside of your kingdom, your highness, it seems it's awfully lonely on your throne."

Tildie looked out the window, seeing nothing, really. Considering queens, Sissy was the reigning one of speaking uncomfortable truths. Tildie had finally reached the place where she was ready to face them. She needed to look those painful realities in the eye. But even after steeling herself for this day, it still hurt. "It was Ben. There. Now can we bake some cookies?"

Sissy followed her, incredibly, in silence.

The afternoon came and went, and when early evening arrived, the house smelled of cinnamon and ginger with a touch of cloves. Cooling racks loaded with cookies stacked four deep lined the counter. The cutters were in the dishwasher, along with the rest of the mess. Sissy gave her a hug and said, "You did good today. See you tomorrow."

Tildie made her list for the following morning. She would get up extra early and start whipping egg whites and confectioners' sugar into royal icing. They'd finish the icing and decorating early afternoon, then the cookies would dry before evening. She could stack them in containers without them sticking to each other.

She decided she would call Carol and Lindy first thing in the morning, too. They'd have a decorating marathon. She was singing along with the Christmas music on the radio, just wrapping up her best bluesy version of Santa Baby, when Jack scratched at the door. As she walked across the room toward him, Karen Carpenter began singing. Tears welled in her eyes. "Have myself a merry little Christmas? God, I'm trying. I'm trying..."

Waiting outside while Jack did his business, she took in the beauty of December moonlight, and the haunting memories it brought. The clarity of the night reflected in her thoughts. She looked up at the stars and whispered, "I'll always love you, Harp. The loneliness is killing me. And you know, Jack isn't going to live forever." She reached down and patted his head. He looked up at her, cocking his head to the side at the mention of his name. She shivered. "Time to go inside, buddy."

CHAPTER SEVEN

When Tildie woke, it was still dark, but a seam of light creased the eastern sky. Her first thought was that in the commotion of the last couple of days, she hadn't checked the mail.

She got up, slipped on her robe over her flannel pajamas, and headed for the kitchen. Coffeemaker first. Then Jack followed her out the door into the frigid dawn. They walked to the mailbox, with Jack marking every bush and shrub along the way. "Thank heaven you stay on top of things, Jack. Or the other dogs in the neighborhood might forget who owns this place." One thing about Jack, her sarcasm never seemed to insult him in the least. Another reason hanging out with dogs was better than hanging out with people.

Standing at the mailbox, light down the road at the neighbor's house caught her eye. Christmas lights blazed along the edge of the roof and on all of their shrubs. She picked up the wad of envelopes and ads, and then she started humming jingle bells while she hurried back into the warmth of home.

She dressed while Jack waited, watching. Always watching. His head rested on Harp's slippers. They lay where he'd last slipped them off the night before his heart attack. Each time she cleaned, she lifted them to vacuum, and then replaced them neatly as if she hadn't disturbed them. It was silly, she guessed. But it always brought her some comfort.

There were days when she felt it was all out of control. It hurt to keep living. And the few little things that remained unchanged, like the slippers, and Harp's hunting coat on the hook in the mudroom, helped her get through it. She could never explain to Sissy why those things mattered.

She had tried her best, and thought she'd gotten through one day when she told her, "They belong to yesterday's normal, and sometimes I need that."

Sissy's reply was swift. "Yesterday's gone."

Maybe it was time to move them to the closet. Or even to Goodwill, along with his other clothes she hadn't been able to part with. She chided herself. Someone else could be wearing them, maybe keeping warm on a cold night. She made a mental note to pack up all his coats, gloves, and hats, and to donate them to a charity that distributed to the local needy.

She checked her pantry and her fridge to see what she had on hand to fix for lunch. Glancing at the clock when she finished her coffee, she saw it was still too early to call her friends and invite them over.

She went through her mail. Shame welled up in her as she sorted out a stack of Christmas cards. She recalled the cards she'd received the last few Christmases. Unacknowledged. Unanswered. Not that cards were meant to be an exchange, but sending a card back was the nice thing to do. At least that's what her mom had taught her.

Message after message asking her how she was doing, and each one lightly stepped around the obvious. She wasn't doing well. Her husband was gone. Permanently. He died. Part of her went with him. And it was probably the best part of her. She brought her hands up to her face and bawled like a baby. When no more tears came, she gathered up a dishcloth and ran cold water on it, then held it against her eyes.

When was this going to end? She'd been plunged into the pit of despair. She'd stopped going to church – so angry at God for taking him from her. And she'd avoided anything resembling fun, thinking she just needed to stay home and heal. She'd spent three years merely going through the motions. Existing.

Well, she was doing better, a little better anyway. At first it had been unbearable. But now that she really thought about it, she was almost back to taking part in life beyond her front door.

Maybe healing doesn't just automatically come. Or maybe it's there, but you have to reach for it? Maybe you have to just move on through the hurt.

She went back to the closet where she kept her Christmas things. Rooting around in the bottom of it, she came up with a box of cards and her Christmas address book. *Time to take a step. Time to send some cards. No candy-coating the messages.*

After an hour – and two more cups of coffee – she finished the last message. She addressed the red envelope and tucked the glittery greeting inside. Then she applied two Christmas stickers to the seal on the back. A glance at the clock – she had just enough time to drive to town and mail them, then get back before Sissy showed up.

While she waited in line at the post office counter, she called Lindy and Carol. It was all set. Cookie day for four. When she stepped outside, Jack barked a greeting from the driver's seat. He scooted to the other side when she opened the door. "Time to decorate the cookies. And who gets to eat the broken ones?" Jack wagged his tail. "Jackie boy does."

While she drove home, she couldn't help but notice that the clear sky was fading, being replaced with a thickening layer of gray. "I guess a storm really is coming..."

CHAPTER EIGHT

"Lindy, I must say, you have such an odd sense of what colors things should be. Your cookies don't look right."

Tildie narrowed her eyes at Sissy. "It's called creativity. Go ahead and give it a try."

"This is Christmas. That's no time for creativity!"

Tildie rolled her eyes, and the other three laughed.

Sissy said, "Creativity or not, you got any wine? I could go for some mulled wine."

Tildie jumped up from her chair. "Let me check." She brought back a bottle of Lambrusco and four wine glasses. "The good news is I have wine. The bad news is that we're drinking it at room temperature because it wasn't chilled, and I'm not warming it because I have no mulling spices."

Sissy said, "Now that's a surprise. The Grinch is missing an integral Christmas ingredient." Sissy rolled her eyes.

Tildie leaned over and put a bright red spot of icing on the tip of Sissy's nose. "I'm not missing Rudolph this year."

Carol feigned a straight face while she shook her head from side to side. "And this is all before we've had any wine."

Tildie poured while they all giggled.

At 4:00, after Christmas hugs, Carol left. Lindy walked out the door, two steps behind her. "I want to get home before dark."

Sissy closed the door, turned to Tildie, and said, "Wimps. Carol needs to tell Alex that he can learn how to at least open a can of ravioli. I've never seen anyone run after their husband like that girl does. You don't see me racing home before it gets dark. And Phillip's dinner can wait. You won't get rid of me so easily."

"Wimps? I think Carol's lucky."

Sissy's smile faded. "I'm sorry. I wasn't thinking."

Tildie did her best to smile when she said, "It's okay. I have to get through it. That's all."

"I'm proud of you. That sounds corny, but I really am. I can't imagine what it feels like. I..."

"No, you can't. I could never have imagined..." Tildie walked back into the kitchen. "How about a cup of tea, like old times?"

"That sounds wonderful."

They sat at the table, a bone china teapot full of steaming Earl Gray tea in front of them. Their dainty cups and saucers matched the pink rose print of the pot. With tea perfectly sweetened, and a plate of broken cookies at the ready, Sissy said, "Do you remember when we did this at your house when we were in what, sixth grade?"

"Yep. And this is the same tea set we used." Tildie broke off a nibble of cookie and threw the rest to Jack.

"Oh God, we felt so grown up. I still can't believe your mom turned us loose with your grandmother's tea set." Sissy's hand flew and Jack caught another cookie.

"She always said that the good china should be used. And that it was the memory of the people who used it that made it special – not how it shined while it was sitting on a shelf."

Sissy nodded her head slowly. Her thoughts seemed to be miles or years from where they were. "Do you remember the pearls? I do. Your mom lived what she said. And while I think about it, how smart was she? She let us wear her pearls, and tonight, years and years later, we're recalling that memory."

Tildie's eyes brimmed full. "I miss her. And I miss dad." She left Harp's name unspoken. "Why does it have to be this way? Why do people have to die?"

Sissy didn't try to answer the unanswerable.

Tildie sobbed for a minute, grateful for the touch of her best friend's hand – and the comfort it brought. Then she gave herself a mental slap, sat up straight, wiped her eyes, and said, "I want to go through the fudge recipe and take stock of the ingredients. Just making sure I have everything for tomorrow."

After that was finished, Sissy looked soberly at the living room window where Tildie and Harp's tree always stood. "Are you sure about not having a tree?"

"I think so. Besides, it's pretty late to find a decent one."

"Okay, but your house could use a little more Christmas. Where do you keep your decorations? Not in the garage, I hope. It's too cold out there."

Tildie walked toward the hall. "They're in here, in the guest bedroom."

At 7:00, Gene Autry was serenading them while they hung wreathes on the front windows. Sissy reached into the box of ornaments and when she pulled out her hand, she wore the look of eureka! "What is this? Huh? Huh?"

"No! I mean it Sissy. There's no reason at all to hang mistletoe."

"Awe, c'mon! I'll even give you a smooch beneath it." Then she winked at her.

"Really, must you?"

Sissy grabbed a chair from the table and pulled it beneath the light hanging in the entryway. She stood on it, teetering while she reached for the bottom finial.

Tildie hurried to her. "I may as well hold you so you don't fall. You're stubborn as they come."

Sissy wrapped the wire around the light and then leaned on Tildie's shoulder while she stepped down from the chair. "There. Ready for visitors."

As if on cue, there was a knock at the door. Sissy opened it. "Ben! What a surprise." She turned toward Tildie and stared her down while she said, "I had no idea you were stopping this evening."

Tildie pulled her away from the door. "Please, come in Ben."

Sissy followed them to the kitchen and took a seat. It looked like she couldn't get her eyebrows to go down where they belonged.

Tildie handed a plate to Ben. "Help yourself. Pick out what you like and I'll wrap them up for you."

His easy grin lit up his whole face. Heck, it lit up the whole room. "You did a great job decorating these. Some are too pretty to eat."

Sissy snorted. "Yeah. Take a bunch of the ones that Lindy did. You won't feel guilty eating them. Whoever heard of a green Santa or a blue reindeer?"

His laughter was so genuine, it made Tildie ache somewhere deep inside. It had been so long since a man's laugh rumbled in this house. She scolded. "Sissy, I think they're pretty. She's not afraid to paint outside the cookie-decorating box. That's all."

"Maybe. But I'm going to take the cookies I decorated. I don't want those crazy colors. And you know what? It really is time for me to go. I'm sure Phil is starving by now. It's a good night for pizza, huh?" She winked at them, gathered up her coat, and came Tildie's way. She hugged her. Then she headed for Ben.

He stopped what he was doing and gave her a hug. "Nice seeing you again, Sissy."

She said, "You know, if I could drag you over to that mistletoe, I'd give you a big old Christmas kiss."

His eyes followed the direction she was pointing, and then he grinned. "You'll never change, will you?"

CHAPTER NINE

Tildie closed the door behind her friend. She rubbed her arms. "Cold out there, huh?"

He set down the plate of cookies and said, "Yeah. Noticeably colder. Now they're saying it might be snow instead of rain. The wind's picking up, and not a star to be seen." Then he looked around and said, "What happened to getting a tree? You never called."

"I just had a bad day. And I'm not sure who I'd be decorating it for anyhow, you know?"

"Well, for you. I remember how much you loved Christmas."

She exhaled. "It's just not the same now." Jack sat next to her, watching Ben. His tail was doing a lazy, lopsided wag. It didn't go unnoticed by Tildie. It seemed to go with his lopsided grin. Maybe he was meant to be Ben's dog all along. "Would you like some coffee? Hot cocoa? Tea?"

"Do you have decaffeinated? It's after 6:00, and I'd never get to sleep if I drank full strength.

I do have the lower octane," She winked at him and continued," I'm the same way now. Regular coffee makes me so restless during the night. But I sure love my caffeine in the morning."

They took seats across from each other and nibbled on cookies – with Jack getting double tosses. One from Tildie. One from Ben. And so it went.

The evening was passing in a haze of laughter, memories, a few tears, and the reminder of how much history they shared. The clock chimed 11:00 and Ben said, "I'd better be going. Don't want the neighbors talking," He looked out the front windows. "Nothing to see but darkness out there. You really don't have close neighbors, do you?"

"Nope. One of the things Harp liked best about it."

Ben grabbed another cookie and broke it into tiny pieces. His demeanor had changed. He cleared his throat. "Just one thing, Til, before I go. I've wanted to talk to you for a long time about Charlene."

The cookie suddenly felt like grit in her mouth. "There's really nothing to say."

He lowered his chin and looked into her eyes. "There is. Years ago, when you first began avoiding me, I couldn't imagine what I'd done. I questioned Harp about it. He told me he didn't know. For years, he kept up the denial. All that time you steered clear of me. I kept thinking that it made no sense, because whatever made you mad enough to shut me out of your life wasn't bad enough for you to keep Harp away from me. After Harp retired, he finally gave in. I don't know if you knew this, but he admitted to me about his drunken confession to you."

She froze in her seat, and words failed her. It was just as well that she was speechless. She wasn't thinking straight right now, and anything she'd say would no doubt be the wrong thing. No, Harp had never told her he'd fessed up to Ben.

"I want you to know. No, I need you to know that my marriage was over a while before she left. I mean months. We'd seen a counselor—in another town. We didn't need the wagging tongues here to make things harder. And then..."

She found her voice. "Hey, I'm sure you had your reasons for what happened. But it's done and over with."

"We did have our reasons, but what I want to be sure is that you know you weren't one of them."

"I really don't think this is any of my..."

"Til, listen to me. Please. I need to say these things. What you do with the information is up to you."

She nodded. What else could she do, short of taping his mouth shut or shoving him out the door?

"That New Year's Eve that..."

"Stop. Please, Ben..." She couldn't... No, she wouldn't talk about that night.

"Please, let me have my say..."

She stood up. "No. Ben, I'm done listening. I don't know what I was thinking. I'm not ready for this. I'm tired."

"Til, I–"

"Please. Go."

Jack raced to the door and started whining. When Ben moved his direction, he ran back toward him and jumped up, planting his paws on Ben's waist.

Tildie snapped, "Jack! Down!"

He got down, but he went into herding mode, darting from side to side between Ben and the door, trying to head him off.

"Jack, come! Now." The dog had never once ignored her, but he sure was tonight.

Ben bent down and hugged him. "I gotta go, buddy." With that, he let himself out.

Tildie snapped her fingers at Jack, but he stood at the door whining.

"What is wrong with you? Get over here."

Jack lay down, curling into a ball in front of the door.

"Fine. Do what you want. I'm going to bed."

CHAPTER TEN

The wind-chimes singing on her back porch woke Tildie sometime in the middle of the night. She lay in bed listening. Her mind roamed through years of memories, of other storms, other Christmases. She'd checked out of celebrations three years ago, and she wasn't doing so well trying to find her way back in. Taking a vacation this week to ease herself into some of the Christmas hoopla was starting to look like a failure.

Thirty years ago, on that New Years Eve, she'd sworn to herself that if her marriage was going to last, and if Harp and Ben's friendship was going to last too, she had to avoid Ben for the rest of her life.

Ben and Harp had been plastered, and Charlene was even worse; she couldn't stand. When the wee hours of the morning came, Tildie was the only one fit to drive.

When she watched Ben and Charlene stagger up their sidewalk, she was relieved to have them out of the car. Charlene had called Ben every name not fit to be heard by ladies and children. And each one had been delivered in that drunken, excruciatingly slow delivery. Some were so garbled, only imagination could make sense of them.

Then Tildie drove her husband home.

Husband. What a word. What a feeling. She had a husband, once. She'd never, ever forgot how it felt. Like her life and her heart were so tangled up with his, that she'd stopped knowing where she left off and where he began.

She could picture him on that New Year's Eve, half sitting, half falling onto their bed. Then he'd said it. Strangely, there'd been no animosity in his voice. His words were a slurred, half-joking interrogation. "What do you think of Ben? Would you ever leave me for him?"

She'd laughed while she answered him. "No, and why on earth would you ask such a thing?"

"Because he's smart. And he's – I mean this in a totally un-gay kinda way. He's good looking," Drool ran out of his mouth onto his pillow. "If God was fair, he'd have made two of you."

"What? What kind of gibberish is coming out of you, Mr. *Drunk* Harp?" She'd pulled off his shoes, then his socks.

"He said you're the most beautiful girl he's ever seen. And he meant you're a beautiful person. That was it. He didn't want me to take offense – like he was checking out my wife. You know? Get it? He meant that your heart was beautiful. But he wasn't telling me nothing I didn't know. You are beautiful, my Matilda Janson." He grinned. His was no Benjamin Draper grin, but it was wonderful. One that never failed to melt her heart. He'd dozed off then, but woke in a couple of minutes. "He said him and Charlene are calling it quits." Then he dozed off for the twelve-hour hangover sleep.

All these years later, Tildie thought about Harp's words. Though he'd been three sheets to the wind, she considered that weird thing about drunks; after they'd opened enough bottles, they opened the confessional. She recalled how her dad – who'd been raised by his alcoholic father, used to say, "No truer words were ever written than those put down in alcohol based ink."

She had been the cause of Charlene losing her husband. Worse, she'd caused two little girls to grow up without a mom. Maybe she wasn't completely at fault for that. Lord knows, many women have left a man without leaving their kids too. Then again, how would she have felt if it had been the other way around – Harp saying those things about Charlene? Would she have left him?

When the alarm went off, she lay in bed, tired from her restless night. She rehashed what Ben had said about the end of his marriage not being about her. Maybe he was telling the truth. Maybe there was something she didn't know about the whole thing. And maybe, just maybe, she should let Ben have his say – to get whatever weight he carried, off his chest.

She groaned, talking to the empty air. "It's too fast, Tildie. Just slow down, because it's all a tangled mess – Harp, and Ben, and Charlene. She decided that her best plan was to hibernate until after the first of the year. That should be long enough for this emotional circus to pack up tents and leave town.

She heard Jack scratching to be left outside. Sleepy-eyed, she walked through the living-room. When she opened the door, a gust of cold air hit her in the face. Bits of snow flew at her. "Oh boy Jack, looks like the weather's moving in. Harp's forecasting still works."

She stood in the front yard, waiting for him to return from his rounds. Lights appeared down the road and then a turn signal started flashing. Her heart sped up. It was Ben. She hugged her robe against her and called for Jack. Then she ran her hands through her hair. God, she looked like hell. No one had ever accused her of being a natural, morning beauty. She retreated to the front steps to wait for Ben.

He wrapped a muffler around his neck before he opened his truck door and then dashed for the house. "Morning Til. I forgot my cookies last night."

"C'mon in. I'll put on some coffee." Jack dashed inside as soon as Tildie opened the door.

"I really didn't come over to impose, just to pick up my cookies."

"You're not imposing." When he stepped inside, she closed the door while she asked, "Did you sleep good?"

"Not really, to be honest."

She motioned toward the table.

He pulled out a chair and sat, never taking his eyes off of her.

She dumped the water in the coffeemaker and pushed the button. "Yeah. If I'm being totally honest too, I tossed and turned most of the night."

"You do believe me, right? What I said last night about you not being the reason Charlene left?"

Tildie sat across from him. She clasped her hands together on the table. "I don't know what to think."

"Do you feel up to hearing a little bit more of the story?"

"Ben, I really think none of this matters in the long run."

"It matters to me, and I hope that maybe, given time, it'll matter to you too."

Butterflies took flight in her stomach. And there was a war going inside of her too. In spite of the words escaping her lips, it already did matter to her. But this was so fast. She jumped up and got their coffee. "How about eggs?"

"Nope. I came hoping to talk. The coffee is more than I expected."

She grabbed milk from the fridge, and the sugar bowl, and then sat down again.

"Til, Charlene left because she wasn't happy. And I wasn't happy either. The counselor really helped. But not in the way we thought she would. She opened our eyes. We both could see that we were horribly mismatched from the get-go."

"I see." It was her stock answer for uncomfortable conversations.

"It took professional counseling to make me admit to myself that Charlene was not, and was never going to be the girl I wanted. I tricked myself into believing it. And it went both ways. She wanted the wedding, the nice house, the man with good money coming in. But when the kids came along, it got real for her. She didn't like the life."

"She was a fun person. I always liked Charlene."

"She was fun when she was fun. And when she wasn't, she made life miserable. But hey, I don't claim I was much different. Life wasn't fun for either of us, so we were both busy making everyone miserable. But it's all history, now."

Tildie stirred milk into her coffee, lightly clicking the spoon on the side of the cup. Any noise to not be hearing what Ben was saying.

"The counselor got through to me. I needed to quit living the misery of my mistake. I couldn't have who I wanted. She was taken. You see, years ago I got a soft place in my heart for a girl, but I was too stupid to act on it. And after I missed my chance with her, no one could ever get to that place again."

Tildie's face went hot under his intense gaze. "Ben, I don't know what to say. What do you want me to say? I don't know how I feel about all of this. It's been thirty years since she left. Thirty years I've been busy blaming myself for your children not having a mother. I...I... Ben, maybe you should go."

That he was hurt was clear. He opened his mouth to say something, then closed it, slid the coffee cup back toward the middle of the table, and stood.

Jack went haywire. He pounced against Ben, nearly knocking him back into his chair.

Ben regained his balance and gave Jack a quick pat on the head. "Gotta go, buddy."

Tildie started to stand but Ben said, "I can let myself out. I hope you have a good Christmas, Til."

She nodded at him. "Thanks, Ben, and the same to you and yours." She turned away and looked at the clock, the wall, anything that kept her back toward him – and kept him from seeing the tears sliding down her face.

CHAPTER ELEVEN

She was on her third batch of peanut-butter fudge. Jack was still laying at the door pouting–and for no good reason, she thought. Maybe it was stupid to even continue with the fudge. She really didn't feel like visiting anyone to hand it out. And from the look of the weather, Sissy wasn't going to be coming her way either. The weatherman said this storm could hang on until Christmas day.

She stuck the candy thermometer in the pan after wiping stray sugar grains from the side. Then she walked to the window facing the front yard. Snow blew in sheets. Great gusts of wind rattled tree branches and set the wind chimes to a cacophony. Jack whined at the door.

"What's upsetting you, Jackie?" She ruffled the hair around his neck and ears. "Come over here." She sat on the couch and invited him up beside her. She cuddled him, and he licked her face and whined. "Is it the storm? I know you don't like thunderstorms, sweetie, but I've never seen you get worked up over a winter storm."

Jack jumped down from the couch and went to the door. He cast a look her way, then scratched the kick plate. When Tildie opened the door, a gust blew snow inside at her. Jack darted out. She grabbed the broom and started sweeping the worst of the snow from her front porch. When her fingers couldn't take the cold, she hung up the broom and called for Jack. She squinted her eyes, trying to see out through the horizontal snow. Jack was nowhere in sight.

She went inside and put on her coat and a pair of gloves. She slid the hood up and zipped the jacket tight to her chin. Then she went outside to call Jack again. The only answer was the strange hush of snow being tossed around by powerful gusts.

She walked out her sidewalk, what was visible, anyway. It was blown clear in places, and drifted a half-foot deep in others. "Jack!" She saw where his tracks vanished, drifted over, right next to the road. She felt sick. What if something happened to him? She had to find him. The weather was brutal, and even with his thick fur coat, he wouldn't survive the storm. He was a pussycat when it came to being outside.

She hurried back into the house, grabbed a scarf and changed into her winter boots. Then she grabbed her car keys. Her last stop was in the kitchen to shut off the stove. The fudge could wait. She had to find Jack.

She drove around the block, first, coming back past her house. She slowed, hoping to see him on the porch, waiting for her to let him inside. *No Jack.* Back down the road she turned right instead of left. It didn't look like a plow truck had been through yet. She was driving while watching, trying to look at fields and yards, when a truck came barreling down the road toward her – and he liked his half of the middle. She edged farther to her right. It was hard to tell where road stopped and ditch started. Then the car slid off the road. When she gassed it, the tires spun but it didn't move.

She pulled out her cell phone. Maybe Sissy's husband could help her get the car unstuck. Tears of frustration and fear ran down her face. What if she lost Jack for good? By the time Sissy answered her phone, it was all Tildie could do to talk.

"Hey, calm down, Tildie. I can't help if I can't understand."

Tildie swallowed hard and counted to three. "Jack is gone. He ran away. Maybe he was chasing an animal, I don't know. I went out to look for him and I've wrecked the car into a ditch. Some truck ran me off the road."

"Are you all right? Are you hurt?"

"No. I'm fine. But my car isn't. And God only knows where Jack is." She cried again.

"I'm calling Phillip. Don't feel bad. It's a short day for him today, anyway. And I'll be right there. I don't want you to freeze while you wait for him. I'll tell him to call a tow truck. Anything else you need?"

"Jack. I need my Jackie back."

"We'll look for him. My little all-wheel drive eats up snowy roads. It'll get us where we need to go, okay?"

"Okay. Sissy? Thank you."

"Hey, that's what friends are for. I know you'd do the same for me."

CHAPTER TWELVE

Three hours later she had a call from the garage. The undercarriage was dinged up pretty good. The ditch was so low that her car had been resting on its frame. The wheels didn't even make contact in the ditch. The mechanic wanted to give it a thorough look over before it was declared safe.

When it started to get dark, Sissy told Tildie, "Listen, I know you don't want to hear this, but I think it's time to get you home. Jack might even be there waiting."

Tildie thanked Sissy. "I'm so grateful, Sissy. I really don't know what I'd do without you in my life."

When they pulled up to Tildie's house, it was dark. Even without the porch light on, it was obvious there was no dog pacing outside, hoping to be let in.

Sissy shut off her car. "You know, Tildie, Jack is a smart dog. He's probably inside somewhere. Some softhearted soul has him warm and dry and fed."

When Sissy unbuckled her seat belt, Tildie said, "Go home, Sissy. I'll be fine. I am so, so thankful for all of your help today. I can never tell you how much it meant to me, going out on those treacherous roads." She leaned across the seat and hugged Sissy.

"Are you sure you're okay?"

Tildie swiped at tears with the back of her hand. "Yes. I'm fine."

Sissy put the key in the ignition. "If you need anything, an ear, a shoulder...a ride anywhere, call me, okay?"

She nodded at her friend. She didn't dare chance trying to talk. The dam would have burst.

CHAPTER THIRTEEN

The house was dark, empty, and lonely. Tildie lay on the couch. Outside, wind jangled chimes, and snow made a whooshing sound against the windows. She hadn't cried so many tears since Harp died.

She glanced at her cell phone. It was 3:30 AM. Christmas Eve. Another one without Harp, and now without her dear Jack. She reconciled herself to the likelihood that he was dead. If he wasn't, he would have come back home. He might have been hit by a car. Lord knows, if he dashed in front of one on these roads, it wouldn't have been able to stop. As cautious as she was behind the wheel, she'd even managed to slide on the ice, right into that ditch.

"Jack, oh Jack," she whispered, "If you're alive, please find someplace protected from the snow and wind." Harp wouldn't be exactly proud of her, the way she had taken care of his dog.

She got up to use the bathroom, and when she passed Harp's side of the bed, she stopped in her tracks. His slippers had been moved. They were nowhere in sight.

* * * * *

She didn't know how fast or slow time was passing later as she lay in bed, still unable to sleep. She listened to a branch clicking against the house, a dry, rattle-bone sound that sent shivers down her spine. The wind alternated between moaning and silence. Tugging the blanket closer, she looked for Jack on the foot of the bed. He wasn't there. Hurt washed over her.

She studied the landscape through the window. It was hauntingly unfamiliar under drifts of new snow. She closed her eyes and hugged her pillow. Words whispered into the night. "*When two roads part, the travelers' journeys don't end. They simply diverge into new adventures.*" They'd been spoken by Harp's voice.

When the alarm went off, she lay in bed in the tail end blackness of the long, winter night. Her dream came back to her. It had to be a dream, right? But it had felt so real...

Her thought train was running out of control. Everything in life was interconnected, she decided. Harp. Jack. And the connections didn't break when someone died. They're as alive as loved ones kept them, even if their paths did diverge. Another round of sobs made her ribs ache. She finally dozed, waking up when a plow truck went by.

After lunch already? She kicked the afghan off of her legs, trying to shake some life into herself. She couldn't believe it was 1:00 PM. She rubbed her eyes. They felt puffy. *Jack.*

She pictured him when Harp brought him home. Ben had already given him a bath and fed him. And she remembered thinking Harp would have been a good father. But some things just weren't meant to be. Harp often commented about Ben's children, that they were good kids. Tildie hadn't seen them since they were little. And now they were grown up with kids of their own.

Harp always said that Ben was a great dad. In some ways, she wished it had all turned out different. After she and Harp found out they couldn't have children, it would have been nice for both of them to be part of Ben's kids' lives. She sighed, deep and heavy. She'd kept her distance from Ben, not wanting to cause problems in Harp's friendship with him.

Ben. Charlene left him because she wasn't happy. Not because she thought he was in love with another woman. All these years she'd had it wrong.

Ben had never been anything but good to her. Even when they were kids, he never let the neighbor boy bully her. She never told a soul that he even played dolls with her a time or two. How would life have been different if he'd been the one to write that note to her in seventh grade? Silly thoughts.

No, they weren't. Even at the funeral, it was his shoulder she cried on. He probably grieved more than anyone else in the world, save for her. If she was ready to move on, she couldn't imagine anyone Harp would rather have her spend time with.

God, she was so lonely she ached inside. She loved Harp, and she always would, but Ben wasn't asking her to stop loving him. She didn't have to stop, to spend time with Ben. Maybe that was the twisted logic she'd been struggling with. The survivor never has to stop loving their mate in order to move on.

She thought wistfully about love. How if there was real magic in existence, it was love. Love never died. And there was always more love to go around, like that cheesy saying about the more you give it away, the more you have. She'd never given it much thought, but it was the truth. The times in her life she'd reached out to others, the more love she'd gotten in return.

The phone startled her. When she answered it, a man's voice inquired, "Mrs Janson?"

"Yes?"

This is Crosskey's Garage. We gave your car a good look-over. We didn't find any real damage. A little superficial stuff, some scuffs. It's ready."

"Oh, thank heavens. How much is the bill?"

"Boss says to tell you 'Merry Christmas'. We're getting ready to close. Wayne – who works here—rides with Bill. They both live out your way, so Wayne said he'd drop it off for you on his way home. If you're okay with that."

"Oh my goodness, I am. Thank you so, so much. And merry Christmas to you too." She'd be able to drive around and look for Jack one more time.

She'd no more than hung up when her cell phone rang. "Tildie? Sissy here. I just talked with Marylou Perelli over on Madison Lane on the other side of town. She said they had a black and white dog show up last night. Sure sounded like Jack. Her husband, Morty – you know him I think. He used to coach the little league team for Wagner's. Anyway, they have a beautiful house and no animals allowed, but it must have been the Christmas spirit. Morty put the dog in the garage – of course, it's heated. Jack slept next to their Escalades. They fed him beef and gravy and gave him water. When Morty opened the door to check on him this morning, he bolted."

Tildie's hand was over her mouth, trying to soften the noise from her sobbing. "Oh, thank you God. He survived the storm. He survived the night. Thank you, Sissy. This is the best news ever."

"Do you need me to pick you up, and go searching again? Just for a little bit. The kids come over this evening, and I can't miss them. But you're welcome to join us."

"The garage is dropping off my car in a little bit. I'm good. I have to go! I love you, Sissy. Thank you again."

She got up, showered, dressed, and had coffee, which was the best java she'd tasted in years. At least in the last three years.

She hurried, putting together plates of cookies with a few pieces of fudge in each. She was going to give them to Wayne and Bill. It was a nice thing they were doing.

Next, she started to pack up the fudge she'd finished making before Jack disappeared. And then she was going to fill plates with cookies. She might have to wait until after Christmas, but she would deliver cookies and fudge. She was going to crawl out of her self-imposed confinement of grief.

Then she thought about Ben, and her mind went straight to the brown sugar pudding. She checked her pantry once again. Brown sugar. Check. Raisins. Check. Butter. Flour. Vanilla. Baking soda. She had it all. She'd make it tomorrow and take it to Ben's. Not only would she visit with his mother, but she'd get to see what kind of adults Ben's children have become. And she'd get to meet the grandkids Harp was so fond of.

The mechanics showed up within the hour, after which she took several trips across town to Madison Lane. She circled that neighborhood, looking. She was driving past St. Joseph's church and could hear them singing *Oh Come, Oh Come Emanuel*. Any sense of despair left her. Somehow she knew Jack would make it home.

When she pulled into her driveway, it was getting dark. She looked at the windows in the front. Why did she have to be so stubborn? A tree would have been nice. Oh well. Next year. She knew she was going to be strong enough. This was the beginning of getting on with her life.

She still had the key in the door when she heard a vehicle slowing. She turned to look. What she saw sent a wave of joy rushing over her. It was Ben.

When he opened his door, a black and white shadow of fur leapt out and raced to her. She went down on her knees, right on her snowy front porch. "Jack, oh Jack. Thank God you're home. Ben, thank you for bringing him home to me!"

Ben trudged through the snow to her. "Got any hot coffee tonight? Sure could use some. And no decaf. I got a lot of work ahead of me." He reached down and grabbed her arm, helping her to stand.

"For you, for the man who brought my dog home, anything."

His lopsided grin lit up his face. He held the door for her while Jack rushed past.

"She started toward him after removing her jacket. "Here. Let me take your coat."

"I'm going to need it for a little bit. Where's your tree stand?"

"My what? Why?"

"I've got a tree to haul in now, so if you don't mind, I'll leave my coat on."

She couldn't stop smiling. "I can't believe you brought a tree."

He gave her an exaggerated wink. "I figured since I was on my way over anyhow."

She headed toward the guest bedroom. "It's here, in the closet, on the top shelf."

He stood behind her, looking over her shoulder at the boxes bearing C-H-R-I-S-T-M-A-S in big red letters. Nudging her aside, he said, "Let me get them down from there."

CHAPTER FOURTEEN

Three hours later, Perry Como sang "Oh Holy Night" as they hung the last of the tinsel garland. Jack lay in his bed by the fireplace, watching them.

"How about coffee or hot cocoa now?" He followed her to the kitchen. "I want to get organized for my early morning baking."

"Don't you ever quit? It's Christmas, for Pete's sake."

She opened her recipe box, sorted through them, and then lifted one of the cards for him to see. "In my mom's handwriting. I haven't made it in years."

"I'm drooling. I love brown sugar pudding."

"As you've already said," She laughed. "I was going to bring it to your house tomorrow, if the invitation is still good. I'd like to see your mom and your children – and meet your grandchildren."

He took a step toward her. "I'd like that. Very much."

Jack walked around the corner and stood at the door, whining. They both went toward him at the same time. Tildie said, "Do you need to go out, Jackie?" She opened the door, but he didn't budge. In fact, he sat and looked up toward the ceiling. They both looked up at the same time.

Her heart started racing.

Ben rested his hands on her shoulders and leaned down, so close she felt the warmth of his breath when he said, "Did I ever mention that I think mistletoe is one of the best parts of Christmas?"

She smiled while heat spread to her cheeks.

The next moment was pure bliss. A sweet kiss full of endless possibilities. Tomorrow looked brighter. Tomorrow had hope.

She took a step back and said, "Whew! I think I'll leave the mistletoe up all year."

"I think that's an excellent plan."

She brushed her hair back out of her eyes and fanned herself. Then a question came to her. "How did you know that Jack was missing? I mean, how long did you drive around looking before you found him?"

His brows furrowed. "I didn't have any idea he was missing. He just showed up on my doorstep this morning."

Realization hit them both. Their heads turned to where he sat with an impossibly obvious, knowing look on his face.

Ben half whispered, "Wow..." Then added, "He couldn't have... Could he?"

She shook her head from side to side. "He must have, I mean, there's no other way to explain..."

"He's invited to dinner tomorrow too."

Tildie leaned down and hugged him. "Merry Christmas, Jack. Thank you..."

The End

ABOUT THE AUTHOR

Teresa K. Cypher wears a lot of hats, but her favorites are those of a wife, mom, grandma, and writer. She lives in a little stand of woods between cornfields and soybean fields in western PA. During the day, she works in a bio-lab, keeping an eye on micro-organisms on microscope slides and on petri dishes. In the evening, she writes romance of the Sweet, possibly Sci-Fi, or even Fantasy variety. She is a co-founder of Weekend Writing Warriors.

Teresa has garnered deep inspiration from the myriad genres she reads. That includes everything from Star Wars to Cinderella to Arthurian legends. Though it sounds cliché, she truly believes that love does make the world go round

When she's not spending time with her family, or writing-with her faithful Cocker Spaniel, Leo, at her side, you can find her online.

Website: http://dreamersloversandstarvoyagers.blogspot.com/
Facebook: https://www.facebook.com/authorTeresaCypher/
Twitter: https://twitter.com/Teresa_Cypher

Jack and the Christmas Journey in the *Have Yourself a Merry Little Romance, 2015 Holiday Collection* is Teresa K. Cypher's debut story with Victory Tales Press.

Return Engagement

M. C. Scout

Dedication:
*To all of our service men and women—at home and
abroad, past and present—thank you for your service.
To their families, thank you.
Enjoy the holidays.*

CHAPTER ONE

"Are you sure we can pull this off?"

"Of course. Everyone I've talked to is on board. They all love the idea."

"I sure hope so."

"Trust me, we'll pull it off. All you need to worry about is your part in this."

Tanner Armitage had a great deal to worry about in order to pull off what he hoped would be the surprise of a lifetime for his girlfriend of four years. *Thank God for my brother!*

Chapter Two

Near Fort Bragg, North Carolina

Brynn Josephs went through the mail finding the usual—bills and junk mail. The last envelope piqued her curiosity. Opening it, she pulled out a pair of tickets to an ice hockey game scheduled for Christmas Eve. She hadn't ordered any tickets since the only one she went to games with had been stationed in Kabul, Afghanistan for the past twelve months.

She pulled out her cell phone, tapped a number in speed dial then waited.

"Armitage."

"Zach, it's Brynn."

"What's up, kiddo?"

"I just got a pair of tickets to the Christmas Eve game. Do you know anything about it?"

"No, though I had planned to ask you if you wanted to go."

"And you know my answer."

"Come on, it's Christmas Eve and I'm in goal. Gotta have at least one fan on my side."

"What about your family?"

"You know them—they have that big get-together before they head to Christmas Eve services."

"I don't know. Who would I go with?"

"Good question," Zach Armitage replied. "Just out of curiosity, where are the seats?"

"Ice seats, I think."

"Then go. In fact, I'll take you out to dinner after the game."

"I don't know..." she said with slow hesitation.

"It's the Christmas game. There's always something special going on at that game."

"But..."

"Trust me, Tanner would not want you sitting home alone."

"But, if he calls..."

"Didn't he say he had patrol duty that night?"

"I think he did."

"Well?"

She didn't answer him right away, knowing Zachary Armitage waited for her to say something. "Okay, I'll go," she told him after a few moments.

"Good," he said. "I'll be in touch, and if you don't find someone to go with then I'll take you to the game."

"But you have to be there early, don't you?"

"Won't be a problem."

* * * * *

Zach breathed a sigh of relief. If Brynn had turned down the tickets, he would have had to figure out some other way to get her to the rink for that one game. With her finally agreeing to go, it made things all that much easier to take care of.

When his twin brother had told him the idea he'd had for Brynn's Christmas gift, Zach had wholeheartedly jumped into the planning process. Ever since they'd started going together a few years before, Brynn had become more of a sister to him than any of his brother's other girlfriends. The family knew the relationship had become serious when they'd moved in together shortly after Tanner had been assigned to Fort Bragg, and just before his recent deployment overseas. *Besides, her father's a ranking Army officer so she understands...*

He went to his desk and pulled out a list he'd been putting together and checked off *getting Brynn to game. One down, so many more to go...*

CHAPTER THREE

Kabul, Afghanistan

Tanner Armitage picked up his orders. His leave would start in a few days so he put his things together.

"Hey, Sarge, I hear you've got thirty comin' up," Joey Norton said.

"Fortunately, I got it when I did," Tanner said.

"Got any plans?"

"One or two," Tanner said, inwardly smiling. He'd made a vow to himself not to tell anyone in case Brynn didn't like the gift. As the time drew closer to giving it to her, the more nervous he became.

"Hope you enjoy it. Unfortunately, I haven't been here long enough to get leave."

"You'll make it," Armitage said. "In fact, you'll be going home before you know it. You've got what, six months?"

"Six months out of nine left," Norton said. "Some days it feels like it's six years though."

"We all feel like that at one time or another. Trust me, you'll make it."

"If I don't see you before you leave, have a merry Christmas."

"You too."

Norton left him alone to finish packing what he could. He checked his watch, grabbed his rifle and headed to see his commanding officer. *Leave could not start soon enough...*

* * * * *

Walking out of his commanding officer's office after their meeting, Armitage felt an overwhelming sense of relief. After pulling a few strings, his captain had been able to arrange a hop on a military transport direct to Fort Bragg. Besides the fact it would save a great deal of time and a lot of aggravation, this way would make it a lot easier.

He knew if he tried to purchase a commercial flight home, it would be expensive considering the high cost of travelling on the days immediately ahead of the Christmas holiday. On top of that, he would have ended up flying into Charlotte or Fayetteville and would have needed to have someone pick him up, which inevitably could lead to the secret getting out.

As much as he appreciated the fact that there would have been a crowd waiting for him—family, friends and the veteran motorcyclists who turned out to greet returning service members—he didn't want it. At least, not this time—maybe at a later date but not now. Tanner Armitage needed to slip in under the radar, so to speak. *This is the only way...*

With the flight leaving the next day, he returned to his corner of the base and finished packing his things. He figured he would be returning at some later time but knew not to leave anything behind. With his luck, they'd deploy him somewhere else and he'd have to arrange to have things either shipped home, or brought home by another returning soldier. Bringing everything home would turn out to be the best thing to do.

Once he finished, he went to grab something to eat. Afterwards he'd sleep. He had a big day ahead of him and everything had to be right.

CHAPTER FOUR

Fort Bragg, North Carolina

The plane touched down at Fort Bragg the day before Christmas Eve. Tanner Armitage had been fortunate getting a hop back to the States instead of taking a commercial flight, which would have been time consuming. A once in a lifetime chance, he'd jumped at the offer, grateful to his commanding officer for arranging it plus whoever above him approved it.

Grabbing his pack and duffel, he stepped off the plane and headed to where he'd parked his car in a lot adjacent to the airfield. He'd left his Chevy Camaro there figuring it would be safer than having the car sit at the apartment. While he trusted Brynn to take care of it, they'd agreed it would be one less thing she'd have to worry about during the year he served overseas. Of course when the idea had come up, he had no clue what his plans would be once he returned home.

"Need a lift, sir?"

"Thanks," he said as he accepted a ride from one of the mechanics who worked on the planes.

As soon as he got to the car, he put his duffel on the back seat and his pack in the trunk. Going to the front of the car, he popped the hood. After a year, he wanted to make sure nothing furry had taken up residence in the engine compartment. Satisfied nothing had and that the engine looked in good order, he crossed his fingers and tried to start it. After a few tries, it finally turned over and he breathed a sigh of relief.

Driving out of the lot, he headed over to headquarters to report in. Before doing so, he requested housing at the BOQ—Base Officers Quarters—for twenty-four hours.

"You're in luck, sir, we have an opening," the lieutenant said.

"Great," Armitage said as he filled out the required paperwork. "I've been looking forward to a hot shower since I left Kabul."

"Here are the keys. Do you know where you're going?"

"Yes, I do and thanks," he said. "By the way, is Major Kemper in?"

"Just stepped away from his desk. Give him a call in fifteen."

"Thanks again."

Armitage left the office, drove to his quarters and found the room he'd been assigned. Once inside, he dropped the duffel by the bed and went to the window. He opened it and breathed in the fresh North Carolina air. *It's good to be home...*

After checking his watch, he pulled out his cell to call his commanding officer on the base and advise him of his whereabouts.

"Glad to hear you made it home safely. As soon as you can, come see me."

"I'd like a shower and a clean uniform..."

"Fine, I'll be expecting you, then."

"Yes, sir."

Armitage ended the call and sighed. *So much for relaxing...*

After taking a shower and dressing, Armitage left his quarters and went to report in with his commanding officer.

* * * * *

"Sergeant First Class Tanner Armitage reporting, Sir."

"At ease," the major said after the requisite salutes had been taken care off.

Armitage relaxed his posture and waited for Kemper to say something.

"Good to see you, Armitage. Your flight?"

"Not bad, sir."

Armitage handed a copy of his orders to Major Kemper and waited.

"You've got thirty days—why are you here and not at your off-base housing?"

"I haven't told anyone I'm home yet, except my brother."

"Why—there's no trouble at home, is there?"

"No, I plan to ask Brynn to marry me and I wanted to surprise her."

"And how do you intend to do it—or shouldn't I ask?"

"At the Christmas Eve game tomorrow night. Zach's been doing my leg work for me here, and my part's been getting home and picking up the ring."

"I see," Kemper said. "That explains base housing. You had me worried."

"Sorry, sir. Figured it would be easier this way. If Mom finds out, there will be no secret."

"I hear ya. Mothers have a way of being overly emotional when their children are away from the nest too long. My wife is a prime example. When our son went off to West Point, she didn't handle his absence well at all. When we went up to the school for a visitation, she calmed some but she still hadn't accepted that her first born had left home."

"Mom could have been happier when I enlisted but she's come around—especially once she realized and accepted I've made this my career."

"She still misses one of her children—it's a parent thing..."

Armitage laughed. His mother had been strong about his decision in front of others but once when she had him alone, she confided to him that the idea of his going into the service terrified her. They'd talked for several hours until he'd calmed her. She put up a good front but he knew it still bothered her.

"Well, you've got thirty days of freedom unless we need you. Good luck and, if everything goes as you want it to, congratulations."

"Thank you, sir."

"Dismissed."

"Yes, sir."

Armitage left the office, slipped into his car and drove through the main gate of the base. He turned onto the main highway and headed to a small store on the outskirts of town. Once he found it, he parked the Camaro and went inside.

Opening the door caused a small bell to ring, letting the owner know a customer had entered the store. Looking around, Armitage didn't see anyone.

"Mister Jacoby?" he called as he closed the door behind him.

"One moment."

A few minutes later, an older man came out of the back room and stood behind the counter.

"Tanner...or is it Zachary?" he greeted.

"After all these years and you still can't tell us apart?"

"Since your brother isn't military..."

Armitage laughed, the old man's amusement obvious.

"I came to pick up the ring," he said, suddenly suffering a major case of nerves as the time drew nearer.

"It's a beauty," Jacoby said. "The picture you sent me gave me a good deal to go on. I hope you like it."

Jacoby handed him a white gold ring with a diamond solitaire setting. Armitage nodded as he looked at it closely.

"It's perfect—nice and simple yet elegant."

"I agree. Some of the ones I've seen being advertised in Tiffany's and other jewelry outlets have turned me off. Way too much, but this one states a great deal while being understated."

"Like I said—perfect. I really appreciate you working with me on this. It couldn't have been easy."

"I like a challenge and I loved doing it for you. Your family has always been good to me so it's been my pleasure."

He handed Jacoby his credit card, signed the receipt and left the store with Brynn's Christmas gift. *Hopefully, she'll say yes...*

* * * * *

Armitage drove back to the base then went to the mess for a quick bite to eat. Once he had, he stopped by the base store and bought some beer and some food for later on, then returned to his quarters.

Once inside his room, he put the beer in the small refrigerator and then kicked off his boots. Changing into a Tee-shirt and sweat pants, he sat on the side of the bed and pulled out his cell phone. Pressing a number in speed dial, he waited for the call to connect.

"Where are you?" his brother asked.

"At the base."

"So you're back on American soil in one piece."

"Yep, and it feels really good."

"I can imagine."

"Is the secret still safe?"

"Yes, it is. No one suspects a thing. I've got the family set up in one of the private boxes so Mom can see everything. They thought it would be different to go to the game and then they'll go to services. Brynn has no idea..."

"Outstanding," Tanner said.

"Now comes the game and then it's on you to do the rest."

"You do realize I'm nervous as hell about this?"

"And so you should be—it's a big step for you both. Besides, I'd hate to see all this fall apart because something went wrong."

"What if she turns me down?" Tanner asked hesitantly.

"She won't—trust me, bro."

"Always have, always will."

CHAPTER FIVE

Brynn spent the last day before Christmas Eve buying last minute gifts and tying up loose ends before she took a week off between the holidays. One thing she had learned early on—take that week off in case the emotions go the wrong way and you want to be alone.

Growing up with a father who travelled a lot between deployments and meetings at various bases, she'd gotten used to the military way of life. It didn't bother her as much as it had her mother but then again, growing up with that being a major and very influential part of life, she had to become accustomed to it.

With this being Armitage's first deployment since they had moved in together, she didn't know how she'd handle his absence. She knew she didn't want to miss his calls or the times he found the chance to talk with her on SKYPE. The ability to do that made his deployment easier to handle than it had been for her mother. *I couldn't have handled letters, and once in a great while phone calls. How did she do it?*

Wrapping the last gifts and putting them under the tree she'd decorated a few days before, had put her in the holiday mood, but without Tanner, Christmas would not be the same. She wanted to deal with missing him without having to put on a happy face with her co-workers.

She thought about the hockey game and decided that it probably would take her mind off the fact that Armitage would not be home. Zach—his twin brother—had to have been the one who'd sent the tickets and she felt grateful for his thoughtfulness. Ever since she and Tanner had started going out, Zach had been a huge supporter of the relationship and by doing this one small thing for her, she felt like she had family.

She thought about her parents—her father a lieutenant general based in Germany and her mother who followed him everywhere— the epitome of a military officer's wife. She admired them both and hoped she could live up to her mother's example. *So far, so good...*

Her cell phone lit up a second before a ringtone of Frank Sinatra's *That's Life* started playing—her mother's favorite song. *Talk about timing...*

"Hi, mom," she said as she put the phone on speaker.

"How are you, Brynn?"

"Fine. How are you and Dad doing?"

172

"He's at some meeting—as usual. I'm curled up under a blanket with a glass of wine watching it snow."

"At least one of us gets a white Christmas..."

"I'd rather be there with you but –"

"Mom, it's all right. Zach got me tickets to the game tomorrow night which should be fun."

"Have you heard from Tanner?"

"Not yet. He may be out on patrol and when that happens, he calls me after they get back."

"Tell him to have a merry Christmas for us. I mailed your gifts but obviously they haven't arrived yet."

"I would have let you know."

"I know, dear."

They talked for a while longer before wishing each other a merry Christmas. Brynn ended the call, happy to have heard from her mother. On a whim, she called the manager of the complex they lived in to ask if anything had been delivered for her.

"I had just picked up the phone to call you," she said. "Two boxes arrived earlier from Germany."

"I'll be over in a few minutes to get them," Brynn advised before thanking her. Quickly, she slipped on a pair of flats and grabbed her keys and phone. While she walked to the office, she texted her mother telling her the boxes had arrived.

Collecting them, she returned to the apartment, opened them and put the gifts under the tree with the others. She pointed her phone at the tree and snapped several pictures knowing at least one would be sent to Armitage.

A fleeting hint of loneliness touched her. *Please let me get through this...*

Chapter Six

The day of the game, Brynn set out what she planned to wear. She chose a red silk blouse, her favorite pair of black jeans and her favorite pair of boots. She smiled remembering the day Armitage had bought them for her.

They'd been in Raleigh for the weekend with plans to attend a Carolina Hurricanes game. Before the game, they went to a nearby mall and did some shopping. Passing a leather store, they went in and she immediately fell in love with a pair of soft leather boots that she could wear with the pants leg tucked in. Tanner bought them for her and she wore them all the time.

After taking a shower, she dressed in a robe and then dried her hair. While not usually unruly or a problem, for some reason it took longer to take care of her long brunette tresses. As soon as she liked what she saw, she finished dressing then went into the living room to wait for Zach to pick her up, which did not take long.

She opened the door after he knocked and welcomed him in. He gave her a hug and they held each other.

"Are you all right?" he asked.

"It's beginning to set in that he's not going to be here for Christmas. I really thought I'd..."

"Don't worry. The family's here and you know Mom will make sure you don't have a chance to feel lonely."

"I know but..." she began. "Mother would not be happy with me for not being stronger."

"You are strong, kiddo. Not every person handles separation the same way."

"How do you deal with it considering how close you two are?"

"I miss the hell out of him and to be honest, if not for cell phones and the Internet, I'd probably be a basket case."

She hugged him again.

"Thanks," she said.

"For?"

"Being here."

"Anytime, kiddo," he said. "Anytime."

Brynn grabbed one of Armitage's jackets and they left for the Crown Coliseum in Fayetteville. She knew she had time to kill before the game since Zach had to be at the arena early for warm-ups and anything else the hockey team did prior to a game. *Maybe I can find a game on my phone to play...*

* * * * *

Half an hour after they left, a key slid into the lock and unlocked the door. With his arms full, Tanner Armitage slipped inside and looked around in the remaining light of the day. Setting down the vase of roses on the dining table, he carefully made his way through the apartment to the bedroom.

Stowing his rucksack in the corner with his duffel on top, he went over to the bed and grinned. Soon, he'd be sleeping in his own bed for the first time in over a year and hopefully with Brynn curled next to him. When not planning his surprise on his free time, he'd done nothing but think of her—missing her like he'd missed no other person in his life.

Brunette with very dark brown eyes, Brynn Josephs had been the best thing to happen to him. She'd come into his life at a time when he'd damned near sworn off women thanks to being dumped by a girlfriend who expected him to give up the Army. When she ordered him to make a choice, he'd made it and she walked out of his life in a huff.

Better off without her and the attitude, he concentrated on training and ended up in Spec Ops, which he loved. Having no connections at home made it easy to deploy for various lengths of time—at least until he'd met Brynn.

She'd changed his mind about abstinence and they'd been together ever since. Of course, being a military brat helped their relationship immensely. Coming back to the present, he glanced at his watch—something he'd been doing every few minutes though time had still not sped up. If anything, it seemed as if it had slowed down. *What should I expect?*

Knowing he needed to get to the arena, he quickly took a bag of rose petals out of his pocket and spread them on the quilt. In the space between their pillows, he laid an envelope with his Christmas card inside and a long-stemmed red rose then stepped back.

"Perfect!"

He left the room and headed to the kitchen to get something to drink. While he wanted a beer, he needed to be sober for what he intended to do. *There will be enough time to celebrate or drown my sorrows later...*

Pouring a glass of iced tea, he drank it, then rinsed the glass out and set it on the counter. He walked back into the front room and gazed at the beautiful Christmas tree sitting in the corner. He could see a great deal of love and attention had gone into decorating it. His eyes travelled down the length of the tree from the star on top to the presents sitting underneath it.

Like he had when he and Zach grew up, he wanted to shake the boxes to see if he could guess what might be hidden inside under all the pretty wrapping. Checking his watch again, he changed his mind then left for the one date he could not be late for.

The butterflies in his stomach grew worse. *Hopefully, this is normal...*

* * * * *

At the coliseum, Tanner parked the Camaro next to his brother's Ford pick-up in the player's lot—another part of the arrangements. He walked into the player's entrance then down the corridor to the locker room where he would keep out of sight until the time came to pull off his part of the plan. The butterflies turned into dive bombers.

Looking at the clock above the doorway, he sighed. Still two hours to go and it felt like it would take forever to pass. *Damn, I hate waiting like this...*

As the players came into the locker room, they welcomed him home. When they had all arrived except Zach, the coach welcomed Tanner home and wished him luck.

"We're all pulling for you, Tanner," he said, the team loudly agreeing.

"Now, about tonight's game..." the coach began.

* * * * *

Zach Armitage had been given the time to speak with Brynn about the first intermission shoot-out. He found her sitting in her seat playing a game on her phone, the arena still quiet before warm-ups and the opening ceremonies.

"Hey, what's up?" he asked as he sat next to her.

"Not much," she answered. "I've never realized what goes on before a game. I've been watching the guys working on the ice and it's as if they could do this in their sleep."

"Some might," he agreed. "I remember one of the guards telling stories of stopping people trying to smuggle stuff through the gate. He said his wife told him she heard him saying 'I'm sorry, no cans, bottles or alcoholic beverages permitted in the arena'."

"Seriously?"

"Yeah, it happened years ago when they took a more active part at the entrances. Tanner did it for about a year before he went into the service. He didn't like it that much though."

"Why?"

"Things changed with procedures and in some cases, not for the better."

"Wow."

"He really loves what he does right now and I admire him for the devotion."

"It takes a lot to sign a *blank check* to the country, considering they never know what's around the corner."

"I hear ya," he agreed.

"So what's brought you out here—don't you have a meeting or something?"

"Coach and I agreed that I should come out here and give you a heads up on the first intermission."

"What do you mean?"

"They have some holiday entertainment while they set up the shoot-out in one half of the rink. I think it's a tiny tots game. Anyway, four people take shots at the goal and whoever scores gets a special prize."

"And I need to know about this—why?"

"You're the last one to shoot tonight after a teen and two younger kids."

"Me? How?"

"Consider it a gift. When they mentioned doing it tonight, I asked them to include you."

"Why?"

"I want you to have a happy memory of this year's holiday since Tanner can't be here."

"I don't know what to say..."

"Merry Christmas, kiddo," he said as he leaned over and kissed her cheek.

"What am I supposed to do?" she asked changing the subject.

"You do remember how I taught you to shoot one-on-one?"

"Yes, I do, Zach," Brynn replied. "But, remember, I'm no Alex Ovechkin."

Zach snickered at her reference to the captain of the Washington Capitals.

"Good," he said. "I'll need to go to the head then I'll be back out to do the shoot-out with you. Remember—keep it low."

"Yes, sir, I will," she said wanting to salute him.

The fact he and Tanner had been born minutes apart made him just as over-protective of her as Tanner. *I guess he wanted to make sure everything would be all right while he went overseas...*

Zach disappeared into the tunnel leading to the team's locker room. As soon as he entered it, he saw his brother.

"Damn, you look good," he said as they hugged each other, the team applauding as the brothers met in the center of the locker room.

"I feel good," Tanner said.

"Glad you're home, bro."

"So am I," Tanner agreed, before asking the question nagging at him. "How is she?"

"Totally unaware of what's going on."

Tanner took a deep breath and let it out slowly.

"Damn, I hope this works."

"Do you have it with you?"

"Of course," Tanner assured him as he held up his hand to show him the ring he hoped Brynn would accept.

"Wow! Not bad, bro," Zach complimented.

"Hopefully, she likes it."

"She will," Zach assured him.

* * * * *

After the first period, the team returned to the locker room. Tanner Armitage met his brother by his locker before Zach took off some of his gear.

"Here's the mask and gloves—now, get going."

"Damn, how long has it been since I've been on blades?" he grunted as he headed toward the door.

"Obviously, too long," Zach answered. "Hey, do me a favor and don't embarrass me."

"I'll try not to."

"I'll hold you to that, bro."

Tanner nodded and put the goalie mask on his head. He pulled down the cage that would protect his face and started heading for the door leading to the tunnel and the rink. He barely heard Zach calling him as he caught up to his brother with his goalie's stick. He stopped and turned.

"Yo, here's my stick. You can give it to one of the equipment guys on the bench on your way off the ice."

Tanner nodded, put the gloves on then took the stick. Leaving the locker room, he received a lot of good wishes from the team which made him feel less nervous about what he intended to do. Gazing down the tunnel, it looked like it went on forever—those feelings he chalked up to nerves. *I've gone on dangerous missions and never felt like this...*

Once he made it to the bench, he waited for his signal to go on the ice. Someone opened the door leading to the ice and he stepped on to the slick surface, then skated in a figure eight to accustom himself to the skates and the ice. He heard the door close behind him—the so-called point of no return. He took another deep breath and waited.

"Ladies and gentlemen, the goaltender for the Fayetteville FireAntz, Zachary Armitage."

The crowd cheered as he skated toward the net.

Here goes nothing...

CHAPTER SEVEN

Having played in goal before he went into the service, Armitage remembered to rough up the ice in front of the pipes a little in order to give him a bit of purchase on the ice. Doing this also helped to calm him, though he knew it would only be momentarily.

Once he'd found it to his liking, he turned to center ice and watched the proceedings. Several people stepped onto a carpet runner leading from the bench to the blue line. The participants ranged in age from a six or seven year old to a ten or eleven year old, and then a teenager. Bringing up the rear, he saw the most beautiful woman in his world—the one he wanted to spend the rest of his life with. He felt his heart beating, the beats likes drums in his ears. *Calm down or you'll screw this up...*

The announcer explained the shoot-out and how it would proceed. While he did, workers set up a smaller goal for the young kids—they would move it back several feet for the teen since they would take no chances that the boy would hit Armitage. Several years back, an eighteen year old boy shot the puck at the goaltender and put a spin on it. It caught the goalie hard in the chest as they had not counted on the power behind the kid's slap shot. They had no clue the kid played on his high school team and had a scholarship to the University of New Hampshire for hockey. Organizers changed the rules after that, though tonight would be different.

Tanner waited, wishing they'd get this part over with. The longer he had to wait, the more nervous he became. *Hurry up...*

Out of the three, only the youngest had scored a goal, winning a promotional prize pack while the other two received food court passes for the next game they attended before the end of the season. They removed the net and then Armitage went into his act—goaltender waiting to be shot on. He took another deep breath and watched Brynn—standing in front of him wearing a team jersey that had *B Armitage* across the back, though he doubted she'd noticed his brother's *gift*.

"Ladies and gentlemen, our final participant is Brynn Josephs. Because she and our goalie are old friends, it's been agreed that she can shoot on him. Are you ready?"

Brynn nodded and took her position. She had three chances to try to score, Armitage waiting impatiently. *Come on, baby...*

Finally, she drew back and shot the puck at him. Armitage blocked it, not wanting to make things seem obvious or too easy.

She easily fired the next shot at him, another easy block. *She hasn't forgotten what we taught her.*

The final puck he allowed past him, the crowd cheering. He bent down, picked the puck up and skated back to where she stood. As soon as he stopped, he handed the puck to her as the announcer stepped back.

Armitage got down on one knee and looked up at her through the protective cage of the face mask. *Please, God, let this go the right way...*

* * * * *

Brynn watched as Zach skated back to her and took the puck out of the basket of his catching glove. She noticed something different about him but couldn't figure out what. It stunned her when he took a knee in front of her like he intended on proposing to her.

"Zach, what the hell are you doing?" she asked quietly, hoping no one could hear her.

He pushed the helmet up to a spot on top of his head, took the gloves off and dropped them on the ice, while pulling off a small item he wore on his pinkie. He looked at her and waited expectantly.

When she looked into his eyes, she realized she gazed at Tanner and not Zach—the only difference between them being that Tanner had blue eyes while Zach had green—the only way to tell them apart.

"Tanner, what..." she started but tears of joy stopped her.

"Brynn, will you marry me?" he asked quickly, forgetting everything he intended to say. *So much for rehearsal...*

Unable to speak and overwhelmed by the sight of him, Brynn nodded. Tanner slid the ring on her finger then stood up. Stepping onto the carpet, he pulled her into a kiss as the crowd roared its approval.

"Ladies and gentlemen, we are proud to welcome home from Kabul, Afghanistan after a twelve month deployment, Army Sergeant First Class Tanner Armitage. We'd also like to congratulate him on his engagement to Miss Brynn Josephs and extend our appreciation to everyone for their part in this joyful time."

"How did you pull this off?"

"How else—Zach did most of the leg work plus making the arrangements for me. The team agreed to help and they got the arena management to give its approval."

"You're..."

"The happiest man in the world right now."

One of the promotions people came over to escort them off the ice. As they neared the bench, the team congratulated them. Zach waited at the entrance to the tunnel then shook his brother's hand and hugged his future sister-in-law.

"It's about damned time, you two."

"I can't believe you pulled this off," Brynn said.

"Not a problem, though I held my breath when he asked you."

"And if I had said no?"

"I would have asked you," he joked.

Chapter Eight

After watching the rest of the game from the seats Zach had gotten them, they headed upstairs to where they agreed they'd meet up with Zach in one of the suites. When they arrived, they walked into another celebration.

The Armitage family crowded around them as they welcomed Tanner home and Brynn to the family. His mother hugged him, tears in her eyes.

"Why didn't you tell me?" Rose Armitage asked.

"I wanted to surprise Brynn and considering how secrets get leaked in this family..."

"What?" his sister, Jordan, asked in mock horror.

"Don't be surprised. You know damned well if I had told anyone but Zach, the entire state of North Carolina would have known and I didn't want my surprise for Brynn ruined. Sorry, but I wanted her to be totally in the dark."

"Definitely worked, Tanner," Brynn said. "I still can't believe it."

Her hand gripped his tightly as if fearing she'd lose him for some reason. He squeezed her hand back, overwhelmed in emotions between being home and the fact she had said *yes* to his proposal. He thought he felt a little apprehension in her grip and took his cue.

"Yo, bro, how much time before we can't go out of the tunnel?"

"Thanks for reminding me. Security'd probably like to go home early."

"If we plan to make it to midnight services on time, we'd better take off, too," their mother said. "Will you be there, Tanner?"

"I need to run over to the base to pick my things up so I doubt it."

"Son?"

"I know but I'm still getting over jet lag and..."

"Dinner is at three. Be there—both of you."

"Yes, ma'am," Tanner said.

Brynn hugged their mother.

"We are so happy for you and to have you join the family."

"Thank you," Brynn said, holding back tears.

The entire Armitage family left the suite and headed for the exit. They hugged each other before the twins and Brynn left for the locker room area.

As they approached the guard on the door, he leaned over to unlock it.

"Good thing you came down when you did. Almost locked you in here."

"Thanks for waiting for us," Zach said. "Merry Christmas."

"Same to you."

The three of them left the coliseum and headed for their vehicles.

"Bro, it's been quite an evening," Zach said.

"I hear ya," Tanner said.

"How can we thank you?" Brynn asked.

"I'll let you know," Zach said as he slid behind the wheel of his pick-up. "I'll see you tomorrow at Mom's."

He backed out of the space and drove off, leaving the newly engaged couple alone by Tanner's Camaro.

Tanner Armitage pulled Brynn Josephs into a deeply passionate kiss, but then leaned back to look at her.

"You have no idea how long I've wanted to do that," he said.

"Oh, I think I do," she said.

He kissed her again then opened the car door for her. Once he made sure she'd settled in, he closed the door then went to the other side and slid behind the wheel. He backed out of the space and headed for the exit, but once there, he turned in the direction leading away from the base.

"I thought..."

"I had to come up with something quick. I couldn't go to services tonight..."

"Why? Don't you always?"

"Yeah, but right now, I'm not up to seeing a lot of people. I pulled this off to be with you..."

"You lied to your mother," she accused as she tried to hide her smile.

"A little white lie meant to not hurt her feelings. I know most of the folks in the congregation and know what they'd do if we walked in there. They mean well, but I wouldn't have seen you for who knows how long, once they fought for my time. I'm not trying to be mean but I've dreamt the last several months of being with you..."

"I'm glad," she quietly said. "I've missed you so damned much."

"Let's go home."

CHAPTER NINE

When he unlocked the door to their apartment, Armitage stepped inside first to make sure no one had entered their home. He took Brynn by surprise when he yanked her inside and kicked the door close. Pulling her into another deeply passionate kiss, the hunger suffered from their year-long separation took over.

"Baby...."

"I know," she said. "I've missed you so much."

"We've got thirty days—any ideas?"

"Plenty," she said as she ran her hand along the strip of Velcro at the front closure of his ACU—Army Combat Uniform. Finding the zipper behind it, she pulled it down, opening the tunic and pushing the sides out of her way.

He snickered when she groaned, but loved the feel of her pulling the Tee-shirt out of his waistband. The mere touch of her fingertips on his body sent his heat level up. The next thing he knew, she had both pieces of his uniform off seconds before she pulled him tight in her arms.

"Brynn?"

"What?"

"Your turn," he gasped as she feathered kisses across his firm chest.

"But that means I have to let go of you."

"You can do it," he coaxed as his body continued to react to the woman he loved.

"If you insist," she said pouting a little.

Slowly Brynn removed the team jersey, finally noticing the *B Armitage* across the back.

"I didn't know my name had been put on the back," she said. "I'll look at it later. I've got more important things to attend to at the moment."

"Music to my ears," he said as he watched her while he finished taking off his uniform.

Moments later, she stood before him naked.

Armitage grinned as he pulled her into his arms, picked her up and carried her into their bedroom. Laying her down on the rose petal covered quilt, he began making up for twelve months' worth of lost time.

Needing to taste her again, he kissed her while his hand massaged her breast. He'd dreamt of this moment, but reality had definitely proven to be way better. The feel of her hands on his back sent him soaring.

"I never realized how much I've needed you."

"As a daughter, I always hated deployments because Dad had to be away from us. Now, I understand what Mom went through. I can't believe I survived this."

"You're special, Brynn."

"Do me a favor," she said.

"Anything," he said. "What?"

"Before you get deployed again, leave me with a baby. I always want a part of you with me."

"Are you sure? We just became engaged."

"I'm very sure."

"Whatever you want, but if you want to change your mind..."

"I won't," she stated emphatically. "I won't. Besides, I went off the pill months ago, figuring I wouldn't be needing it since you didn't expect to be home for a few weeks yet."

"Interesting. Shall we start now?"

"Are you getting deployed already?"

"No, I love you and I'll do anything for you."

"Then let's..."

Armitage groaned as he pulled her tight against him. He could tell she wanted him as much as he wanted her, their feelings driving him to give her what she wanted. He held her tighter, needing the feel of her body surrounding him.

"Tell me what you feel?"

"While you're holding me tight against your hard body, you're filling me completely. I can feel our heartbeats and want more."

"Then get ready for the ride of your life."

"Bring it on Tanner, and don't hold back. A year..."

His lips covered hers as their tongues danced. Hunger took them both over as he pushed her body to the edge and beyond.

"It's good to be home," he whispered.

* * * * *

When they woke later, Tanner's body surrounded hers, prohibiting her from leaving his side. She turned in his arms and gazed at him—his handsome face, his toned body, every tiny bit of him.

He stirred and she pulled him closer for a passionate kiss—one long overdue.

"A hell of a way to wake up."

"Merry Christmas."

"Same to you, baby."

"You definitely planned a unique return..."

"...engagement?"

"Yes," she said thoughtfully.

"I did, didn't I?'

"Yup, and I love you for it."

"You have no idea how I dreaded the possibility of you refusing me."

"Tanner, I love you. Ever since we talked about getting married before you left for Kabul, I've been imagining our life together. No way would I turn you down—especially after what I asked last night."

"About a baby?"

"Yes. I can't even begin to remember my life before you came into it."

"God, I love you," he said.

"Then let's make this a short engagement. I don't want to lose out on what could be by following tradition. I need you, Tanner Armitage, and I can't wait to start our life together as your wife.

"You just made my Christmas by giving me the best gift ever."

"Then you know what to do."

"Oh, yeah."

The End

ABOUT THE AUTHOR

M. C. Scout lives in the Mid-Atlantic region of the United States with her family and deep in the center of Revolutionary history—strange how her love is immersed in the Civil War era and the South. "I grew up learning there is the Northern side, the Southern side and the truth to the Civil War. Finding the truth is fascinating.

She finds her inspirations from many facets of life then weaves them into stories either contemporary or historic in nature. She enjoys many different types of music and books when not writing as well as ice hockey. Her favorite actor – who truly sends her heart racing – is Daniel Craig. "I was one of the ones who didn't want him as James Bond – a huge mistake. The movies and his Bond are phenomenal." Plus, you can also add Alex O'Loughlin and the guys from Strike Back – the show needs more seasons. Her favorite authors are Jackie Collins, WEB Griffin and Vince Flynn.

One of her favorite places to visit is Gettysburg because each time is always different and shows another new side to the times and how they've changed our everyday lives today. Another is the museum at Wright-Patterson AFB in Dayton, Ohio where she loses herself among numerous planes from the past and present. "It's a special place."

One thing she lives by–"if you don't learn at least one new thing a day, the day is definitely wasted."

You can find the author online.
Website: http://cpoff.bravejournal.com

Other M. C. Scout stories:
The Southern Legacies series – The Ghost and the Wolf, His Lady Avery, Wounded Hearts, Redemption in Blood and Midnight Rider.

The Blood Lords series – My Lord Baltimore and My Lord Richmond

Third Time's the Charm

Gerald Costlow

CHAPTER ONE

Trudy grabbed her coat and was out the classroom door as soon as the closing bell rang, ignoring the students who were heading her way with expected complaints about the assigned book reading over the Christmas Holiday. She pushed through the surge of teenagers digging through hall lockers in order to reach Brian's office before he left.

She was still too late. She looked at the locked door and considered trying to text his cell phone, but she'd already done that an hour or so ago. In fact she'd tried to track him down several times over the past few days, ever since their last date, but didn't want to appear desperate. The gym teacher couldn't have gotten far. She sprinted down the now empty hall and made it to the parking lot in time to see Brian scraping the ice off his car window while it warmed up.

"Brian!" she yelled, waving. "Wait up!"

The handsome gym teacher paused as she came over. He didn't look happy to see her. Maybe he had something else on his mind. It was rumored their basketball team didn't have the talent to make it to the championship this year. "I just wanted to let you know how much I enjoyed our last date," she said. "How about to pay you back, I fix you a home-cooked meal for the next one? Just let me know when you want to come over. I have the house to myself for the entire holiday." She grinned. "I figure for our next date, maybe we should be someplace more private. You know what they say: third time's the charm."

Brian looked uncomfortable. "Uh...Trudy, I've been meaning to talk to you. My ex-girlfriend and I, well, we've been talking and... Look, she agreed to take me back. We're going to try to make a go of it this time, maybe even get some relationship counseling. Sorry. I was going to tell you during our last date, but—"

"But you were too busy shoving your tongue down my throat." She held up a hand and squeezed her eyes shut. "No, we're both adults. All we did was go out on a couple of dates and neck in the car. I guess it just wasn't meant to go any further. Merry Christmas. Good luck with your girlfriend."

She turned and walked across the lot to her own car, jamming her cold hands into her pockets and fumbling for her keys. She slid into the seat and started the car. Then, under cover of the frosted windows and loud car radio, she let it out, screaming and beating her fists against the steering wheel in frustration.

Three dates! All I ask for is three dates. Three lousy dates before I get dumped. She leaned forward and pressed her forehead against the cold plastic of the steering wheel. Brian hadn't been the man of her dreams, for sure. His idea of a great date was dragging her to a hockey game or watching a boxing match in a sports bar. Still, he was patient enough not to demand sex right away while persistent enough to let her know when she did give the green light, he was going to take charge and want lots of it, just the way she liked. But for that, she needed a man who stuck around for more than two dates. She had a firm "Third time's the charm" rule, and she wasn't desperate enough to break. Yet.

Hell, I'd even settle for a man who's lousy in bed, if he's willing to learn.

Trudy drove the short distance home. She parked on the street in front of her house since her new stepmother's car filled her old parking spot in the driveway. Somehow this last accommodation summed up all the problems in her life lately. Dad's new bride had certainly made herself at home in the past week. On top of everything else, she'd had to listen to their bedsprings squeaking at night while bemoaning her own dry spell. Whatever reservations Trudy had about the wisdom of her dad getting married, she had to admit Patty was giving the old man what he needed. She hadn't seen him so mellow in years.

The front door opened as Trudy reached for the doorknob and a plump, short woman stepped through. "Thought I heard you pull up," Patty said. "I have to run back to the office for a few minutes. There's always some last minute paperwork can't wait until after the holiday. We ordered pizza. Money's on the table." Trudy started to slip past her but the woman grabbed hold of her arm. She looked directly into Trudy's eyes. "Thought so. The jock you've been dating broke up with you, or my Sherritt blood is lying to me. I'm so sorry, Hun. You want to talk about it? I can come back inside for a while. The office can wait."

"No, you go ahead. Thanks for asking." Trudy had tried to hate Patty, but the woman was too damned nice.

She found her father packing the last of the presents from under the tree into a cardboard box. "Some of those have my name on them," she reminded him. "I'd still like to open them on Christmas morning. I can pull up a video link on your smartphone if the Appalachia wilderness has internet where you're going."

"First, the bed and breakfast I booked has wireless," he said. "Sherritt Holler isn't Dogpatch. They even have satellite television and indoor plumbing. Second, you're coming with us. Patty had a feeling whatever plans you had for a happy holiday would get shut down today, and I'm not having you moping around an empty house crying 'cause your man dumped you."

"And you took her word for it?"

"Was she wrong?" he stopped and looked at her.

"Well, no. The skunk decided to go back to his ex. Patty must think I'm a loser who can't keep a man for more than a couple of dates. Turns out she's right. You married a smart woman this time."

Her father stepped forward and pulled her into an embrace. She took a shuddering breath and hugged him back, remembering how years ago, as a rebellious teenager, she would have been stupid enough to pull away.

"You're not a loser," he said. "I don't want to hear you call yourself that again. From what I can tell, half the time you're the one dumping them after the first few dates, and for good reason. Remember what I taught you: third time's the charm!"

"I love you Dad. If Patty makes you happy, I'll make room for her. Maybe she'd prefer having you to herself for your first Christmas together? Call it a second honeymoon."

"I already paid for your room and it's non-refundable," he replied. "This was her idea. She knows she can't take your mother's place, but she thinks you two can be good friends once you get to know her. Speaking of your mother, a package arrived today. It's on your dresser." He picked up the box of gifts. "Try to make do with one suitcase and a makeup kit, and they also have stores there so you can buy anything you forget to pack. I have to fit everything into one car."

Trudy went upstairs to pack, glad she didn't have to spend the holiday break alone. On the other hand, meeting the bunch of hillbillies Patty called family didn't much appeal to her, either. She picked up the small package, surprised to see it was mailed from Ireland this time. The last letter she received came from Nepal, where her *mixed-up Mom in search of herself* had taken the vows of a Buddhist nun and changed her name once again to something Trudy couldn't be bothered to memorize.

Why Ireland? Is she a druid now? There was a heavy silver necklace wrapped in tissue paper along with the letter. The necklace had a lifelike silver rabbit as a pendent. My Dear Charm, the letter started off as always, making Trudy grit her teeth. Her middle name might be Charmain, but the day her mother signed the divorce papers and left to join a cult was the last time anyone went around calling her Charm. Her mother went on to say she was teaching meditation retreats at some Buddhist temple in Ireland for the next couple of years, and how wonderful the head honcho was. Trudy barely glanced over that. Buddhists in Ireland? The world's getting smaller every year. Then she got to the point in the letter where her mother explained about the necklace.

It was the strangest thing, little Charm. I was doing some walking meditation and came across a young man sitting alone on a bench. A local lad. Rather handsome, if I was being honest. Anyway, we exchanged greetings and he asked me where I was from, with my strange accent. We got to talking about America and perhaps I went into too much detail about the pretty young daughter I left behind who is all grown up now. Anyway, the stranger told me he'd always wanted to travel abroad. Then he handed me this pendent and asked if I would send it to you. He took off while I was examining the wonderful craftsmanship so I didn't get his name. I showed it to the head monk who said the stranger gave it to you so it would be dishonest for the temple to keep it. Namaste, my daughter.

Not the strangest letter Trudy had ever received from her wacko mother. It was a very nice necklace, if a person had a thing for rabbits. She almost dropped it in the trashcan like all the other trinkets her mother had sent her over the years, but thought again about the Irish man who'd sent it. He sounded like the sort of man she was desperate to find. Maybe this would bring her luck. She slipped it over her head and pulled her travel bag out from the closet.

She was trundling the bag down the hall toward the stairs when she passed her father's open bedroom door and spotted the big book on the bed. Normally she wasn't the nosey type, but as an English Literature teacher and keeper of their home library, she thought she knew every book in the house by sight. She went in to examine it, expecting to see Patty had brought with her a cookbook or perhaps a large family Bible.

Sherritt Book of Spells? Patty was always making references to her Sherritt blood like it was something special. She looked inside the title page. Private printing, but professionally done. This one had a publishing date from over a hundred years ago so it must be a family heirloom. It even had an index, with titles like "Truth Spell" and "Potion to Arouse a Man's Loins" scattered among pages of spells for charming honey bees and potions for removing warts. There was no sorting by topic she could determine. Typical amateur mistake.

On a whim, Trudy scanned the index and an entry caught her eye. "For the Spurned and Lovelorn," she read. "Page one-thirty-two. That's for me. Do they have a fix for a horny girl that doesn't require batteries?" She flipped through the pages.

"Take a token from a handsome rogue. Place it close to your heart. Bring up your Talent and say the following: When first we meet, a friendly greet; the second tryst, only kissed; for love to stay, third all the way (See Potion for Preventing Pregnancy, page twelve)."

She laughed and looked at the index again. "What absolute nonsense."

"Aye, lass," said a man's voice in a strong Irish brogue behind her. "It's old magic, and the oldest magic is made from only the best quality nonsense."

Trudy whipped around to discover a tall young man with wavy red hair had snuck into the room. The stranger gave her a wicked grin and reached out like he was going to grab her breast, but only touched the silver rabbit nestled in her cleavage while she stood there in shock. "I've given you my heart," he said. "What will you give me in return, little Charm?"

"I didn't hear you come in," she told him. "Who told you my old nickname?"

"Why, I heard it from – Oops! Gotta go. I'm looking forward to knowing you better." She blinked and the stranger was gone, disappearing into thin air as Patty and her father came into the room.

"Thought I heard your voice," Patty said with her usual good cheer. "Pizza's here. You on your cellphone?" Then she stopped when she saw Trudy with the book. "Oh, dear." She came over and took the book from her hands. "Did you read one of the spells? You've gone all pale. Here, better lie down before you pass out. Henry, fetch a cold washcloth, would you?"

Trudy struggled to make sense of what just happened. "What the hell was that?" she finally got out. "Who was that man? What was he talking about, giving me his heart? How'd you make him disappear?"

"What man?" her father said, putting a cold washcloth on her forehead. "I didn't see or hear any man. You were standing here talking to yourself."

"It's probably nothing to worry about," Patty said. "You must have a touch of natural *Talent,* like your father. The spells can have side effects if you're not a trained Sherritt witch. Do you have a headache?"

"I feel fine. A bit shook up. Are you telling me you claim you're a real witch and you think those spells actually work?" Trudy started to get angry. "Just like Mom, believing in supernatural crap like chakras and ghosts. Great. Dad went and married another wacko."

"Settle down, honey," her dad said. "It's not like that at all. Patty is about as down to earth as they come. She and her family aren't part of that New-Age stuff your mother was into. We were getting ready to sit down and talk to you about it tonight. Figured it was time."

Patty leaned over and adjusted the washcloth. "That's why I had the book out. I was going to show it to you. Why don't you tell us which spell you tried and about the man in the room. Maybe that will give me a clue what happened."

"I know what I saw, so something strange is going on." Trudy rubbed her eyes, took the wet cloth from her forehead, and sat up. "I'm famished. I want a slice of pizza in my hand before I say another word."

* * * * *

Trudy went through about half a large pepperoni while explaining what happened, beginning with her mother's letter and ending with the man promising to see her again. She didn't mention how the memory of his wicked grin and his hand reaching for her chest made her heart flutter. "Too bad the handsome rogue my mind invented is just my imagination," she concluded. "That must be a popular spell for young witches. I wouldn't mind getting him alone in my bedroom."

Her father cleared his throat and Trudy's face reddened when she realized what she'd said.

Patty looked again at the letter Trudy had brought down. "Our spells can't create people out of thin air. At least, not that I know of. I need to see how strong your Talent is. It's a simple test." She held her hand out. "Take my hand, look at me, and tell me what you hear."

Holding the woman's hand felt good. "What am I supposed to be hearing?" she finally said. "Dad's stomach is gurgling where he shouldn't have eaten spicy sausage pizza. He needs to take an antacid or he'll be up half the night. Is that it?"

Patty pulled her hand away. "You should have heard my voice in your head if you had any Talent at all. Your father can hear me if I shout loud enough. Trudy, honey, you don't have a bit of Talent. The spell shouldn't have done anything."

"So it really was all in my head? I swear he was as real as you sitting there." A horrible thought crossed her mind. "Dear God, maybe I'm schizophrenic. It happens sometimes at my age, you know."

Her father reached over and put a hand on her knee. "Pumpkin, will you relax? Schizophrenia is inherited. There's none of that in your family, and that includes your mother. She's goofy but never claimed to hear voices. We've all seen things we can't explain. Once as a young man I was camping with some buddies and saw a hut on giant chicken legs walking across a field in the distance. 'Course I was high at the time."

"Not helping," Trudy said. "The last time I got stoned was in college. Mom was the one into that sort of thing." Then an idea hit her and she looked at the letter again. "Could there be something on the letter? It does feel like I have the munchies. She wouldn't have done it on purpose, but... Damn! I have a habit of licking my finger when I turn a page. Am I tripping?"

Patty and her dad both started laughing. "I handled the letter, too," Patty said. "If that's what it is, Henry is going to have a wild time tonight. I'll let you know." She shook her head and stood, collecting the empty pizza boxes to throw away. "My Sherritt blood is telling me there's more to it than a brain hiccup or accidental acid trip. It'll take someone wiser than me to figure it out. Fortunately, tomorrow morning we're driving down to see someone wiser than all of us combined. Wait until you meet Gran."

CHAPTER TWO

The bed and breakfast turned out to be one of those huge multistory houses built when having money meant living on the right street and being able to hire servants to take care of a house full of children.

She'd been given a crash course on Smithville and the nearby Sherritt Holler on the long ride down, including the fact that East Tennessee had unpredictable weather so one never knew if it was going to be a white Christmas. It turned out this was one of those years when the occasional dusting of snow didn't stick around and the unseasonable 50 degree temperature seemed like a tropical heat wave to Trudy.

The young woman who opened the door was a surprise, since she was dressed in a hooded white robe cinched at the waist. "You must be the Macalester party," the woman exclaimed, ushering them inside with a wave of her long, floppy sleeves. "We've been expecting you. I'm Marian Graford, owner and operator of the Smith House, along with my husband Mark. Excuse the outfit, but our church is putting on a live manger scene for the Christmas light show and I just finished the sewing. Since I can supply my own baby, we're drafted to be Jesus and Mary for the news cameras today. Not to worry; plenty of room at this inn."

Patty stuck her hand out and Marian took hold of it, stood silently for a minute and then nodded. "Nice to see Sherritts from out of town making the effort to visit. I'll show you to your rooms. My husband and I came for Christmas several years ago and fell in love with the area. We moved here and bought the bed and breakfast. Mark would help carry your bags, but he disappeared into his workshop earlier and insists on not being disturbed."

She prattled on, while she led them up the wide staircase. If Marian was this talky all the time, Trudy had a suspicion why her husband insisted on being left alone once in a while.

"For the newlyweds," Marian said, ushering them into the first room at the top of the stairs. "We call it our Honeymoon Suite because it's got a private bathroom and a special, heavy duty king-sized bed guaranteed not to squeak."

Patty chuckled while her father checked the view out the window and pretended he didn't hear. Trudy was led to a small room at the end of the hall with barely enough space for the single bed, dresser, and nightstand inside.

"Missus Macalester said you've just learned about the Sherritts," Marian said. "It was only a few years ago when I discovered my heritage, so I know what a shock it can be. This house has a history, if you're interested in such things. The website only tells part of it. We even have a little museum. Oh dear, Nan is waking up from her nap. Hope you enjoy your stay. Refreshments and conversation in the drawing room most evenings." She disappeared down the hallway and only then did Trudy hear a baby start crying.

Trudy had several hours to kill before they were supposed to pile into the car and start the round of visits. She closed the door and took the scrap of paper out of her pocket with the spell copied onto it. Her hallucination seemed to avoid being seen by strangers so Patty had suggested she find some privacy and try the spell again. If nothing happened, it might mean she didn't have to worry about her handsome rogue appearing out of nowhere and ravishing her in her sleep.

She looked at the comfortable bed she happened to be standing next to while preparing to read the spell. *Or maybe I'm hoping for a bit of ravishing.* Then the silliness of it all struck her and she crumpled up the note and threw it in the wastebasket. She was getting as bad as her mom, believing she could summon magical lovers.

I need some fresh air.

The air didn't feel so warm once she walked far enough down the street to catch the steady breeze off the surrounding mountains. The Literature Teacher in her couldn't stop thinking about the spell book. She wondered how many generations of Sherritts had copied and recopied those spells and faithfully prepared potions as instructed. Now she wanted to study it. Even nonsense could be fascinating.

By then her steps were taking her past a huge old cemetery surrounded by tall stone walls. She sat on a handy bench just inside the gate and wondered if Patty would let her do some research. The spells were obviously designed for easy memorizing. Trudy would bet she could recite it from memory.

"Let's see... Token next to your heart, Talent up, blah blah. Then recite when first we meet, a friendly greet, the second...tryst, only kissed. For love to stay, third all the way. I wonder when tryst was in common usage?" She searched through her pockets for a pen and paper to write a note to check.

"It's Old English," said the man with the Irish accent. "Tryst started off meaning a hunter's cabin in the woods. A popular place to meet in secret, it was. I could recite it in Gaelic, if you like."

Trudy tilted her head back, squeezed her eyes shut and took a deep breath. "I'm not going to faint," she said. "I'll accept magic works and freak out later."

"Not even a little swoon? That's a shame, that is. I was lookin' forward to catching you in my arms. Then I'd get to loosen your girdle. Now I'll have to get you out of your clothes the hard way."

She looked at the man who had appeared next to her on the bench. It was the same man from before, with the same wicked grin. This time he wore a heavy knit turtleneck pullover and the breeze ruffled his curly hair. She reached over and poked him on the arm.

"Oh, aye, I'm as solid as a rock, I am, little Charm. Especially where it counts." His wicked grin flashed again. He yawned and stretched and put his arms across the back of the bench behind her, scooting an inch or so closer. It was such an obvious move. Trudy had to laugh.

"Slow down, Casanova. You're the guy my mother wrote about? My name is Trudy, not Charm. Tell me who you are – what you are – and what the hell is going on. Why me? I want the truth."

He looked at her with exaggerated surprise. "So it's the truth you'd be wanting? You're a remarkable woman indeed, Trudy Macalester. Call me Pook. Let's find a spot more private so we're not interrupted. This isn't my first tryst in a graveyard. It's a fine place for lovers to meet."

Since the last thing she wanted was for him to disappear again, she let him take her by the arm and lead her deeper into the privacy of the stones. "Let's get something straight," she told him. "I haven't yet agreed to be your lover and if you try anything I know how to hurt a man. Pook is a funny name. Pook...as in Pooka?" She fingered the rabbit pendant. "You're a Pooka, like in the movie?"

He groaned. "I'm not a Pooka; I'm *the* Pooka. My name isn't Harvey and I'm not a six-foot tall rabbit and I can't stop time. Technically, I'm a fairy."

"No stopping time? I'm disappointed. What can you do, Mister Pook?" He took the opportunity to slide an arm around her while they were walking. "I mean, besides charm a girl out of her panties."

He threw his head back and laughed; a high-pitched twitter she didn't expect. "Lord, what fools these mortals be," he said. "True magic is dismissed while parlor tricks amaze. Why you? When your mother described you so beautifully I knew we were destined to be lovers." His hand slid further down and cupped her behind, letting her know all these questions hadn't sidetracked his goal one bit. "As for what I can do, I have a deserved reputation as a great lover. I've also been known to change form. I'll give you a horseback ride by the light of the moon, if you'd like. I'd love to feel your heels kicking my side."

Oh, the Hell with it. The spell does say we're supposed to kiss. She stopped him, grabbed hold of the front of his pullover, and planted her lips on his. He responded to her need and his fingers knew the right spots to touch on her body. If she'd summoned him in the bedroom earlier, clothes would have started coming off and that would have been it. As it was, she had to eventually call a truce and cling to him with her face pressed against his chest, legs trembling.

"Raspberries," she murmured. "Fairies taste like raspberries." Then as her brain started working again, something he'd said triggered a thought. "The thing you said about fools and mortals. That's Shakespeare. Pooka... Pook... Am I talking to the famous Puck?"

Pook's reaction startled her. He clamped a hand over her mouth and made shushing sounds while he looked around them, like he was expecting to be attacked. "Please, please don't say that name again," he whispered. "King Oberon can hear it being spoken and know where to find me."

Trudy pulled the hand away and stepped back. "I knew it was too good to be true," she said. "You're a criminal, or at least a trickster. What did you do? You escape from some fairy prison?"

"Nae, lass," he said. "I've done nothing to be ashamed of. The King now forbids me to cross over to this world. I could not abide the boredom of the twilight land another moment and snuck away from the court. It's not the first time. As long as I'm careful and return soon, no harm done."

"Uh, huh. Define soon. I'd rather not wake up the next morning and find a note saying, Gotta go, thanks for the great sex."

He shrugged his shoulders. "Last time I stayed fifty years. Anything longer is taking a chance." Pook stepped forward and took her hands. He looked serious for a change. "I want more than one night with you. Let me prove I can be the lover of your dreams. When you tire of me, give the necklace back and tell me to leave. You'll never see me again."

She didn't know what to do. Her body ached from wanting his fingers to explore further and she could still taste raspberries, but this was way too much craziness to digest all at once. "I studied Shakespeare so I know about your fairy tricks. No dreams and no messing with my head. If I decide to invoke the spell again, and I said *if*, then you have my permission to take me in your arms and have your way with me. I'll be the lover of *your* dreams."

Pook made his twitter laugh and pulled her back into his arms. "Trudy Charmain Macalester, I have tumbled many a woman with no thought of tomorrow, but never someone like you. You're special."

They began another round of exploring each other's bodies. Then she heard someone call her name. She was leaning back at the time while he nuzzled her cleavage, so when he disappeared it caused her to fall backwards onto her butt.

"There you are," Marian exclaimed, appearing from around a tall headstone and pushing a stroller. "Thought I heard your voice. Baby Jesus and I are on our way to put in our tour of duty at the manger. Patty asked if I saw you, to remind you it's time to go eat dinner with her clan. Why are you sitting on the ground?" She went over to help Trudy up. "Did you have a tumble?"

"Not yet," Trudy said, "but I'm definitely considering it."

CHAPTER THREE

Patty gave her a knowing look when she returned, but fortunately seemed to understand Trudy wasn't ready to talk about it. The more she got to know Dad's new wife, the more she liked her in spite of the weirdness. Trudy was still mad at her dad for not filling her in on that whole Sherritt witch business before the wedding, but had to agree with him, Patty and her mom were about as different as night and day.

Trudy was put in charge of making sure the pies Patty had baked and brought along remained safe on the back seat as they headed out for the family gathering. The winding road into Sherritt Holler took them past fields and farmhouses and several small country churches. This valley was almost a cliché of rural America, complete with a faded Mail Pouch Tobacco sign painted on a barn and shot-up stop signs used for target practice.

"So this is where Sherritt witches come from?" she asked. "I feel like I'm in a Stephen King novel. Everything appears normal but I'll discover people are being sacrificed in the corn fields at night to their god."

"More like the Sherritt witches were being sacrificed by the normal people to their god," Patty said. "Our ancestors were chased halfway around the world by people who insisted we must get our powers from the Devil. There's still a few churches around here that won't let a Sherritt through the door, so don't go spreading the word about how special we are, all right?"

"You got it." Trudy didn't want to hurt Patty's feelings, but she wasn't about to embarrass herself by telling people how her new stepmother was a witch. She rode the rest of the way in silence while thinking about her options on the fairy lover front.

The GPS eventually led them to a large farmhouse with several other cars parked in front. Some kids came running up to greet them and she was kept busy for a while being introduced to the Sherritt clan. These did seem like friendly people who were eager to welcome a new husband into the extended family. Henry was nabbed by the men and taken to the barn, where she supposed some sort of secret bonding ceremony was taking place involving cold beer, smelly cigars, spitting for distance, and declaring your allegiance to various sports teams.

As for the women, they all took turns greeting her with hugs and admiration that she chose teaching as a career, and regret she hadn't found a husband yet. They assured her that she was still young so not to worry too much and by the way they happened to know several young men who needed a wife. It was no different from greeting a bunch of parents at a PTA meeting, but Trudy couldn't seem to relax and enjoy the attention this time. They evicted some children watching cartoons from the couch, sat her down and put a cup of coffee in her hands. Then the rest of the women got on with preparing the meal and catching up on family gossip while Trudy watched.

It was only then Trudy realized what it was about these Sherritt women making her uncomfortable. She'd already figured out their handholding hid a private conversation. Patty and the other witches continued to occasionally pause and touch each other on the arm in silence while fussing around in the kitchen. There was a secret conversation going on, and she wondered how much of their gossip was about a stepdaughter who talked to imaginary men.

She heard a door open and shut, and a teenage girl came strolling out of the hallway holding a cup and plate. "Gran says if you try to give her decaf again she'll kneecap you next time you come in range of her cane. Also we're finished with her bath so you can go on back now."

Patty put down the big spoon she'd been using to stir something on the stove. "The red-eye gravy needs to simmer a while. Come on, Trudy. Let's pay our respects."

Trudy expected an ancient, bedridden crone. The room did have an unoccupied hospital bed. A woman wearing a tailored pantsuit sat in a recliner, holding a hand mirror and applying lipstick. Her hair might be pure silver, but she still showed signs of having been a stunning beauty. This woman should be shopping Fifth Avenue, not hanging out in a place called Sherritt Holler.

"Patty, it's wonderful to see you again," the woman said, holding her arms out. "Come give Grandma a hug."

"It's good to see you up and about," Patty said and came over for the hug. "I was telling Henry just this morning how much I adored the quilt you sent us for a wedding gift. I can't make up my mind whether to display it or lock it away. It must be worth a fortune."

"It's supposed to go on your bed. Your Great-Grandma didn't spend all winter sewing it by hand so you could pack it away in a closet. Now let's see this new stepdaughter. Come a little closer, Hun, so I can get a good look at you. I'm Jillian Jack, Patty's Grandma so that makes me your new Great-Grandma. Call me Gran."

"Hello, Gran," she said. "I'm Trudy. Pleased to meet you." She was a bit surprised to discover she actually meant it.

Gran squinted at her. "Nope, not a bit of Talent, but you're neck deep in some sort of magic. The tea leaves this morning told me you needed my help."

"Uh... You can see my problem by reading tea leaves?" By this time, Trudy was willing to believe these women flew on broomsticks.

"Well, mostly I learned all about you from Patty calling me last night and repeating everything you told her. She's worried to death but hides it well. Let's go for a walk. The doctor says I have to exercise this new hip or it won't set right and Ellie here keeps me on a tight schedule."

The teenage girl had come back in and stood holding a jacket while tapping her foot impatiently. "Blame Mom," she said. "She told me if I get this grouchy old bat out of our house and back into her own home by the end of the year, I get a new smartphone for my birthday."

Gran laughed, pushed herself out of the chair and let Ellie help her with the jacket. "See why I picked them to stay with while I'm healing? Ellie, you've earned some time off. I'll grab Trudy's arm if I need help."

Trudy felt like she was escorting royalty as they marched past the rest of the witches and out the front door. Gran had a sturdy cane in one hand and barely limped as they strolled down the path.

"Now," Gran said, "I told Patty to get you to try the spell a second time. Your young man showed up again, or I'm not a Sherritt. What did you learn?"

"He tastes like raspberries," Trudy answered without thinking, then felt a blush come on while Gran laughed. "I know it sounds crazy," she continued, "but he claims he's a Pooka. *The* Pooka. A fairy. He's hiding out."

"You don't say. Thought we left those troublemakers behind in the old country. That explains it. The spell is powered by fairy magic, then, not our Talent. Have fun. Legends say fairies are fantastic lovers." They'd reached a small clearing with a huge old oak tree in the center and Gran stopped. "Far enough. Let me rest a minute and we'll head back."

"Well, it doesn't explain anything to me," Trudy said. "Can I do magic or not? If I read another of those spells, will it work?"

"Depends on if you're wearing the necklace. I can feel the magic in it from here. Fairies don't give gifts lightly. When he called it his heart, he meant it."

Trudy fingered the pendant and thought back to everything he'd said. "According to the fairytales, this will give someone power over him if it falls into the wrong hands. Why would he take the chance?" Then the reality of how she'd been used became clear. "Why, that liar! I'll bet King Oberon already knows he snuck off, and Pook was desperate to get out of the country without being spotted. Destined to be lovers, my... He would have settled for anyone with a mailbox."

Gran leaned on her cane and shook her head. "My dear," she said, "I've had two husbands and a dozen lovers in my long life, and they were all liars. The question you should ask yourself is, does he mean well? I'm not sure I'd want a man who couldn't be bothered to flatter me outrageously by telling me what I want to hear. Fairy or mortal, he's still a man."

Trudy sighed. "Thanks for the advice, Gran. It means more than you know. Now let's get you back before people come looking for us."

"Not yet." Gran stepped closer. "That wasn't the advice the tea leaves showed me you needed. Dear, there's no excuse for what your mother did to you back then. A twelve-year old girl couldn't hate her mother for leaving because she loved her, so she blamed herself. You've never stopped blaming yourself. Give yourself permission to hate your mother for what she did. She earned it. Only then will you be able to forgive her."

Trudy was still hanging onto Gran and sobbing when she heard Ellie's voice.

"Thought so," Ellie said. "Gran, why is it every time you drag someone off for a private chat, they end up crying on your shoulder?" She took each of them by an arm. "Miss Macalester, you can freshen up in my room. And if any of my aunts ask you what's wrong, feel free to tell them to mind their own business. I swear, a Sherritt witch is about the nosiest creature on God's earth. So what was all the crying about?"

* * * * *

They made it to Ellie's bedroom without being waylaid by the women, although Patty came over and handed her a handkerchief without comment. "So Pookas are real," Ellie said, holding the necklace up to admire the pendent. "A giant rabbit with the hots for you? Eww." She handed the necklace back.

"Don't go by the movie," Trudy said, slipping it back around her neck. She blew her nose one last time. "Pook is a charming, good-looking ginger. Very charming."

"Huh. Might try the spell for myself. Think you could ask him if he has any cute friends?"

Ellie might be young, but she had an easy, non-judgmental way of talking. Trudy liked this girl. She was the rare kind of teenager that made teaching high school rewarding, but she was still a teenager. "How old are you?"

"I'm sixteen. I know all about protection, if that's what you're worried about."

"How about we keep in touch, and in a few years if you're still interested, we'll see." She pulled out her smartphone. "Send me your contact info."

"Hey, is that the new iPod? I want one of those. What apps do you have on it?"

She was showing Ellie some of the features when someone called out dinner was ready. The food was a country feast and after a brief prayer of thanks, the bowls and plates started making the rounds. Gran presided at the end of the big dining room table. Trudy and her dad were given the seats of honor closest to her. The women took turns grilling her dad about his life. She had to step in several times and draw their attention away so the poor man had a chance to chew his food. Sherritt witches really were about the nosiest creatures on Earth.

Once they were down to the desert and coffee stage, it was Gran's turn. "So, Henry," she said. "Did the menfolk welcome you into the Sherritt clan? Don't worry; I'm not going to press for details. They're quite a bunch of jokers, aren't they?"

Her dad laughed nervously and looked around at the men who stared at their plates and pretended they weren't listening. "They're a great bunch, but I have a feeling they love pulling the leg of the new guy. I think maybe I shouldn't believe half of what they told me."

"But you know some of it has to be true so you paid attention. Patty, you've got a smart man here. I like him."

Trudy happened to be looking in Patty's direction and spotted the huge look of relief on the woman's face. She realized then this entire Christmas trip must be so the head of this extended witch family could pass judgment on her choice of husbands. She wondered what would have happened if her dad failed the test.

The assembled clan started packing up leftovers and giving Gran kisses and hugs goodbye. From their remarks, they were headed out to drop off care packages at the homes of the less fortunate and more antisocial kin living further out on the ridge. That left her and her parents alone with Gran and Ellie to relax over coffee. Gran refused to lie down in spite of Ellie's most lethal glare, but compromised by stretching out on the couch.

"Any questions for me?" Gran finally asked. "You're family now, so don't be bashful. You know we're witches. Patty would have told you some of it."

Her dad stood examining a wall full of family pictures. "If I may ask, is Gran the title of the oldest witch, or does the coven get together and elect a leader? Are you in charge?"

Ellie seemed to think this was funny.

"There's older witches," Gran said, "and there's some couldn't care less for what I have to say and the feeling's mutual. Anna was Gran before me. Before she died, she said it was my job now to look after the Holler whether I liked it or not. That's her over on the wall next to the Christmas tree in the corner."

Trudy looked at the picture. There was a close resemblance between this Gran and the stately mature woman smiling in the picture, except for the hair. The picture showed a woman with wavy green hair and flowers woven into it, wearing a matching green dress of shimmering satin.

"She died her hair green?" Trudy asked. "Not that I'm criticizing. It looks lovely on her."

"As a young witch she fought the spirit of the mountain to save the life of the man she loved. Get Trudy to tell you the story sometime. The spells she used were so powerful, it changed her. Her hair stayed green until the day she died. Ellie, hand me the journal."

Ellie brought over a thin volume and handed it to Gran, who opened it to a page already bookmarked. "Anna had random premonitions and visions of the future and jotted it all down in this journal. A few of her entries are spells or advice I'm supposed to pass on to the right people at the right time. Trudy, my Sherritt blood is telling me this one's for you. Here, I copied it out."

She took the card. In a precise penmanship not taught anymore in school, Gran had written: *From distant land he comes to stay, but hunters come to take him away. If lovers would continue to play, Sherritt Holler saves the day.*

"So is this a spell or advice?" Trudy asked.

Gran chuckled. "Beats me. Might not have even been meant for you. No harm keeping it in mind."

Patty came over and gave her Gran a peck on the cheek. "We've got to head out," she said. "I promised an old friend I'd stop by tonight."

They were heading back toward town when her dad said, "Pumpkin, we'll drop you off at the bed and breakfast. I have to endure being shown around like a prize hunting trophy on display, but you don't. You can relax in bed and read a book or something."

Patty reached around and handed Trudy their room key. "And in case you do something instead of read, we decided to trade rooms with you for the night. I already explained to Marian that you might have a visitor and she's fine with it. Says if he stays for breakfast she's going to charge extra, though."

Trudy accepted the key without a word, embarrassed beyond measure at the matter-of-fact way these Sherritt women dealt with an active sex life.

If lovers would continue to play? You betcha.

CHAPTER FOUR

Trudy sat on the bed and fingered the necklace. She felt as nervous as the night she'd planned on losing her virginity to her high school sweetheart. Up until now, she'd been pretending she hadn't made up her mind on whether or not to summon Pook for the third time. She finally had to admit there was no way she could pass this up. She really did like the man...Pooka...whatever, and wanted to get to know him in every way.

She took a deep breath. "When first we meet, a friendly greet; the second tryst, only kissed; for love to stay, third mumph—"

Lips locked onto hers and a raspberry flavored tongue got in the way of completing the spell. She fell backwards on the bed with Pook on top. He looked at her with one of his patented wicked grins while he unbuttoned her blouse. He'd appeared wearing only a pair of trousers, to save time.

"All right, you big liar," she said. "Third time's the charm, like I promised. Now confess. You didn't need the spell to show up in the first place, did you?"

"Well now, lass," he said, "how far would a man bent on seduction get, if he didn't wait for an invitation?" He pulled her shirt open and reached for her bra, but then stopped and looked puzzled. "Does it slip over your head? I swear you ladies invented undergarments just to vex a man."

"Tell you what, stud," she said, pushing him back for now. "You sit here and watch how quick I can get out of these."

Instead of quick, she gave him a bit of a show, figuring a man who'd never seen a modern bra had missed out on the invention of the striptease. He stared with wide eyes in silence, the growing tent in his pants doing all the talking for him. When she was down to practically nothing, she stood next to the bed and slowly pulled her panties down. She knew what was coming next.

"Uh...what's that, darling?" He pointed to her tattoo down there. "A little man with a green hat and...a shamrock?"

"A souvenir of my college days," she told him. "It's Lucky the Leprechaun, from the Lucky Charms cereal box. My boyfriend at the time thought it was cute to ask if he was getting lucky tonight and since my nickname was Charm, well..."

"I love it," he said, pulling her onto the bed next to him and bending over to plant a kiss on her belly. "It speaks to me."

"When Lucky speaks, he says, 'You're always after me Lucky Charms, they're magically delicious!'"

"I'll be the judge of that," Pook said, and slid further down.

"Well, if you – Oh! Right there!"

For love to stay, go all the way? She clutched the back of his head. *Just try to stop me now.*

* * * * *

Trudy sighed and stretched out on the big bed. It had lived up to its reputation as being guaranteed not to squeak. Pook had also lived up to the reputation he bragged about. Multiple times.

"My dry spell is officially over," she said. "When it rains, it pours."

"I find it hard to believe a lovely lass like you doesn't have a line of men begging for your affection," Pook said. "Not that I'm complaining. Now that you have me, you don't need anyone else."

"I don't want anyone else. None of them have your magic tongue. Heh. I mean touch. Speaking of magic, does this mean I have to go around telling people I have a magical invisible boyfriend? I'll end up in a loony bin like Elwood P Dowd." She did her best Jimmy Stewart impression. "Then I introduce them to Harvey, and he's bigger and grander than anything they offer me..."

He rolled over and traced a line down her stomach, giving her goose bumps. "Darling, I have to confess–" He was interrupted by a high-pitched scream and then a woman yelling from somewhere in the house as a baby started crying.

Trudy jumped out of bed and looked around at her scattered clothes. Her bra had ended up hanging from the ceiling fan. She grabbed the sheet off the bed to wrap herself in and ran to see what was going on. The yelling came from downstairs, in the nursery. She found Marian clutching her baby to her chest and holding a fireplace poker, looking like she was going to beat the stuffing out of a big chair in the corner.

"It's behind the chair," she told Trudy without taking her eyes off it. "I don't know what it is. Some kind of monkey. The scream came from that thing. It got caught in my protection spell while trying to climb into Nan's crib."

Pook walked into the room while holding his pants up with one hand. He reached behind the chair and grabbed the intruder, picking it up by the neck while it hissed and struggled. He gave it a shake and it hung there limp, glaring at them with big black eyes. It looked vaguely like a cross between a monkey and a frog.

"It's a boggart," he told them. "They're known to snatch babies from their cribs to sell at the Seelie market. If it's here, then I'm in big trouble. Who are you working for, ya varmint?"

"The Wild Hunt sent me to give warning," it said. "They arrive when the sun sets. Let me go, and I'll swear on my true name to never set foot in this house again."

"Swear to return directly to the court and never set foot on this world again."

"Ya drive a hard bargain. Aye, I so swear. I'll be looking forward to watching ya stand before our King. He won't be so forgiving this time."

Pook tossed the boggart out the nursery door and it scampered off. "You won't see this one again. I don't know how the King tracked me down. I was careful not to let anyone see me, leave alone speak my true name. No sense hiding now. Nice to meet you, Marian. You have a lovely baby and I'll make sure nothing bothers her while I'm around."

Marian cleared her throat. "I wasn't going to mention it, but someone was yelling 'Oh, Puck! Oh, Puck!' a while ago. The walls of this old house are a bit thin. So you're her mystery lover? Pleased to meet you, too, and well done."

Trudy and Pook looked at each other. "I'm so sorry," she told him. "I don't remember doing that."

He took her in his arms. "I was a bit distracted at the time, myself. It's not your fault, lass. They would have found me sooner or later. I was hoping for later. At least you get to call me Puck and introduce me to your friends now – if I'm still around after tonight."

"Who's hunting you down?" she asked. "Why would they warn you? Are they friends of yours?"

He walked over to the window and squinted up at the sky. "The Wild Hunt is nobody's friend. They give their prey a head start because they enjoy the chase and they're certain of the outcome. The sun is already low. If I start now, I'll be able to make them work for their reward. They'll find out the Pooka is not so easily caught."

"Not so fast!" Trudy said. "Let me think." She looked at Marian, busy changing her baby's diaper while it kicked and gurgled. "I think Gran knew this was going to happen. Maybe even Anna. Are they really that good?"

Marian gave her a big grin. "More than you know. The stories I could tell. My Sherritt blood is saying you need to trust your instincts. According to legend, Anna had to fight the mountain itself to save her man. Maybe she's reaching through time to help you do some fighting of your own."

That settled it. She pulled the sheet tighter around her shoulders. "Puck, you're not going anywhere without me. We need to get to Sherritt Holler. Marian, we need to borrow your car."

"Mark has it. He's gone Christmas shopping. I'll give him a call on the cellphone and check with the neighbors. It might take a while."

"So it's sanctuary we'll be heading for?" Puck asked. "That's the spirit, lass. You point me in the right direction and I'll get us there. Put on something warm and meet me out back."

* * * * *

Trudy ran out the back door while pulling on her cap. She stumbled to a halt at the sight. A horse stood in the back yard, a beautiful chestnut stallion with the setting sun gleaming off his long red mane. Marian was already on the porch, holding her heavily swaddled baby to her breast and admiring the animal. Puck was nowhere to be seen.

"I promised you a ride," the horse said in Puck's voice, turning his head to look her up and down. "You'll be needing a chair to climb on. Hurry up, lass. Time's wasting."

"Bareback? Maybe with a saddle. I owned a pony as a child."

"You won't fall off. Trust me."

Like I have a choice? Once she settled onto the wide back, Puck gave a shudder and it felt like his hide turned to Velcro. "Turn right at the light," Marian told them. "Then it's a straight run. Don't stop until it turns into a dirt road and you pass a sign saying welcome to Sherritt Holler. There's a rest stop just past that where you can make a stand."

"We can do better than that," Puck said. "Not even the Wild Hunt can match me at cross country. Point out the direction of this valley."

Marian pointed toward a gap in the mountains as the setting sun disappeared completely. Puck took off with a bound and if he hadn't glued her to his back, it would have been the end of her ride already. The rest of the trip became a teeth-jarring, terrifying series of jumps and hard landings and sudden spurts of acceleration in the dark. All she could do was hug Puck's neck and hope she didn't soil his sleek hide with the contents of her stomach before this was over.

They were on a straight stretch when she heard the unmistakable sound of a hunter's horn. It sounded close and spurred Puck into a faster gallop. Then he finally stumbled to a halt and stood taking deep, gasping breaths. The light above an outdoor toilet told her they'd reached the rest stop. She slid to the ground and massaged feeling back into her legs and butt as his form shimmered and the old Puck appeared before her on hands and knees.

"I'm...spent," he gasped out. "It's up to...you, lass. Prepare yourself."

Half a dozen horses bearing riders pulled up in front of them. The hunter's clothes were made from different types of animal skins sewn together like a patchwork quilt, their hair and beards long and unkempt. The one in the middle wore some sort of helmet with antlers stuck to it and held a horn in his hand, while the others held bows and spears. He must be the leader.

She dug the paper with the spell out of her pocket and held it up with shaking hands. "From distant land he comes to stay, but hunters come to take him away. If lovers would continue to play, Sherritt Holler saves the day," she read. Then she looked around and picked up a hefty branch to use as a weapon. "Anna, I could use your help about now," she called out.

The hunters ignored her. "So, the chase ends with a scared rabbit cowering in the dirt," the leader said, looking at Puck sitting on the cold ground. "Hardly a hunt at all. You're ours, now."

"He's mine," she told the hunters. "You can't have him."

That caused them all to start laughing. The leader finally waved his hand for silence. "I never thought I'd see the day proud Puck hid behind a strumpet," he said. "The court will never let him live it down. Is it trial by combat then, wench?"

"Who calls me from my slumber?" said another voice in the night. The woman who stepped out of the shadows had long green hair woven with flowers, a matching green gown, and a timeless beauty. "Who disturbs my winter sleep with talk of Kings and courts and combat? Who calls upon my name?"

The hunters started whispering to each other. "So that's who you were invoking," the leader eventually said, shifting nervously in his saddle. "We have no quarrel with you, Anu, and none with your worshipper."

"You think not?" Anna said. "You've trespassed upon a sacred valley, so I definitely have a quarrel with you. You do not belong on this world, elf. I should tell the ground itself to open up and swallow you."

Trudy was flabbergasted at the exchange. This apparition didn't sound like a Sherritt witch at all.

"As I said," the hunter repeated, "we have no quarrel with you, fair Anu, or Anna, or whatever name you go by in this land. We will take our rightful prey and depart so you may slumber undisturbed until the land warms in the spring."

"Um... Anna, they're talking about Puck," Trudy said. "The man I love. They want to take him away."

Anna looked over at Puck, seeming to notice him for the first time. "This is Puck? Your reputation has reached even my ears. So you have played with this girl's affections? No, I believe this elf will stay here. He has trespassed also, and must be punished. Your punishment will be..." Anna folded her arms and pursed her lips, then nodded her head. "You will give your heart to this mortal woman forever, for her to use and abuse as she pleases; a toy to her whims. Do you swear on your true name to accept this fate? I might think of something worse if you refuse."

"Not even Puck deserves that," the hunter said. "Have mercy and let us kill him before we leave."

"'Tis a heavy sentence," Puck said, with a gleam in his eye, "but one I have earned a thousand times over. I swear on my true name to accept the punishment, if Anu will let the Wild Hunt return to our fair land to tell the King of my sacrifice."

Anna waved her arm in dismissal, and the assembled hunters bowed their heads in homage to the bravery of Puck before fading into the night. Trudy stood there still clutching the branch, confused and a bit angry. It felt like she'd just been insulted by everyone.

"Oh now–" she began.

"Hush!" Anna said, holding up her hand. "Are they truly gone, Puck?" she asked.

"Gone and with the door locked tight," he said, getting up from the ground and brushing off his pants.

"Thank goodness," Anna said. "I'm about to fall down. Ellie, dear, you can come out now."

Anna reached up and removed a green wig to reveal white hair as Ellie ran out of the dark with a cane and a helping hand. Gran limped over and sat at the picnic table. "Good thing I lost some weight recently," Gran said. "Anna's old dress is a tight fit. Ellie, fetch the car." She turned back to Trudy and Puck. "We parked down the road a bit."

"Hold on," Trudy said, "everyone shut up for a minute!" She sat on the bench and put her head in her hands, trying to think. Puck came over and put his arm around her. "Would someone please explain what happened before I start screaming?" she said. "The message wasn't from Anna?"

Gran patted her on her knee. "The message was real, but Anna would think poorly of me if she had to show up personally to handle that bunch. Besides, Ellie needed to see me in action. She might be Gran one day. I told her to look into the tea leaves and tell me when and where we'd be needed tonight, and here we are. A bit of green dye and some plastic flowers in an old Halloween wig, being careful to stay in the shadows, letting their own imagination fill in the gaps, and I had them quaking in their boots."

"But, that was the Wild Hunt!" Puck said. "Feared across a dozen realms as the most determined pack of killers to ever exist."

"It was a pack of fairies acting like bullies," Gran said, as Ellie drove up in the car. "I know how to handle bullies. We'll give you a lift back to Marian's place – unless you prefer another horseback ride on a cold night." Ellie came over and helped Gran get into the warm car.

Trudy took Puck by the hand. "I don't want your heart if you think you're being punished."

He shook his head and the old wicked grin came back. "I love you, lass. For better or worse, in sickness and in health, I want to be with you. Use and abuse me as you will. I'm looking forward to it. I actually enjoyed you riding me over half the county. Maybe next time you can use tackle and spurs?"

"You want it, you got it." They walked to the car hand in hand. She looked up at the clear night sky sprinkled with stars. "Feels like a dream already. A midwinter night's dream. Tonight, the high and mighty elves were brought low by a crippled old woman in a wig, a teenage apprentice, and a girl just trying to get a date." She leaned over and gave Puck a kiss as he fumbled with the car door.

"Lord, what fools these fairies be."

The End

ABOUT THE AUTHOR

Gerald Costlow currently lives and plays in Michigan and has published many short stories and a few novels over the past ten years or so. He is currently working on a series of paranormal adventures set in 1920s Appalachia with occasional detours as the muse strikes. Visit the author at: http://theweaving.blogspot.com/ http://www.amazon.com/Gerald-Costlow/e/B00A9I8ZAU/

Stories by Gerald Costlow published by Victory Tales:

Appalachia Sherritt Witch Series:
A Distant Call~ Published in *2011 Mystery/Suspense Collection* and now available as a single. (The story of Anna)
Deal With the Devil ~ Second in the Appalachia series.
Crazy Jack ~ Novel length and third in the Appalachia series.
Ring for a Lady ~ Published in *Fated to Be Yours, 2015 Collection from the Heart* and available as a single. Fourth in the Appalachia series.

Modern Day Sherritt Witch Series:
Family Heirloom ~ *Published in 2012 Christmas Collection* and available as a single. First in the Modern Day series. (The story of Marian)
Magic Words ~ Second in the Modern Day series.
Man of Her Dreams ~ Published in *2014 Autumn Collection* and available as a single. Third in the Modern Day series.

Other stories set in the Sherritt Witch universe:
The Sherritt and the Sharpshooter ~ Published in *Be My Always, 2015 Summer Collection.* Set in pre-Civil War Kentucky.
Legacy ~ Published in *Myths, Legends and Midnight Kisses, 2015 Collection.* Set in 1950s Sherritt Holler.

Other Titles from Victory Tales Press

A Summer Collection Anthology
A Halloween Collection Anthology: Sweet
A Halloween Collection Anthology: Sweet
A Halloween Collection Anthology: Stimulating
A Christmas Collection: Sweet
A Christmas Collection: Sensual
A Christmas Collection: Stimulating
A Christmas Collection: Spicy
A Valentine Collection Anthology: Sweet
A Mystery/Suspense Collection Anthology: Sweet
Spring/Easter Collection Anthology: Sweet
Historical Collection Anthology: Sweet/Sensual
Western Saga Anthology: Sweet/Sensual
2011 Christmas Collection Sensual/Spicy
2011 Christmas Collection Sensual/Spicy
2012 Fall/Paranormal Collection: Sweet/Sensual
2012 Christmas Collection: Sweet/Sensual
2014 Summer Collection: Sweet/Sensual
2014 Autumn Collection: Sweet/Sensual
2014 Christmas Collection: Sweet/Sensual
Fated to Be Yours: 2015 Collection of the Heart
Be My Always: 2015 Summer Collection
Myths, Legends, and Midnight Kisses, 2015
Halloween Collection

Please watch for future releases from *Victory Tales Press* at victorytalespress.com.

Made in the USA
Charleston, SC
19 December 2015